"Over There Near the Fireplace, the Tall Gentleman with the Black Hair. That Is Randy Ketcham."

Sara looked to where her grandmother indicated and felt the blood drain out of her face. He was considerably older than she, probably in his early thirties. He was indeed exceptionally tall, and his thick black hair was pulled back into a queue. He wore a perfectly fitted dove-gray coat that showed off his broad shoulders and narrow waist. The unmentionables he wore of the same dove-gray exhibited a pair of well-muscled legs. He moved with the languid grace of a born athlete. The frothy white cravat was a perfect foil for his dark complexion and strong features. This was the man she had dreamed about ever since she was old enough to know that the species came in two sexes. She noticed that he was approaching them and she hastily turned away, afraid that her feelings might be too obvious. She took a couple of deep breaths as she heard a deep, melodious voice directly behind her.

"So you are the mysterious Lady Sara. . . ."

Dear Reader,

We, the editors of Tapestry Romances, are committed to bringing you two outstanding original romantic historical novels each and every month.

From Kentucky in the 1850s to the court of Louis XIII, from the deck of a pirate ship within sight of Gibraltar to a mining camp high in the Sierra Nevadas, our heroines experience life and love, romance and adventure.

Our aim is to give you the kind of historical romances that you want to read. We would enjoy hearing your thoughts about this book and all future Tapestry Romances. Please write to us at the address below.

The Editors
Tapestry Romances
POCKET BOOKS
1230 Avenue of the Americas
Box TAP
New York, N.Y. 10020

Pride and Promises

Adrienne Scott

A TAPESTRY BOOK
PUBLISHED BY POCKET BOOKS NEW YORK

An *Original* publication of TAPESTRY BOOKS

A Tapestry Book published by
POCKET BOOKS, a division of Simon & Schuster, Inc.
1230 Avenue of the Americas, New York, N.Y. 10020

ISBN: 0-671-52354-6

First Tapestry Books printing November, 1984

10 9 8 7 6 5 4 3 2 1

To my family,
who believed in my cannon

Prologue

Somerset, 1784

LADY OLIVIA LIVISCOMBE, THE DUCHESS OF Darnton, clutched her swollen stomach and moaned pitifully. The midwife, sitting by her side, mopped the perspiration that was streaming down her face with a delicately embroidered lace handkerchief. Her beautiful black hair, normally so elegantly coiffed, now lay in damp tangles across the white satin pillowcase. Her face was as white as the satin.

"Hang on, now, dearie," the midwife was saying in a falsely hearty tone. "Yon babe is sure to put in an appearance soon."

The young duchess moaned again. "But it has been hours already."

"I know, dearie, I know. It is often that way with the first one. You wait and see. The next won't be nearly so hard." Even as she spoke, a frown crossed her wrinkled old face. She had delivered thousands of babies and knew all the signs of a troubled birth. This case was bad. She had wondered for several hours now if the duchess was strong enough to have this baby and if she herself would be able to save either mother or child.

Another pain shot through her wracked body and Lady Olivia screamed, gripping the midwife's hand as though it were her only link to this life. The spasm subsided, and there came a quiet knock on the door. The midwife again mopped the duchess's feverish brow, then opened the door and slipped quietly out.

"How is she?" asked the duke.

She looked sympathetically at the tall, elegant man. He was almost as pale as his wife and there were lines of strain around his eyes. "I fear for her, M'Lord," she said in a hushed voice. "She weren't strong to begin with and this labor's goin' on much too long."

"Is there nothing you can do?"

She laid a withered, coarsened hand on his elegantly clad forearm. "We can but pray, M'Lord." With that she reentered the room, closing the door silently behind her.

The candles were guttering in the sconces and a weak sun was trying in vain to lighten a cloud-laden sky. The duke sat in the library, holding a half-empty brandy glass in his hand and staring blankly at the dying embers of the fire. He could hear his wife's screams in the room above and every one seemed to sear through him. He prayed from the depth of his being that his beautiful lady would survive. Never again would he let this happen. He would be celibate the rest of his life if it would prevent her from experiencing this torture. The child seemed insignificant at this moment. Of course, he wanted an heir, but without one his young brother would inherit and Charlie was a responsible, conscientious young man. He would make a good landlord and a worthy successor to the title. The duke hoped that if the child did survive it wasn't a girl—that would just be too unfair. Another scream sounded above, more protracted. They were very regular now and he anticipated them. But suddenly there was silence. He jumped up, dropping the forgotten glass to the floor, and ran up the stairs. A maid was just coming out of the room. As she closed the door behind her, he heard a slap and a different cry—shrill and hearty.

"Well?" he said.

The maid looked up at him, a weary expression on her pinched face. "The babe's doin' fine, M'Lord," she replied, dropping a stiff curtsy.

"I can hear that," he said impatiently. "How is my wife?"

"She be alive, M'Lord," the little maid said in frightened tones. "Let me get Miz Jenkins for you. She'll know." She slipped back into the room.

Within moments, the midwife appeared. "Well, M'Lord, the good Lord heard our prayers. You have a fine, healthy baby daughter."

He stared at her for a long moment as the words sank in. "A girl?" he asked disbelievingly. "Sure to God, no."

Mrs. Jenkins looked at him sadly. She knew well the importance of heirs. "Yes, M'Lord, but it is a healthy babe and I think she'll be a fine-looking woman. I've seen enough of 'em in my life to know, and lived long enough to see how they turn out."

"And my wife?" he asked in a dull voice, ignoring her comments.

Her sympathy deepening, she said, "She's alive, M'Lord, but exhausted. As I said afore, she's not strong and this were a terrible ordeal. We can only wait and see now."

He nodded to her and turned back toward the stairs. "And all for the sake of a girl. Damn, damn, damn," he muttered. He returned to the library, sinking back wearily into his chair.

All day the midwife tended the duchess. The doctor was summoned, but he explained to Lord Darnton that there was nothing anyone could do now and that Mrs. Jenkins knew more than he did about this sort of thing.

The day passed slowly. Lord Darnton went to his wife's room once an hour to check her progress. The report was always the same—she was asleep, but that was a good sign, it would help her regain her strength.

He took his dinner on a tray in the library. He hardly touched the food, but the bottle of claret helped revive him a little. He continued his hourly checks, but still there was no change.

Nightfall brought rain. He listened to it beating against the windowpanes, and the wind slapping the branches of the old gnarled oaks against the casement windows. The weather was a perfect reflection of his emotions. He poured himself a glass of brandy and watched dully as a footman built a fire in the magnificent marble fireplace.

He was sitting quietly, staring at the flames, when there came a knock on the door. "Come in," he called.

Mrs. Jenkins pushed open the door and crossed the room to stand in front of him.

He jumped to his feet. "Is there any change?"

"No, M'Lord," she replied. "I come about the babe."

"Oh," he said, all interest dying out of his voice. "What about it?"

"M'Lord, we need a wet nurse and soon. The wee thing has to eat and her mother is not up to it yet." And never will be, she thought sorrowfully.

"Let it starve," he said harshly. "What do I care?"

She understood his feelings far too well to take umbrage at this callous statement. This was not the first time she had been in such a situation and for once was thankful for her advancing years and the wisdom she had gained. In her business, she saw an equal amount of pleasure and pain.

"Lady Darnton would care," she said calmly. "She carried yon babe for nine months and gave nigh twenty-two hours to bring her into this world. It is for us to make sure her labor was not in vain."

The duke put his hands over his face in a gesture of despair. "Yes, Mrs. Jenkins, you are exactly right. Do you know someone who would be acceptable?"

She thought for a moment. Like the duke, she had had no sleep for three days and her brain was foggy. At last she said, "I delivered a girl in the village last week. It were a sad case. The father had abandoned her when he found out she was with child—they weren't married, you understand—and turned out the babe was stillborn. She has plenty of milk in her paps and her folks would be glad to be rid of her. If you've no objection, I'll send round for her at once."

"Yes, that will be fine," Lord Darnton replied. He had not heard a word she had said but was aware that she had offered a solution.

"Thank you, M'Lord," the midwife said as she left the room. "I'll let you know if there is any change in M'Lady's condition."

An hour later he heard the door knocker. He opened the library door and saw the butler greeting a young girl, obviously from the village. A footman came to lead her upstairs. He guessed this must be the wet nurse and was obscurely grateful that she had been instructed not to use the servants' entrance. Even if he had no interest in the infant, the nurturer of the only child of the seventh Duke of Darnton should not be treated as a common servant. He returned to his chair to continue his vigil.

The clock had just struck two when there came another knock on the library door. "Come in," he called wearily.

It was the little maid with the pinched face. "M'Lord, Miz Jenkins wants you to come up at once," she said, breathlessly.

He leapt to his feet and ran across the room. He took the stairs two at a time, but when he reached his wife's bedchamber he hesitated. His first thought had been to burst straight into the room, but suddenly a feeling of dread washed over him. He knocked at the door, not even aware that he was holding his breath. It opened at once.

"Come in, M'Lord," Mrs. Jenkins said. Her face was a mask of sorrow and weariness. "She is awake and wishes to see you."

He entered the room, making his way slowly to where his beloved wife lay on the huge bed. In the flickering candlelight he could see the pallor of her complexion and the huge dark shadows under her blue eyes. She was clad in the white lace nightdress he had bought for her on their honeymoon just nine months before, and her long, slender hands were clasped across her now flat stomach. She looked at him as he crossed the room, her eyes filled with love and exhaustion.

He sank down on his knees beside the bed, grasping her hands in his. "Oh, my dearest love," he said hoarsely.

She smiled at him and he sensed that there was something otherworldly about her, as if she had already died and was returning to earth for this one last encounter.

"My Lord," she replied in a faint voice. They looked at each other for a long moment, then she continued. "I know that I shall not see the morning light and I wished to say good-bye."

He laid a finger gently over her pallid lips. "Nonsense, my love. You will see the morning and many more to come! Hush now. Just conserve your strength." The look on his face was

7

so intense that she knew he was willing her to live. But she also knew with a quiet serenity that she was slipping away from him.

She shook her head sadly. "No, dearest, my time has come. Where I am going now you cannot join me, at least for a while." She paused for a moment, trying to summon her fading strength. "I only ask that you look after our baby. I am sorry I could not give you the boy you wanted . . ." She stopped again and took several shallow ragged breaths. He could almost see her life ebbing away.

"Do not say any more, my sweet. Rest now. We can talk later."

"There will be no later," she said. "Please, John, I beg of you, do not hate her. She cannot help being born a female."

"I will try," he replied earnestly. "But it will be hard for me to love anyone who takes you away."

"I understand, but please give her a chance." Her voice was growing fainter and he leaned closer. "And, John?"

"Yes, my love?"

"Call her Sara. It is my very favorite name."

"She will be Sara Olivia," he replied.

She closed her eyes then and sank deeper into the pillows. "Please, John," she said so softly that he could barely distinguish the words. "Do not shut her out."

They were the last words she spoke. Moments later the haltering breath stopped and Lord John Liviscombe, Duke of Darnton, was holding the lifeless hands of his eighteen-year-old wife. He hung his head and bitter tears burned his eyes. Mrs. Jenkins, who had been standing by the door during this heartbreaking exchange, came forward and laid her hand gently on his shoulder.

"Would you like to see your wee babe, M'Lord?" she asked softly, hoping the tiny life would help mitigate the agony she saw in his sagging head and quivering shoulders.

His immediate reaction was to say no—he hated this creature—then he remembered her last words, "Do not shut her out." Her last request. He would try, that was all he could do.

"Very well, Mrs. Jenkins," he said, rising to his feet. He moved more like an old man than like one in the prime of his youth.

She led him into the antechamber where the village girl was sitting in a chair, gently rocking a cradle. Pain washed over him as he gazed down at the sleeping infant. There was a cloud of dark hair around her tiny face and her small hands were curled into fists. She was covered by the blanket her mother had so diligently embroidered for her through the long months of her pregnancy. It was that blanket that sent all the memories of his beloved Olivia flooding through him.

He turned abruptly and strode from the room. He spent the remainder of the night in the library, staring into the fire. In the morning, he sent a message to his lawyer, then made arrangements for the funeral, scheduled for the following day.

A bleak, rainy morning saw the interment of Lady Olivia Liviscombe, Duchess of Darnton, in the family vault at Langton in Somerset, the principal seat of the Liviscombe family for five generations.

After the ceremony, Lord Darnton summoned his servants together. "I shall be leaving for London on the morrow, and I shall not return. My lawyer, Mr. Kirby, will arrive within the week to schedule a baptism for the child. It will be christened 'Lady Sara Olivia.' Mrs. Darrell," he said, turning to the housekeeper, "I will provide whatever nurses and governesses are required. Mr. Kirby will make sure you have everything else you need."

With that, he was gone. The servants all turned to look at each other. The gentry had strange ways, as they well knew. Their hearts went out to the duke in his sorrow and bereavement, but they were unable to forget the poor baby girl who lay sleeping in her tiny cot, blissfully unaware of the pain that her entry into the world had caused. Of one accord, they bowed their heads, each vowing to do his utmost to shelter the Lady Sara from life's trials and sorrows.

Chapter One

Somerset, 1800

THE SUN WAS JUST BEGINNING TO LIGHTEN THE
eastern sky. The night had been unseasonably
hot and her maid Agnes had left the draperies
open to allow some cool air into her bedchamber. But even with that, she had not slept well
and was just as glad to see the day break. At
least she could get up now and do something.

She stretched luxuriantly in the satin-
sheeted bed, then sat up abruptly. Today was
her birthday! She was sixteen. The thought
was a source of both excitement and pain.
Birthdays should promise pleasure and surprise. All her neighbors had big celebrations
for their children on this occasion. For herself,
a birthday only meant the visit of her father's
lawyer.

From a very early age Lady Sara Liviscombe
had realized there was something odd about
her life. Of course, she adored Fenton, her

11

butler, and Nana, her old nurse, who had come when she was weaned from her wet nurse, and had stayed on long after the girl had any real need for her. And she loved old Mrs. Darrell, though her fierce protectiveness was a little frightening.

But despite the loyalty and affection of those around her, there was always something missing. It was Nana she had first approached with her problem when she was four.

"Nana?" she had asked in her small, high-pitched voice.

"What be it, sweetings?" the large, rawboned woman answered as the two cleaned up the sewing room where they had been making clothes for the child's doll.

"How come I don't have a mama?"

Nana had been expecting this question, but she was still uncomfortable now that she was faced with it. She took a deep breath. "Yer mama died when ye was born," she said, hoping the child would understand.

She thought about it for a moment. "You mean like Boots?" she asked at last, referring to the housecat who had been killed by one of the stable dogs earlier in the year.

Nana nodded. "Like Boots."

"Oh," Lady Sara replied and turned her attention back to her chore.

The nurse breathed a quiet sigh of relief. That had not been nearly as bad as she had feared.

"What about my papa?" the child asked next. "Did he die like Boots, too?"

This was the question Nana had dreaded.

How could she explain that her father lived a brief two-day trip away and had not visited his daughter once in her four years of life? She decided that honesty was, in this case, definitely not the best policy. "No, sweetings, yer pa is alive. It's just that he lives far away and is a very busy man."

"Oh," Lady Sara said again. She never mentioned the subject to Nana again, but she was very subdued for the next several days.

The nurse spoke to Mrs. Darrell and Fenton about what she had said and they all agreed that her response was the best she could have made.

It was nearly a year later when Sara asked Mrs. Darrell about her father. The two had been in the creamery at the time, watching the scullery maid churn butter.

"When will Papa come see me?" she had asked, grabbing the housekeeper's hand in a gesture of insecurity.

She looked down at the pretty little face looking so innocently up at her. "I'm not sure, My Lady," she replied. She only used the girl's title when she was angry or upset.

Lady Sara knew this and was surprised. "Have I made him angry?" she asked, bewildered.

"No, not angry, my pet. It's just that your father is a very busy man. I know he will come when he can. You must be a big girl and try to understand."

"Where does he live?" she asked next.

Mrs. Darrell felt even more uncomfortable. "In London."

The girl nodded and again the subject was dropped.

She never again discussed her missing parents. This fact worried her loyal retainers. They talked about it often and thought it unhealthy that she did not show more curiosity. But privately they were relieved. It was a terribly difficult situation and they realized that she was an intelligent girl who would not long be put off by lies.

When her first governess had arrived to begin instruction in reading and writing, the first question Lady Sara had asked was where London was. The governess, pleased with her curiosity, brought out a map of England.

She indicated where they were in Somerset and where London was located.

"Have you ever been to London?" Lady Sara asked.

"Yes, I come from London."

"How long does it take to get here?"

"It is a two-day trip, though some people who have a lot of money take three days, but that means a second night of lodging."

Lady Sara nodded solemnly. "Thank you," was all she said.

Twice a year, once on her birthday and once on Christmas, Mr. Kirby journeyed into Somerset to present her a check for £100. It was an enormous amount of money to give a girl who had no reason or need to spend it. The lawyer never stayed long and never mentioned her father except to say that the check was indeed from him. Since the time she had learned to write she had penned back a polite thank you, but these letters went unanswered. And so her only knowledge of her parents was the portraits hanging in the library and what she read about her father in the newspapers.

He was indeed a very busy man. He was a prominent figure both in the House of Lords and in the social world of the *beau monde*. His name was linked romantically in the gossip columns with many of the most beautiful women in the *ton*. Attracting almost as much attention was his young sister, Lady Alberta Watson. "Bertie," as she was called in the press, was a true dasher. At thirty, she had buried two husbands, both quite elderly and extremely wealthy. Now she flagrantly enjoyed all the advantages of being beautiful, rich and widowed. There had been a younger brother, Lord Charles, but he had been killed in a hunting accident two years before. She also knew through the newspapers that she had a grandmother, the Dowager Duchess of Darnton.

Since she had first learned to read, she had clipped out all the articles that mentioned her mysterious family. Unbeknownst to her retainers, she kept a huge scrapbook with the articles carefully pasted in. Sometimes when she was feeling lonely she would draw it out and try to imagine what they were like.

She often wondered why the rest of her father's family ignored her as well. She sensed somehow that her father's feelings toward her had to do with the death of her mother and maybe she could understand that if he had loved her very much. But what about her grandmother and aunt? And she knew nothing at all about her mother's family.

She was sitting in the small dining room eating toast and sipping hot chocolate when her governess entered. She looked up from the newspaper she was reading. "Good morning, Deb," she greeted. "Sleep well?"

"No, not really," Deborah replied, pouring herself a cup of coffee from the pot on the sideboard. "It was so warm last night. How about you?"

"Same problem. Let's walk down to the pond this morning."

"All right. It is much too warm for lessons today."

Despite Lord Darnton's lack of attention to his daughter, he had been extremely careful in her upbringing. He had made sure that the servants at Langton were of the highest caliber, and he personally selected the governesses entrusted with Sara's instruction. They had all been well-educated, gently borne women who, for one reason or another, had no inheritance and a very real need to earn a living. There had been three. The first had stayed for five years and then married the village curate. Lady Sara still saw her every Sunday. The second had only remained for a year before being called home to tend a dying father and take responsibility for raising her three young siblings. The current governess, Deborah Sanders, had arrived when Sara was ten. They had gotten on well right from the start.

Now, however, Deborah was preparing to

leave Langton. Her dream had always been to open a school for the village children. She had shared this dream with her pupil and the two had spent hours discussing ways in which it could be financed. Sara longed to give Deborah all the money her father had given her but she knew the governess would never accept it. At last they had worked out a scheme in which Sara would put up even money to what Deborah had saved. She now had sufficient funds to lease a building recently vacated in the village. Living quarters were included and, despite Sara's having asked her to stay on, Deborah thought it would be better to live at the school. She could not afford a carriage and it would be too long a walk during inclement weather. Sara had offered her the use of the carriage and a footman, but Deborah had firmly declined. She had, however, readily accepted Sara's offer of assistance in fixing up the school, and the two had spent many pleasant hours cleaning and revamping the building and ordering furniture and supplies.

The villagers, for the most part, were delighted to have their children learn to read and write and had gladly pitched in with the more difficult work. The school was set to open in less than a month and Deborah had been promised a good enrollment. A few villagers might even send their daughters.

Now as the two women sat in the small dining room, Sara began to laugh. Deborah looked at her in surprise. "Something amusing in the papers today?"

"Oh, the gossip columns, of course. Listen to

this. 'And no day would be complete without another outrageous prank from our beloved Bertie. Informed sources say that she borrowed Lord M———'s phaeton to participate in a race from Haymarket to Newcastle. We understand that the Dowager Duchess of D——— and Lady M——— were not best pleased about this incident.'" Sara laughed again. "'Not best pleased' indeed. Oh, Deb, can you imagine? I would dearly love to meet my aunt Bertie."

Deborah looked disapproving for a moment, then joined in Sara's laughter. "She does sound like a dasher. Remember the day she went riding astride in Hyde Park wearing her late husband's breeches?"

"And the costume ball when she dressed as a harem girl and wore no underclothes?" said Sara.

Deborah put on her best governessy expression. "I should not be encouraging you, Sara," she said at last. "Your aunt Alberta is not a proper example for a young girl."

"Oh come, Deb," Sara said, a wicked look in her eye. "I am not all that young, you know. In fact, I am sixteen."

The governess smiled at this hint and said, "I did not forget." She reached into the pocket of her skirt and pulled out a small box which she presented to her pupil. "Happy Birthday, Lady Sara."

She watched as the girl delightedly opened the box, realizing suddenly that the awkward, gangly child of ten whom she had first come to teach had indeed grown into a woman. And a beautiful woman she was. Tall and slender, with dusky black curls and eyes of a deep blue, she moved with an innate sense of grace and breeding and her manner hinted of intelligence and wit.

"Deb, it's exquisite," she said, picking up the beaded reticule. "Whenever did you find the time to do it?"

Deborah grinned at her. "I have my ways. You get so caught up in your reading that I actually worked on it in the same room with you and you never noticed."

Sara hugged her and kissed her cheek. "Thank you so much. You are wonderful."

Deborah laughed. "I do not know about that but I am glad you like it. And now we can start for the pond. I will ask Cook to send a picnic down in a few hours."

"Oh that would be fun. Shall we take our watercolors?"

"Yes, I think we should. I would like to hang a few more pictures in the school."

They were soon on their way, carrying their watercolor boxes and chatting amiably.

"I am going to miss Langton," Deborah said wistfully. "It is so beautiful."

And indeed it was. As befitted the principal seat of a duke of the realm, the estate was vast. Fortunately, the Liviscombe men had always been prudent investors and good landlords. Consequently, there had been enough funds to keep it in prime condition. The main house was built in the Palladian style. The golden brick facade had mellowed through the years and now appeared warm and inviting. The vast expanse of well-manicured lawn swept down to a stream that was arched by a wooden foot bridge.

They followed the path by the stream through the deer park until they came to the ornamental pond that had been created by the fifth Duke of Darnton. In the middle of the pond he had built a small island and added a gazebo surrounded by lush foliage and hanging baskets filled with colorful flowers.

They set up their easels and stools and began to paint.

"You will come back to see me often," Sara said. "And of course you can spend your holidays here. We shan't be that far apart."

Deborah looked at her for a moment. "I am afraid it may not be that simple."

Sara glanced at her in surprise. "What do you mean?"

She was silent for a moment, wondering if she should say any more. "I may as well tell you. You will know soon enough anyway." She took a deep breath, then continued. "When I decided to open the school, I wrote your father and told him that I would be leaving in the fall. I also indicated that I saw little point in hiring another governess. You have all the accomplishments that a young lady of your station needs and are more than ready to assume your proper position in society. I recommended that he make other arrangements for your future."

Sara looked bewildered. "But what other arrangements can there be?" she asked.

"That I cannot tell you," Deborah replied, "because I do not know myself. I presume Mr. Kirby will tell us when he arrives today."

Sara was silent for a long while thinking about this odd turn of events. She had never really thought about the future but somehow had assumed it would be much like the past. She suddenly felt confused and more than a little frightened.

A footman arrived shortly after noon bearing a basket containing baked chicken wings, meat pasties, a wheel of cheese and peaches. He set up a small table for them and laid out the repast.

Nibbling on a chicken wing, Sara looked across at her companion. "You have met my father, have you not?"

"Yes, I have," Deborah replied, uncertain why she would ask the question now after all these years.

"Tell me about my family."

The governess looked uncomfortable. "You probably know as much as I do from reading the papers."

"No, I do not agree. There is too much that simply does not make sense. I have given the matter a great deal of thought, as you might expect, and have come to some conclusions, but there is much I do not understand."

"Like what?"

"My main assumption is that my father loved my mother very deeply and somehow holds me responsible for her death. Is that correct?"

Deborah nodded solemnly. "And for the fact that you were not born a boy. Since the death of Lord Charles, he has no direct heir."

Sara digested this for a moment. It had not occurred to her before, but she realized the truth of it. "Yes, I see. But tell me why my aunt and grandmother have ignored me also. They were not in love with my mother."

Deborah lowered her eyes. This was going to hurt the girl and she did not want to be the one to tell her. Damn the duke, she thought inelegantly, not for the first time. How could he have been so thoughtless? "They do not know of your existence," she said finally in a quiet voice.

Sara dropped the chicken wing. "What?"

"When your father returned to London, he said that you had been stillborn."

There was a long silence during which Deborah focused on slicing the cheese wheel. At last she could not stand it and looked across the table. Sara was sitting absolutely still, her head bowed and tears coursing down her cheeks. Deborah jumped up and ran around the table to throw her arms comfortingly around the girl. "Oh, Sara," she murmured, "I am so sorry. I never wanted to be the one to tell you."

"Does everyone here know?" she asked in a choked voice.

"Yes," was all Deborah could say.

"I see." She pulled a handkerchief out of her pocket and wiped her face. "Thank you, Deb. I am glad you told me." Regaining her composure with an effort, she asked, "What about my mother? Did she have any family?"

"Yes, a brother who is widowed with four small children, and a spinster sister who resides with him."

"Where do they live?"

"Up north somewhere. I am not completely certain."

"And they, too, think I died." It was a statement more than a question.

"Yes."

"This has been most enlightening. Now we had best get back to our painting. It will soon be time to return to the house for Mr. Kirby's visit."

A look of concern crossed Deborah's face. She wished that the girl had just let herself cry it all out rather than withdrawing this way. Damn the duke, she thought again.

They were seated in the Green Parlor waiting for Mr. Kirby's arrival. Lady Sara had changed into a blue-striped day dress that enhanced the exotic color of her eyes. She had brushed her hair until it shone, the black curls forming a perfect frame for her heart-shaped face.

Fenton entered, an odd expression on his face. "My Lady," he said, clearing his throat, "His Lordship, the Duke of Darnton."

She looked at him, stunned. "The duke? My father?" she gasped. "Send him in." She rose uncertainly to her feet. Why had he not warned her? She wondered if she looked all right. Why had she worn this old gown? What had happened to Mr. Kirby? A million thoughts jumbled through her brain as she waited to greet the father she had never seen, except in the portrait in the library.

As he entered the room, they stared at each other for a long moment, like opponents. He was tall and slender, his brown hair thinning slightly and streaked with gray. His bearing was straight, almost regal. There were dark shadows under his eyes and it was obvious from his pale complexion that most of his activities were nocturnal. He turned even paler as he beheld the girl in front of him—a stunned look crossing his somewhat harsh features. She was the absolute image of her late mother and he felt as if he had just encountered a ghost. This was the last thing he had expected—the one time he had seen her, she had been a wrinkled infant just a few hours old. For the first time in his life, he was at a complete loss, struggling for words.

It was Lady Sara who pulled together her composure and approached this man who had ignored her all of her life. She held out her hand and curtsied demurely. "Good afternoon, Father," she said in a stilted tone. "We were not expecting you. Will you join us for tea?"

"Yes, thank you," he said in a voice that trembled slightly. He took her hand and raised it briefly to his lips.

As she poured the tea, she indicated her governess who was watching them curiously. "I believe you know Miss Sanders?"

"Yes, of course," he said, recollecting his manners. "Good afternoon, Miss Sanders."

"Good afternoon, my Lord," she said, rising to her feet and dropping a curtsey. "I have some duties to attend to if you would like to be alone with your daughter."

"No," he said hastily. "Our conversation will concern you also. That is why I have come." He took the cup that Lady Sara held out to him and sat on the edge of the brocade sofa, obviously ill at ease.

There was an uncomfortable silence for a few moments, then he looked at his daughter and said, "You are sixteen now."

She nodded in confirmation and waited for him to continue. "Miss Sanders has informed me that it is her intention to set up a school and thus will be leaving my employ in the near future." He glanced at the governess, who also nodded confirmation. "She has also said that she feels you no longer need a governess."

Again there was silence. At last he continued, "Since I cannot leave you here alone, I have decided that you shall make your come-out early."

The two women exchanged expressive looks. When he did not continue, Sara asked, "What exactly do you mean, Father?"

He glanced at her impatiently. "Exactly what I said, girl. My mother has offered to sponsor you for the season. We know you are too young, but you have been properly trained and your ancestry and wealth will overcome any objections. You will go to London Friday week. I will make all the arrangements." He set down his teacup and stood up. "And now I must return to London." He nodded to Deborah and again kissed his daughter's hand briefly. "I am sure I will see you there occasionally." With that he was gone.

The two women stared at each other for a moment, then started to laugh. Throwing their arms around each other, they did a little dance.

"I am going to London!" Sara exclaimed. "Oh, Deb, I cannot believe it. This is fantastic! Can you imagine? I am going to have my first season!"

"Oh, love, I am so happy for you. Who would ever have imagined that he would do something so wonderful? And the duchess as your sponsor! After all these years of pretending you did not exist and now this. It must have come as quite a shock to her to discover she had a sixteen-year-old granddaughter." She hoped that it had been a painful interview for the duke, then bit down the unworthy thought.

"Deb, it is beyond anything great! I just wish you could go with me."

"No, my dear," she said. "My school is what I want. But we will stay in touch. I expect at least one letter a week. And I want to know everything—the people you meet, the functions you attend, what you wear. . . ."

They spent the rest of the afternoon and all evening discussing the promised debut and the wonders and delights of London. They talked about the current fashions and pored through the magazines looking for the exact styles that would best suit her features, and the fabrics that would bring out her coloring.

The next few days passed in a whirl. Sara received a letter from her grandmother expressing surprise at her existence, regret that they had never met, formally inviting her for the season, and detailing the travel arrangements that had been made on her behalf.

It was Wednesday night of the week she was scheduled to leave that there came a knock on the door. She had just sat down to dinner with Deborah in the formal dining room when Fenton entered.

"I am sorry to disturb you, my Lady, but Mr. Kirby has arrived and wishes to speak to you."

She looked at him, a startled expression crossing her face. "This is odd," she said. "I expected him on my birthday, not today. Would you send him in, please?"

The little lawyer entered the room, looking uncomfortably at Sara. His expression was even more somber than usual. He bowed to her briefly as she indicated a chair.

"Please sit down, Mr. Kirby. Would you care to join us for dinner? The fare is plain but ample."

"No, though I thank you, Lady Liviscombe," he replied. "I will not be staying long." He rubbed his forehead. "I am afraid I bring deeply distressing news." He paused.

"Pray continue, Mr. Kirby. No reality is worse than dreading the unknown."

He nodded. "Very succinct, Lady Liviscombe." He took a deep breath. "Your father, the Duke of Darnton, was killed in a—a—an accident Monday night," he stammered.

She stared at him blankly for a long moment. She tried to feel something but could not. He was a man she had seen but once in her life. The only concrete thought that passed through her mind was that she would now have to go into mourning and would not have her London debut. She knew the thought was unworthy, but why should she care about the death of a man who had so patently not cared about her?

"How did it happen?" she asked at last, not knowing what else to say. Somehow, expressions of sympathy did not seem appropriate.

The lawyer looked even more uncomfortable. "It is not easy to explain, Lady Liviscombe."

She looked at him intently. Though young, she was no fool and had read enough about her father in the newspapers to know fairly well what went on in his life in London. "I gather it was a duel," she said flatly.

He looked at her, startled. "Yes, that's right."

"So what happens now?" she asked reasonably.

"Now?" he repeated, at a loss for words in the presence of this oppressively collected child. "Well, immediately, your father will be buried here in Somerset in the family tomb on Saturday. I have made arrangements for the body to be sent down. As you are aware, there can be no thought of you going to London. The required mourning period is one year. I have spoken to your grandmother, Lady Darnton, and she is in agreement that since your governess"—and here he glared at Deborah as if she were a traitor—"is leaving next week, you need some female to give you countenance. We researched your family and found that, besides the duchess, you only have two female relatives left. We contacted Eloise Farley, your mother's sister, but she is committed to her brother's family. That only leaves your father's sister." He took a deep breath and wrinkled his brow. "I do not like the idea of that woman being in contact with an impressionable girl, but I see no other course of action. It will only be for a year, until the mourning period is done, and then you will go to your grandmother's for your come-out, as planned."

Again, she stared at him, but this time there was a look of surprise in her eyes. "Bertie?" she queried.

He reddened slightly and stared blankly down at the table, refusing to meet her gaze. "Yes, Lady Alberta Watson," he answered in a strained voice.

She was laughing inwardly, but kept her outer composure. "And when will my aunt arrive? Have you contacted her?"

He was positively squirming in his seat now. "Yes, I have. She will be here on the morrow. It turns out that this is a good time for her to be away from London."

"I can imagine," she murmured under her breath, remembering the story of the race to Newcastle. From all the accounts she had read, Bertie had been entangled with half the male members of the *ton* and periodically had to disappear when the water got too hot. Deborah was looking her disapproval, but Sara was pleased at the prospect of meeting her infamous aunt.

Lady Alberta Watson turned out to be all that Sara could have wanted. She was a tiny, vivacious blonde who burst upon Langton like a small whirlwind. She had a well-developed appreciation for life's pleasures and a patent disregard for society's prohibitions.

Aunt and niece hit it off from the start. Bertie was the worst possible choice for a young lady's mentor. She regaled her niece with accounts of her exploits and filled her head with the most shocking gossip. She was a little daunted by Deborah's unforgiving morality and was glad when the governess moved to her school.

"I do not know how you ever endured that Friday-faced woman," she said to Sara after Deborah left. "She would have driven me to distraction."

"I love Deborah very much, Bertie," Sara said defensively.

"Oh, my dear, I am sure she is a very good sort of person, but I could tell she disapproves of me. I am not all that bad, you know, I just cannot take things so seriously."

Her niece had to laugh at that. "So I have gathered."

Sara had been sorry to see Deborah leave, but she had to admit that Bertie more than filled the void. As the months went on and she spent more time in the company of her aunt, her perceptions of life among the *ton* changed radically. She had been carefully instructed in the strict codes and rules that governed a young lady's behavior. Now she was becoming aware of the reality behind the structured facade.

By the time the mourning period was over, she was convinced that women only married to have the freedom to discreetly keep lovers and that men only married to have an heir, while they not so discreetly kept lovers. Life in London sounded like one huge game of musical beds.

At the conclusion of the year, Sara gave up her blacks and prepared for her journey to London.

"Do you come with me, Bertie?" she asked as they sat at dinner on the anniversary of her father's death.

"No, not now," her aunt said lightly. "For one thing, Mama specifically disinvited me. She believes that my dubious reputation will hinder her attempts to launch you successfully, though honestly, I do not see what that has to do with anything. She entrusts you to me for a full year, then does not want us to be seen together. Honestly, Mama has the strangest ideas."

Sara smiled at this. "I am looking forward to meeting my grandmother. But is there another reason?" she said archly.

Bertie grinned. "The less said on that topic the better. Besides, you are not supposed to know anything about it."

Sara just nodded. "Of course, dear Aunt, I know nothing."

True to form, Bertie had not wasted her time in Somerset. Within weeks of her arrival, she had discovered the most attractive man in the neighborhood and, despite her mourning for her brother, had managed to enjoy herself quite thoroughly.

And so it was that Lady Sara Liviscombe, the only child of the Duke of Darnton, arrived in London, aware of the laws governing polite behavior, but not placing much importance on them. She was worldly and naive, old and young, a woman and a child. She was unfamiliar with society, but very knowledgeable about people. She knew far more than she should have for her age, but had no practical experience. She and the time were ripe for mischief.

Chapter Two

London, 1801

LADY SARA LEFT LANGTON IN THE EARLY MORN-
ing of a perfect autumn day. Though excited
about the prospect before her, it was the first
time she had ever traveled out of Somerset and
she felt a certain trepidation. She was especially nervous about meeting her grandmother.
Although Bertie had tried to reassure her that
the dowager duchess was not nearly the dragon
that the papers reported Sara was not convinced. Not for the first time in her life, she
was grateful she had her own money. At least
she would not have to feel financially indebted
to her grandmother on top of everything else.

She had brought a book to read along the way
but found all the new sights much too fascinating. The carriage that had been sent for her
was well sprung and extremely comfortable, so
the trip turned out to be a pleasure. She had
been instructed to bring her maid, Agnes, but

very few clothes since the dowager duchess suspected she had nothing at all suitable for a season in London. On this score, she was exactly right. Life in Somerset had been very quiet and the newest gown she owned was two years old.

They spent one night on the road in a small inn that turned out to be very clean and pleasant. Again, the duchess had made the arrangements. Sara was increasingly impressed with her thoroughness.

They arrived in London late the following afternoon. Sara was awed by the teeming city. Everything seemed to be in motion. All the noise, bustle and seeming chaos overwhelmed her a little. She had read about this fabled city but had no idea of the magnitude of its reality.

As they entered the outskirts, she was appalled by the poverty, by the despair written in the eyes of the young children. By the time they reached the fashionable districts, she was dazzled by the wealth and elegance. She could not help staring at the beautiful gowns of the women and the magnificent attire of the men. Within a few short miles, she felt as if she had passed through two different worlds.

The carriage stopped in front of an elegant townhouse on Regent Street. The footman climbed down to lower the steps for her. Taking a deep breath, she walked up the front steps and waited while the footman rang the bell. The door opened immediately and a tall, arrogant figure in stark black looked down at her.

"May I be of assistance, madame?" he asked

in ponderous tones as he gazed at the unstylish and ill-clad creature in front of him.

"Yes, I am Lady Sara Liviscombe and I am here to see my grandmother," she replied in a voice that quaked a little, much to her chagrin.

He stepped aside and motioned her in. "Indeed, my Lady. The duchess is expecting you. If you will step this way, I will announce you." He turned to one of the footmen waiting in the hall behind him. "Please see that Lady Liviscombe's luggage is taken to her room and her maid installed in the servants' quarters."

Sara glanced around quickly. The main hall was large with a wide sweeping staircase off to the left leading to the sleeping quarters above. She guessed that the two doors to the right opened on to the parlor and the living room, and the hallway going toward the back of the house led to the dining room and library. Before leaving Langton, she had read up on London and knew that this was a common layout for a townhouse of this style.

The butler led her to the first of the doors on the right and opened it. "Your granddaughter, Lady Sara Liviscombe, has arrived, My Lady," he announced in his pompous accent.

"Send her in, Roberts," replied an imperious voice.

Sara stepped into the room, her stomach filled with butterflies. The room was very dark, the only light provided by the fire that burned cheerfully in the hearth, as if mocking her fears. She stood still, letting her eyes adjust to the dimness.

"Well, come on in, gel," the voice spoke again. "I shan't bite, you know."

She looked toward the sound. Seated in one of a pair of high wing-backed chairs set comfortably before the fireplace was a tiny woman wearing a gown of black velvet, an enormous turban on her head. Sara's first thought was that the headdress was almost as big as the woman. As she approached the chair, she noticed that her face was very wrinkled, but her eyes were a sharp, piercing gray. She had the same aquiline nose that her father had had and Sara guessed that she had been a great beauty in her youth.

"So you are my surprise granddaughter," she said, as Sara curtsied. She looked her over carefully, taking in every detail of her face and figure.

Sara felt more like a horse at an auction than a granddaughter come for the season.

"Hmm," the old woman said at last. "The gown is deplorable, but there is definite promise. Take after your mother—a real beauty that one, but sickly." She paused, reflectively. "You do speak, don't you, gel? Are you some kind of dimwit?"

Her fear was gone now, replaced by a rising anger. "I am decidedly not some kind of dimwit," she replied, drawing herself up to her full height. "I was waiting for you to complete your amazingly rude inspection." She was surprised at her own temerity but resolutely stood her ground.

Lady Darnton stared at her in surprise and then let out a delighted cackle. "So you have spirit, too. Good, very good. Now pull the bell cord and sit down. We have much to discuss."

Sara pulled the cord and Roberts entered immediately, as if he had been waiting outside the door. "You rang, my Lady?"

"Yes, Roberts. You may bring ratafia for my granddaughter, sherry for myself and a plate of seed cakes."

"Very good, my Lady."

As he withdrew, she smiled wickedly at her granddaughter. "Roberts is an excellent butler but so pompous. And now, my dear, tell me about yourself. Your father, when he so gallant-ly told me of your existence"—her voice dripped with sarcasm—"also said that you had been carefully trained in all the social arts."

"Yes, my Lady," Sara replied, her anger dissi-pated, but still feeling uncomfortable.

"Please, dear, not 'my Lady.' Call me Grand-mama or something a little less formal."

She smiled. "Very well, Grandmama."

"That's better. Now where were we? Ah yes, I presume that you dance, do needlework, paint and play the pianoforte?"

"Yes," Sara replied. "I also read, write, speak French and Italian and have a passing knowl-edge of geography, history and mathematics."

Her grandmother looked at her sharply. "Not a bluestocking, are you?"

"Not at all, just well educated."

"Hmm," muttered the old woman. "Well, I think you'll do. How is that scatterbrained daughter of mine? I certainly hope she was not a bad influence."

Sara remembered Bertie and her outrageous

revelations. "She was an interesting part of my education."

"Exactly what I feared."

Roberts entered, followed by a footman who set a tray on the table between them. He served the refreshments and the servants withdrew.

"And now, my dear," the dowager duchess said, sipping her sherry, "we must make our plans. The first thing to do is outfit you properly. We will begin tomorrow." She then proceeded to detail the raiment she considered vital to a young lady's come-out, walking dresses, evening gowns, morning dresses, hats, shoes, gloves, and underclothes.

Sara felt her head reeling. "But Grandmama, I could not wear all of that in a year."

"Nonsense. That is only the beginning." She paused for a moment. "Has Kirby explained the exact circumstances of your inheritance?"

"No. He only said that I have no financial worries and when I am short of funds I am to contact him."

"That sounds like Kirby. Never did think a woman could have a brain in her head. When John died without an heir, the title reverted to my late sister's grandson. Fortunately, the landholdings were not entailed so the title is empty. When John told me about you, I convinced him to write a will leaving you as his sole heir. That means that, upon my death, you will inherit Langton, this place, the estate in Devon and, of course, the family fortune. No indeed, my dear, you have no financial worries. But be aware that many men will pursue you for reasons that are not purely romantic. I am only telling you this so that you will be leery of fortune hunters. And now I am going to rest before dinner. Roberts will show you to your room."

Sara sat on the windowseat of the beautifully appointed bedroom, staring out at the busy street, thinking about what her grandmother had said. She had not suspected she was the sole heir to the Liviscombe fortune, but she realized it made sense.

The next few weeks passed in a whirl of shopping tours, fittings and "at-homes" in which the dowager duchess brought her granddaughter to the attention of the more influential matrons of the *ton*. Soon invitations began to pour in.

The elderly Lady Darnton was delighted at the response. At seventeen, Lady Sara Liviscombe became the darling of fashionable London society. On the occasion of her very first ball, she took the town by storm. From that time on, no ball or route, fete or picnic was considered a success unless she was in attendance. Her beauty, wit, wealth and the slight air of mystery that surrounded her sudden appearance on the scene as the only child of the Duke of Darnton guaranteed her instant popularity.

The season was only a few weeks under way when the Dowager Duchess of Darnton and her granddaughter were invited to a Venetian breakfast held by the elderly lady's dearest friend, Lady Carston. Though well advanced in years, Rosinda Carston was a prominent and influential member of the polite world and only the very best people were invited to her functions. Few ever declined.

Despite the fact that the season was young, Lady Sara was already well known. Toasted and admired wherever she went, she had established a following of eager young men anxious to do her bidding. She enjoyed the attention she was receiving but in the long, gossipy letters she sent to Bertie she invariably referred to her attendants as "friendly puppies" or "adorable children." She had yet to find someone who sparked her wit or intelligence.

For the Carston affair, she wore a very simple morning gown of lilac silk gathered under the bosom by a ribbon of deeper lilac. The flounced hem was edged in the same darker shade. She picked a simple garnet pendant and eardrops for adornment. Agnes dressed her hair to fall loose around her shoulders and placed real lilac blossoms behind her ears. Every time she moved her head she could smell the delicate aroma.

Lady Darnton was delighted by the effect. "Marvelous, my love," she said when Sara joined her in the parlor. "Fresh, young and lovely," she continued, kissing the girl's cheek. "I particularly wanted you to look your best this morning. There is someone I have been anxious for you to meet and I am assured he will be at Lady Carston's this morning."

Sara looked at her, a slightly dazed expression in her lovely eyes. "Surely I have met *all* of the upper ten thousand, Grandmama. 'May I have the pleasure of presenting' is practically my first name."

Lady Darnton only laughed at this. "Let's just say that you have met nine thousand, nine hundred and ninety-nine. There is still one to go."

She peered intently at the old woman for a moment then said, "You are up to something, I can tell. Who exactly is this person?"

"It is a long story, my dear. I will tell you on the way. Do you have your shawl? Then summon Roberts to have the carriage brought round."

They were soon settled in the elegant equipage and the horses given the command to start.

"Now tell me the whole," Sara demanded.

A wistful look crossed the dowager's wrinkled face as she leaned back against the plush blue squabs. "Many years ago," she began, "many, many years ago, I too made my bow to polite society. I was only fifteen at the time. I know you will find it hard to believe but I was quite a looker in my day. Shortly into the season, I attracted the attention of a man considerably older than myself. He was handsome, dashing, intelligent, impetuous—and a rake. He courted me assiduously and I was soon head over ears in love. It was something straight out of a fairy tale. My parents deplored the situation. They had always planned that I should marry the son of our neighbor, the Duke of Darnton. Their reasons were sound—it was a prestigious title and the match would allow the estates to be combined, a strong advantage for both families. Unfortunately, I was young and romantic and while I liked Percy very much— we had, after all, practically grown up together —it was Robert whom I loved." She paused for a moment obviously lost in her memories of the past, a saddened expression settling over her face.

"What happened?" Lady Sara asked gently.

The old woman shook herself slightly and continued. "As it turned out, unbeknownst to me, Robert made an offer for me to my father. It was many years later, after I was settled as a wife and a mother to my own Charles and John, that I discovered the truth of the matter. My father had told my ardent suitor that I was already promised and that the engagement would be announced shortly. He also instructed him not to see me anymore. All I knew was that suddenly Robert dropped out of sight. Distraught and broken-hearted, I did my parents' bidding and within three months was the Duchess of Darnton."

Lady Sara looked at her in outrage. "But how monstrous!" she exclaimed. "You were never even consulted?"

"No, my dear, but in those days, as is still so often the case, the bride's desires had nothing to say to the matter of matrimony. It was the well-being of the families involved that was the uppermost consideration."

"And what happened to Robert? Is that whom I am to meet today?"

Her grandmother chuckled, albeit a little sadly. "Hardly, my dear. Robert married a few years later, then died in a hunting accident shortly after the birth of his son. In due time the boy also married and had two sons. It is the elder of these whom you will meet today. Since his father is dead he has taken the title. His name is Randolph Ketcham and he is the Viscount of Awick."

Sara's eyes opened wide as she stared at her grandmother. She had heard of the notorious Lord Awick at every function she had attended but had never really thought her family would allow her to meet him. Like his grandfather, he was reputed to be handsome, dashing, intelligent, impetuous—and a rake. "But Grandmama," she said in amazement. "Surely this is not the sort of man with whom you wish me to be associated."

The dowager duchess looked at her in surprise. "But why not? It is an old, honorable and exceedingly wealthy family. What objection could there be?"

The girl felt herself color as she lowered her eyes and replied demurely. "But his reputation! Do you honestly wish me to seek the attentions of a— of a—," she stammered to a halt.

Her grandmother stared at her for a moment then broke into a delighted chuckle. "Of a rake, my dear? Come, I thought you had more common sense and that Bertie would have squelched your more squeamish feelings. Our society is filled with people who dislike those whom they cannot manipulate and who resent those with the freedom and courage to do as they please. Randy comes and goes as he chooses and is financially able to do so. I will not gainsay that he is a rake but why should he

43

not be? He is a wonderfully elegant and fascinating man and I think you will like him."

At this point the carriage drew up in front of Lady Carston's opulent estate on the outskirts of London. As they presented their cards to the butler, they were allowed a glimpse into the elegant long hall where the breakfast was to be held. The tables glistened with leaded crystal and silver flatware, and bowls profuse with cut flowers lent color and a delicious aroma to the setting. Many people were already present sipping champagne and chatting happily, adding their own gay colors and scents.

As the ladies proceeded into the hall, they were met first by their hostess, who hugged her friend of many years, then graciously welcomed Lady Sara. "You look lovely today, my dear," she greeted. "Almost as pretty as your grandmother in her salad days. Do come in. I trust you will find my little entertainment enjoyable."

They exchanged pleasantries with numerous friends and acquaintances and accepted glasses of ratafia which they sipped delicately as they circulated about the hall. Soon Lady Darnton nudged the girl and nodded discreetly. "Over there near the fireplace, the tall gentlemen with the black hair. That is Randy Ketcham."

Sara looked to where her grandmother indicated and felt the blood drain out of her face. He was considerably older than she, probably in his early thirties. He was indeed exceptionally tall and his thick black hair was pulled back into a queue. He wore a perfectly fitted dove-gray coat that showed off his broad shoulders and narrow waist. The unmentionables he wore of the same dove-gray exhibited a pair of well-muscled legs. He moved with the languid grace of a born athlete. The frothy white cravat was a perfect foil for his dark complexion and strong features. This was the man she had dreamed about ever since she was old enough to know that the species came in two sexes. She noticed that he was approaching them and she hastily turned away, afraid that her feelings might be too obvious. She took a couple of deep breaths as she heard a deep, melodious voice directly behind her.

"Lady Darnton," he said, executing a low and elegant bow. "I am delighted to see you looking so well. You have an exquisite secret for hiding the years." The old lady only laughed at this and tapped his arm teasingly with her fan.

As Sara turned to gaze up at him, his piercing blue-gray eyes opened slightly from their usual sardonic squint. "And this must be your granddaughter of whom I have heard so much."

Lady Darnton beamed. "Indeed it is. May I have the pleasure of presenting Lady Sara Liviscombe?" She almost choked as she remembered the girl's earlier words then rapidly swallowed and continued. "My dear, I wish you to make the acquaintance of the grandson of a dear friend. This is Randolph Ketcham, the Viscount of Awick."

By now Sara had somewhat regained her composure, but she felt her heart begin to pound as he took her hand and raised it to his lips. "It is a pleasure, my Lord," she said demurely.

"The pleasure is mine, I assure you," he replied, retaining her hand slightly longer than etiquette demanded. "I hope you will do me the honor of being my companion at table."

Her grandmother gave her consent to this as he tucked the girl's hand under his arm and led her away.

"So you are the mysterious Lady Sara. I must admit that I have been extremely curious to meet you. Since my return to town, I have heard nothing but your praises sung."

She looked at him in momentary bewilderment. "I do not fully comprehend your meaning, my Lord," she said. "I do not believe I am in the least bit mysterious. I do however thank you for the compliment and I, as well as every other member of the *ton*, would love to know where you have been."

He stared down at her for a brief moment then laughed delightedly as another couple approached and engaged them in a brief conversation. When they were again alone, he said, "It is a true joy to meet a girl who can actually utter three statements in a row. I knew you would be a cut above the ordinary."

She gazed up at him perplexedly. "How would you know any such thing?" she asked. "And you have not answered me."

They greeted yet another couple, then he led her to the side of the mirrored hall where they could be more private, chaperoned only by a potted palm. "I knew because your grandmother was such a beautiful woman in her day. There is still a portrait of her at Rotham Abbey that I understand my grandfather insisted on keeping despite the objections of my grandmother. You are mysterious because no one ever dreamed that Darnton's child had survived. John was quite a close friend of mine and I too believed that you had died at birth. I must admit I was amazed to learn of your existence and find it incredible that John would have kept you hidden away all these years. Of course he loved Olivia deeply but still . . ." he broke off as he noticed the anguished look that crossed her lovely face. "Oh, I am sorry," he said, taking her hands in his. "How perfectly thoughtless of me. I did not mean to distress you."

She looked down and again felt the color drain from her cheeks. She could not be sure if it was the thought of her father's abandonment or the fact that Lord Awick still had possession of her hands. "That is quite all right," she said quietly, returning her gaze to his, an impish look appearing in her huge blue eyes. "Now you must tell me where you have been. I am sure you know that your whereabouts have been the source of intense speculation."

Again he laughed, "That is a subject that I do not think we should pursue."

Her curiosity piqued, she asked, "Why ever not?" Then she lowered her voice to whisper conspiratorially, "Are you a spy? Have you been to France acting against Bonaparte?"

He only chuckled as he stopped a passing footman bearing a tray and acquired a glass of ratafia for her and a glass of champagne for himself. "Hardly," he said at last, looking a little sheepish. "Nothing nearly so patriotic."

"To America then, fighting the Indians?"

He raised one dark eyebrow. "I was gone only two weeks. You certainly have a romantic notion of my activities. No, not at all. In fact I have not been out of England and, as I said, I do not intend to tell you."

"But why not?" she asked again, gazing steadily at him.

"There are certain masculine pursuits that gently bred young ladies should know nothing about," he replied, a wicked gleam in his eye.

She thought about this for a moment as she recalled the exploits of her father that she had read about in the papers. "Was it a carriage race or a mill or—?"

He held out one elegant hand and gently touched her mouth. "Enough," he said. "Obviously my reputation has preceded me. Come, let us be seated. I believe that breakfast is about to be served."

She started to protest but he had already taken possession of her arm and was purposefully leading her to one of the smaller tables that sat only twelve near the huge stone fireplace where a cheerfully glowing fire was exuding a soft, romantic light.

Lady Carston had taken advantage of the looser formalities of a Venetian breakfast and refused to set out name placards. She claimed it was much more interesting to see how her guests wished to place themselves and that usually the balance came out right anyway. Of course this also meant that a great deal of gossip was given birth at her affairs. This particular morning proved no exception. Everyone in the hall noted that Lord Awick—the professed bachelor and confirmed rake who assiduously shied away from the innocent young girls of his own class—had requested Lady Sara to be his companion and was obviously very much enjoying the situation. This *was* a departure. There would be much tongue wagging and a good deal of speculation at teatime this day.

Awick was perfectly aware of what was happening. He had lived his entire life among these people and knew their every thought and conjecture. But for once he did not mind the inevitable gossip. If Lady Sara lived up to her earlier promise, it was well worth the price in leading questions and innuendoes. As for Lady Sara herself, she was too fresh and new at the game to understand the implications of Awick's attentions. Totally unaware that she and her escort were the object of every eye in the room, she was flattered by the viscount's interest and anxious to pursue their conversation. She had not enjoyed herself so much during her entire stay in London.

As Lady Carston's well-trained and highly efficient staff brought platter after platter of steamed clams, kippered eggs, hot muffins, fresh fruit, smoked ham and a variety of cheeses, Lord Awick and Lady Sara laughed and talked, seemingly oblivious to the people around them.

Lady Darnton watched them closely from her

position a few tables away. Despite her earlier words, she did have some qualms about her granddaughter's association with the viscount —not because she did not trust him but rather because she did not wish the tattle-mongers to begin idle gossip that might eventually harm the girl's reputation if nothing substantial developed between the two of them. She was pleased to note that they had obviously taken to each other. She could not remember ever having seen Awick talk so long or express so much interest in an innocent young girl. She might not have been so pleased were she privy to their current conversation.

"Was it a cock fight?" Sara was whispering.

Awick choked suddenly on a piece of ham. When he had recovered he asked austerely, "Was *what* a cock fight?"

"Why, where you have been," she replied innocently.

"I have already told you, my Lady, that I have no intention of discussing the matter with you. Now eat your breakfast like a good girl."

She looked down at her plate but only chewed her lip thoughtfully. The viscount breathed a barely audible sigh of relief, believing the matter at last closed. He did not know her very well. She gave him a long sideways look, then said knowingly, "You have been on holiday with your latest lady bird."

Once again he choked and at the same time felt color flood into his cheeks. Oh Lord, he thought as the other people at the table turned to stare at him, this dratted girl has put me to the blush. "Will you please keep your voice down if you insist on making comments like that?" he whispered severely. "I do not wish all of London to be aware of *all* my doings."

She grinned at him in triumph. "So I was right!" she crowed in a slightly lowered voice.

"I did not say you were right. I only meant that I do not want statements like that being made as if it were fact and not just a wild guess."

"If you would tell me the whole, I would not *have* to guess," she replied reasonably.

His tone was exasperated as he said, "Honestly, my Lady, why are you so persistent?"

"Because you are so secretive and everyone has been speculating about it. If you had told me at the outset I probably would not have been in the least bit interested."

He stared at her for a long moment noting the roguish look in her eye. At last he lowered his voice even further and said, "I did not want to tell you because it might put your life in jeopardy."

"What?" Her eyes flew wide open.

He felt himself increasingly attracted as he leaned closer to her. "If you promise to keep your voice down and never reveal to another soul what I am about to tell you, I will confide the truth of the matter."

"I promise," she whispered solemnly, unconsciously crossing her heart in the old schoolgirl gesture.

He restrained a laugh as he noticed this, then said, "You have probably heard that I am extremely wealthy and am able to come and go very much as I wish."

She nodded, and continued to stare at him intently.

His voice was now so low that she had to lean closer to him to hear what he was saying. He enjoyed the fresh scent of the lilac and the innocent closeness of her. "Actually, I am the leader of a highly successful smuggling ring operating in Lands End. We bring in brandy and textiles and occasionally perform small tasks for the government."

She stared at him, her eyes and mouth rounded in an expression of horror. "Whose?" she breathed.

"I beg your pardon?" he asked, puzzled by this reaction.

"Whose government?" she whispered.

He glared at her, deeply offended. "Why, ours, of course. What do you think me, dishonest?"

She looked away, confused and uncertain. She certainly had not meant to anger him. "I am sorry," she murmured, refusing to meet his gaze. "I just thought that smuggling was not completely—honest . . ." Her voice trailed off.

He felt a perfect beast as he noted her downcast face. Slipping a hand under the table to take hold of hers, he began "Please, My Lady . . ."

Much to his consternation, Lady Darnton approached them at this moment. Addressing her granddaughter, she said, "It is time we were on our way, my dear. I hope you have enjoyed the morning but we have much to do this day." She nodded to Awick. "As always, it was a pleasure to see you again, Randy."

Equally unhappy at the interruption of this interesting conversation, Sara nevertheless took the hint and, reluctantly freeing her hand, rose. "Yes, indeed, Grandmama. We have much to do." She turned to her companion. "It was a delight to meet you, Lord Awick. I hope our paths will cross again soon. I would sincerely enjoy continuing our discussion. Your—ah—hobby sounds fascinating."

He also rose and again took possession of her hand. He bowed deeply as he said, "I too would enjoy that and feel certain we will meet again. In fact I intend to make it a point that we do."

Lady Sara was unusually subdued on the way home. At last her grandmother turned to her and inquired if she was feeling quite the thing. Rousing herself, she asked, "What do you know about Lord Awick's source of wealth?"

"The source?" Lady Darnton repeated in surprised accents. "Why, it is inherited of course. Whatever makes you ask such a thing?"

The girl was silent for a long moment then said, "Oh, I just wondered. It is obvious he is very well-heeled."

"Exceedingly. The family has been exceptionally prudent in its investments and has never been cursed with inveterate gamblers or loose screws."

"Mm," was all she replied, more curious than ever about the viscount but reluctant to

pursue the matter further with her grandmother.

Lord Awick proved to be good to his word.
The following morning, as the ladies sat at
breakfast, there came a knock at the door.
Roberts entered to announce the arrival of his
Lordship.

Lady Darnton looked to her granddaughter,
who blushed and turned away, then said calmly, "Please show him in, Roberts, and instruct
the maid to set another place at the table." As
the butler bowed himself out, she smiled.
"Well, my dear, you must have made a signifi-
cant impression. It's not like Randy to be up
and about at this hour, let alone to be paying
calls on innocent girls. Play your cards right
and you will have an offer."

Sara stared at her as the words sank in then
abruptly all color drained from her lovely face.
"But, Grandmama," she stammered. "I have
never known a married couple. I have no idea
what is expected of me or how to proceed!"

A flood of sympathy washed through Lady
Darnton at her granddaughter's plaintive
words and again she silently cursed her de-
ceased son as she recalled his cavalier abandonment of her. She wanted to say something
reassuring but Roberts was already showing
Lord Awick into the room.

He bowed to the ladies and kissed their
hands, then asked for the privilege of taking
Lady Sara on a drive through the park.

Lady Darnton gave her permission but asked
the viscount first to partake of breakfast. He

graciously accepted and took the chair next to Sara. As the footman plied him with offers of poached eggs, sliced sirloin, toast and coffee, he regaled them with stories of his family.

"Did you know, my Lady, that Grandfather kept the portrait he had done of you at Rotham Abbey?"

The old woman displayed an uncharacteristic blush. "Why no," she replied. "I had no idea. Did not your Grandmother object?"

"Oh indeed. But you know he had a true stubborn streak."

Lady Darnton only laughed at this.

"I was raised with that portrait," Lord Awick continued, "and I thought that you were the most beautiful woman in the world. That was before I met your granddaughter."

It was Sara's turn to blush, which she did charmingly. "Thank you, my Lord," she whispered.

As they all fell silent, Lady Darnton asked the viscount about his younger brother. Immediately a glow of pleasure appeared in his usually sardonic eyes.

"Freddie is doing fine," he replied. "He is supposedly at Eton except when he gets sent down which seems to be the case more often than not at the moment. He has gotten himself involved in the usual schoolboy pranks that the deans tend to frown upon." There was a definite reminiscent air about him as he said this.

"I take it, my Lord," Sara said impishly, "that you are not a total stranger to those types of pranks."

He laughed ruefully as he said, "No indeed,

but it is not a subject to be discussed over breakfast with two well-bred ladies. If you are finished, I think we should be on our way."

Lady Darnton acquiesced and Lady Sara ran up to her room for her bonnet and wrap. When she had left, the dowager duchess turned to Awick. "I trust everything is as it should be, Randy." Her tone was questioning.

"Indeed," he replied. "I am sure you know my sentiments and that I will not cause her grief. It is too soon to speak but rest assured that my intentions are totally honorable . . . for once."

They both laughed and the subject was dropped. Sara soon returned and the two took their leave. Awick handed her up into his high-perch phaeton, then took his place at her side. As he gave the spirited team the office to start he turned to her and said seriously, "I must admit that I overheard some of the conversation you had with your grandmother while I was being shown in. I never gave it much thought before but I realize now that it must have been very difficult for you to grow up in a world comprised only of servants."

She shrugged lightly. "Oh, maybe in a way. I do not think I ever thought much about it—at least at the time." She was not yet familiar enough with Awick to confide her private thoughts and fears. Uncomfortable with the situation, she changed the subject. "Now tell me about the smuggling business." She gazed innocently up at him.

He turned to her, a slight frown crossing his handsome features. She looked lovely in her morning gown of jonquil satin, the chip bonnet tied rakishly below her left ear with yellow ribbon. She was such a charming sight that he grinned and chucked her gently under the chin. "I believe you know full well that I was roasting you, my dear." As she nodded, he continued in a sheepish tone. "My nefarious pursuits amounted to no more than a hunting expedition with some friends. *Male* friends," he added pointedly.

She looked absurdly crestfallen at this statement. "Oh," was all she said as she looked away.

He laughed again then turned serious as she refused to meet his eyes. "What is it? Do you prefer me to be a romantic hero?"

She thought for a moment then replied with equal seriousness, "Yes, yes, I think I do."

"And what is your image of a romantic hero?"

Again she paused. "Someone strong and kind and intelligent and . . . and . . . oh, I do not think I can describe it."

He slowed the horses and placed one finger under her chin to raise her face to his. They looked at each other for a long moment then he said gently, "Someone who sweeps you off your feet."

She colored delicately and murmured quietly, "Yes."

He smiled at this open disarming statement. "I will do my best."

He turned the horses into the park and they drove along the lane, greeting the other early risers of the *ton*. They spoke of their homes and families and upbringings. At his acute interest and sympathy, Sara found herself opening up and talking of her more secret hopes and fears that she had not been able to speak of to anyone before. Awick sensed that this was a big step for her and was very careful in the way he led the conversation.

At last he returned her to her grandmother's townhouse, promising to meet her that night at the Ailey ball. He asked what she was wearing and she described the beautiful pink gown that Lady Darnton had given her.

That evening as she was dressing for the event, a footman knocked on the door to present her a corsage of tiny pink rosebuds set about with white baby's breath—a perfect match for the gown. The card was simple:

My dear Lady Sara—
A romantic hero requires a charming heroine. I have found mine.

She clasped the note to her breast. This was indeed the man of whom she had dreamed.

Lady Darnton was equally pleased when she saw the corsage and learned who had sent it. She had been concerned at first but as the days wore on and her superior spy network began keeping tabs on Awick's activities, she discovered that since he had met Sara he had given up the lady bird he had been keeping and in fact had foresworn all his more questionable pursuits. It was obvious his interest in Sara was serious.

The members of the *ton* very soon realized

which way the wind was blowing in that quarter. It rapidly became apparent that if Lady Sara was present at a function, Lord Awick would be also. And when they were together, they saw no one else. It was not long before bets were being placed at White's on when the wedding would occur. There was never a question of it.

For Sara, it was a magical time. She was still young enough to be pleased and impressed by her own success and Lord Awick was a figure straight out of a fairy tale. Before her debut, she had attended some of the country balls back in Somerset and met the sons of the local squires, but nothing could compare with the sheer elegance and worldly air of the viscount.

It seemed natural to have him as her constant escort and companion. Rarely did a day pass when they did not attend a ball or play, a breakfast or musical evening. On nice days, he took her driving in the park in his high-perch phaeton pulled by two perfectly matched bays. On wet days, they visited art galleries and museums.

It was evident from the start that the seventy-one-year-old Dowager Duchess of Darnton was not up to the rigors of chaperoning a much sought after seventeen-year-old girl. She had grown to love her granddaughter and trust her judgment and, consequently, allowed her much more freedom than was either usual or advisable. Many of her friends warned her about the girl's frequent lack of chaperone and the inordinate amount of time she was spending in the company of Lord

Awick, a man who had been on the town for years and had developed quite a reputation—one that the matrons loved, but not for their daughters. The duchess, however, though privately agreeing with these comments, would not hear a word against her granddaughter and resolved to be more attentive. Unfortunately, her mental resolves did not always get put into action and Lady Sara continued her constant companionship with Lord Awick.

Despite his reputation, the viscount knew the rules and regulations of the *haut ton* much too well to ever take advantage of one of society's daughters. Light skirts from the demimonde were for that purpose. He, too, was aware that Lady Sara had more freedom than she should, but he was careful to keep his behavior perfectly in bounds. He fully intended to marry her and would allow no gossip about his future wife.

And so through the halcyon days of her first season, Sara lived in the best of all possible worlds. She was young, free, innocent and in love—a highly volatile and dangerous situation.

It was the night of the Tishford ball, the closing event of the season. Throughout the day, Sara had had a premonition that something momentous was going to happen to her tonight. She wondered if it would be Awick's long awaited proposal. She awoke early and found herself unable to eat all day. She began to prepare for the ball in the early afternoon. The dowager duchess had sent for a hairdresser who arrived shortly after Sara had finished a long, leisurely bath. He proceeded to coax and tease her hair until it formed an exquisite mass of ringlets falling gently over her shoulders with one lock pulled bewitchingly forward to nestle just above her breast.

Her gown for the occasion was of a deep blue that brought out the color of her eyes. Her grandmother had shunned the whites and pastels typical of young ladies in their first season. Her granddaughter's coloring was much too vivid to allow such pallid conventions.

Sara added just a hint of color to her lips and cheeks and then allowed Agnes to ease the silk confection carefully over her head. The gown was cut low over her breasts, the tiny puffed sleeves ending just below her shoulders. She slipped her feet into blue satin slippers as Agnes helped her draw on the full-length white kid gloves. She fastened the beaded reticule that Deborah had made for her around her wrist while Agnes clasped a sapphire pendant around her throat.

"Oh, miss!" the maid exclaimed. "You look beautiful!"

She examined her reflection in the beveled mirror and nodded to herself. Yes, this was what she had wanted. She was an interesting mixture of innocence and allure. "Thank you, Agnes," she said. "I appreciate your help. And do not wait up for me. I suspect this will be a late night."

Once again, there were butterflies in her stomach as she descended the stairs. She could not rid herself of the feeling that tonight was going to change her life. She knew she was early and would have to wait for her grand-mother, so decided to go to the library to calm her nerves by reading for a while.

She had just reached the landing when she heard a commotion in the entry hall. The first voice she recognized was that of her Aunt Alberta.

"I know I am not expected, Roberts," she was saying, "but as you can see, I am here. And, of course, I am aware that the Tishford ball is tonight. Why do you think I have come? I would not miss it for the world." Just then she spotted her niece. "Sara, my love, you look enchanting. That gown is just perfect."

She ran forward to throw her arms around the girl, who had tripped quickly down the stairs. Giving her a kiss on the cheek, she said, "Now come help me dress. Roberts, send up my bag at once," she called imperiously, running up the stairs. "Honestly, Sara," she confided over her shoulder. "That man is just impossi-ble. I do not know how Mama endures him. Can you imagine him trying to deny me en-trance to the house I grew up in?"

"But, Bertie," Sara said, following in the wake of this tiny whirlwind. "Does Grandma-ma know you are here? She did not mention that you would be attending the ball tonight."

"Oh, she does not know yet," came the blithe reply. "Fortunately, Georgie Tishford is an old friend of mine—we made our come-out togeth-er, you know—and she sent me an invitation. It would be the height of poor manners not to attend."

They made their way to the room which

had been Bertie's when she was making her London debut. Despite the rift that had developed between mother and daughter, the dowager duchess had always kept the room for Bertie's use whenever she needed it.

Her niece looked at her dubiously as she sat down at the vanity table and examined her reflection in the mirror. Somehow she could not believe that her grandmother was going to be pleased by this latest start.

Glancing at the little ormolu clock, Bertie moaned. "Oh dear, however am I to be ready on time, and where the devil is my bag? Sara, my love, could you ring for your maid?"

Within moments Agnes appeared at the door, carrying Bertie's bag.

"Oh, excellent!" Bertie exclaimed. "Take out the gown, would you? It's wrapped in tissue so it should not need pressing. Wait till you see it," she said, turning to Sara. "It is absolutely exquisite, though I am not sure Mama will approve."

Dear Lord, Sara thought to herself, this is all the situation needs to become a disaster. She knew Bertie well enough to know that the gown had to be positively risqué. It should prove to be a fascinating evening. "Why did you not arrive earlier?" she asked. "If you had arrived yesterday we would have had plenty of time."

"Yes, I thought of that, but then I figured that if I came down just as Mama was ready to leave, she would be too surprised to try to convince me not to attend."

Sara saw the wisdom of this and nodded. The duchess would certainly be surprised, but, she feared, not pleasantly.

Bertie instructed Agnes to take out the slip next and dampen it.

"Oh no, Bertie!" Sara exclaimed. "You know you should not! Grandmama will have a fit!"

Bertie shrugged her lovely shoulders. "But the gown looks so much better that way. Not to worry, my dear, you will see."

Sara's misgivings were increasing by the moment. She had expected the evening to be momentous but not quite in this way. Agnes soon returned with the dampened slip. She helped Bertie out of her traveling dress and into the wet garment. Next she coaxed her hair into a riot of blond curls that perfectly framed her face, while Sara applied rouge to her lips and cheeks. And, finally, they both eased the gown over her head. It was made of a sheer silk in a brilliant tone of coral. It was cut so low in the front that Sara was afraid her nipples would show. The dampened slip caused the narrow skirt to cling seductively to her legs. Bertie fastened a single ruby pendant around her throat that nestled suggestively between her full breasts. She did indeed look beautiful and there was no fear that she would go unnoticed.

She examined her reflection critically in the pier glass for a moment. "Yes, I think that will do," she said with a complacent smile. She turned to her niece. "Shall we go down and face the dragon?"

When they reached the main hall, the butler

approached, looking disapprovingly at Bertie. He turned to Lady Sara. "Her Ladyship is awaiting you in the parlor. Do you wish me to send for the carriage?"

"Yes please, Roberts."

He opened the parlor door for them, then summoned a footman.

They found the duchess seated in her favorite wing-backed chair. She was dressed in a gown of pearl-gray velvet, on her head a black turban with a single white ostrich plume forming a curved arc sweeping down to her shoulder. She looked up and, at first, only saw her granddaughter.

"Ah, lovely, my dear!" she exclaimed. "Just lov—" She broke off abruptly and rose to her feet. "Alberta Carolyn Liviscombe Watson! What in blazes are you doing here? I specifically warned you to stay out of London." She raked over her daughter from head to foot with a withering gaze and a small shudder shook her frame. "And what do you call that getup? You look like a lady bird."

Bertie colored but looked her mother straight in the eye. "I will be all the rage as you very well know, Mama. Georgie Tishford specifically invited me to her ball and I see no reason why I should not attend."

"You know your reputation as well as I do, Alberta," she retorted, "and I do not want you to have a negative effect on my granddaughter's."

"Oh come now, Mama," Bertie replied reasonably. "She has been out for an entire season and has become the toast of the town. Everyone knows she is my niece and that fact has not hurt her at all. Let her stand on her own—no one else can make or break her now."

The old lady thought about this for a moment and begrudgingly saw the logic in her daughter's words. Still, she was unhappy about both her presence at the ball and, more particularly, about that gown. She was going to object again and demand that at least she could wear something decent, but then noticed the set look on her face. Her daughter had a definite mulish streak and was capable of digging in her heels.

"Let's be on our way," she said at last, pointedly brushing past her daughter and heading for the door. "I just hope you do not catch cold, especially with a wet slip," she commented acerbically.

The journey to the Tishfords' was extremely uncomfortable. Mother and daughter exchanged barbed insults while Sara stared silently out the window. At least in the excitement and bustle of Bertie's arrival she had managed to forget her own anxieties. Now she felt them returning. This was the last event of the season. By next week, all the fashionable people would be closing their townhouses and moving to their country estates. If Awick did not propose tonight, it probably meant that he had no intention of doing so.

As if echoing her thoughts, the dowager duchess said, "I intend to close the house next week, my dear. Do you come with me to Devon or do you plan to return to Langton?"

Sara looked at her aunt questioningly. "I would prefer to go home. Do you come with me,

Bertie? If not, I presume I must make arrangements for a companion."

"Yes, indeed," her grandmother commented. "I must admit I had forgotten you would be living there alone. I will find someone for you since I am sure that Alberta has had enough of the rustic pleasures for a while."

Bertie glanced at her searchingly for a moment but saw nothing suspicious. The one piece of information she had carefully kept from her mother was her affair with her baronet. He was, of course, below her station and married, but he was attractive and very masculine and, for the time being, she was enjoying his attentions.

"On the contrary, Mama, I find myself intrigued by the rustic pleasures. And, besides, town life is so flat in the summer." She turned to her niece and grinned. "Thank you, love, for your gracious invitation. I would be delighted to continue my residence with you."

Sara, who knew the situation in Somerset perfectly well, returned her smile. "Excellent. We will leave next week when Grandmama closes the house."

"If you have no objection, I think I will return tomorrow. I only came for the ball tonight and, truly, I do not have clothes enough to stay any longer."

She looked at her aunt knowingly. "Yes, of course. I understand. I will join you there."

The dowager duchess looked from one to the other, aware of an undercurrent, but uncertain what it meant. At that moment, they joined the string of carriages queued up to deposit their elegant, bejewelled passengers to the lushly ornate entertainment rooms of the magnificent Tishford residence.

As they inched their way forward, a gleam of excitement appeared in the old lady's eye. "I love Georgie's entertainments," she breathed, sounding more like a schoolgirl than a grand-mother of one-and-seventy. "You never know what she is going to do, but you can bet it will be spectacular."

At last they arrived at the entrance and the footman lowered the steps. As they walked up the red-carpeted staircase, they greeted vari-ous friends and acquaintances. It was obvious from the flow of people that the evening would, as always, be a dreadful squeeze and, there-fore, a total success.

They gave their names to the butler at the top of the stairs, then proceeded across the foyer to be greeted by Lord and Lady Tishford.

"The Dowager Duchess of Darnton, the Lady Alberta Watson, the Lady Sara Liviscombe," the butler announced in sonorous tones.

"My dear duchess," Lady Tishford said as they embraced. "I am so glad you could come. And Bertie!" she exclaimed as she espied her friend. "I knew you would not let me down. I always count on you to enliven my dull affairs. And that gown! How exquisite! You are a con-stant marvel." She next turned her attention to the youngest of the group. "Lady Sara, may I say you have never looked better?" She pulled the girl close and whispered, "If that does not bring Awick up to scratch, nothing ever will."

Lady Sara blushed slightly but continued on down the receiving line.

At long last, they entered the ballroom. For this occasion, Lady Tishford had decided on a Grecian motif. The main dance floor had been separated from the encircling sitting area by Corinthian columns. Instead of the usual chairs, marble benches had been placed to mimic the Greek forum. In one corner, a mosaic fountain had been built with a statue of Eros spouting champagne. The servants were all dressed in togas and large potted palms had been set strategically throughout the rooms. In addition to the champagne fountain, the footmen also bore trays holding glasses of ouzo and absinthe.

The Liviscombe ladies attracted a great deal of attention as they entered the room. Her cronies were delighted to see Lady Darnton. She was invariably a good companion because of the delicious gossip she imparted. Most of the men and many of the women who were old enough to know her reputation were anxious for a look at the notorious Bertie, who was rumored to have had more affairs than most people had fantasies. And everyone was anxious to see how the newest diamond, Lady Sara, would fare tonight. Bets were running strong that this would be the night that Awick forsook his well-loved bachelorhood and proposed to her.

Consequently, there was a titter of excitement as the three women descended the stairs into the ballroom. The duchess, espying her old friends, immediately admonished her daughter to behave herself and her granddaughter to have a good time, then drifted through the columns to take her place on the marble benches.

Bertie was instantly swarmed by a press of men ranging in age from seven-and-ten to two-and-sixty. All wanted the pleasure of a dance, the chance to bring her a glass of champagne, ouzo or whatever else she would like, or the pleasure of escorting her to the buffet dinner that would be served later on in the evening.

Sara had scanned the ballroom the moment she entered and was gratified to see that Lord Awick was present. He had been watching for her and the moment he heard her name announced began to make his way toward the entrance. By the time she reached the foot of the staircase he was there to meet her.

"You look divine," he greeted, raising her hand to his lips. He held it too long for convention, but she saw no reason to object. "I have been watching for you all evening. I feared you would not come."

She giggled. "We had a little commotion before we left. I am sure you saw Bertie is with us this evening."

He smiled at her. "I believe that 'a little commotion' is an understatement where Bertie is concerned. The dancing is about to begin. Would you allow me to sign your dance card?"

She held out the tiny card that dangled from her wrist and he proceeded to enter his name for every set, including the supper dance.

She looked at it and laughed. "But, my Lord,"

she protested. "You must know that I cannot dance more than two sets in an evening with a man to whom I am not engaged."

He looked at her intently as he swept her up into his arms to start the figures of the first set. "Of course I know that," he said tenderly.

"Then what does this mean?" she asked uncertainly, feeling her stomach somewhere in the vicinity of her throat.

"It means, my dear widgeon, that I am proposing to you. There is no need to say yea or nay. Just dance with me all evening and I will know."

She felt a thrill go through her. This was the moment she had dreamed about ever since she first met this handsome Lord. "I will dance with you forever," she said softly as she put her arms delicately around him.

"Oh, Sara," he whispered, his lips against her ear. "I love you so. I promise you that we will be exquisitely happy."

They danced the acceptable two sets, then he led her to where her grandmother was seated on the marble benches. All the chaperones fell silent as the two young people approached.

"My Lady," Awick said, taking Lady Darnton's hand and raising it to his lips. "I wish permission to ask for your granddaughter's hand in marriage. I believe you know that I am comfortably circumstanced and I vow to do my very best to keep her happy and content."

She looked at him for a long moment, her stern expression betrayed by the twinkle in her eye. At last she said, "You come from a good family, Randy, and I have no personal objection to the match. But Sara is the one who will have to face you over the breakfast table. If this is what she desires, I will put no obstacles in your path."

They both turned to look at her, as did all the matrons sitting within hearing distance. She wanted to sing and dance, to hug everyone in the room in her happiness. Instead, she took a very deep breath and said levelly, "I would be delighted to marry Lord Awick."

"In that case, my dear," Lady Darnton said, a gratified smile on her wrinkled face, "it is settled. Call on me tomorrow, Randy, and we will work out the settlements. In the meantime, you two go and enjoy yourselves."

Awick put his arm around his fiancée and whisked her back to the dance floor. They completed another set, then she asked if they could sit out and take some refreshment. He guided her to one of the marble benches set back between the columns and surrounded by palms. Soon he returned bearing two glasses of champagne. Unfamiliar with the beverage, she downed it in two swallows.

"Mm, that is good," she said, licking her lips. "May I have another?"

"Of course," he replied, unaware that this was her first experience with the surprisingly potent drink.

As the night wore on, they were lost in a world of their own, dancing and drinking champagne. So absorbed were they in each other that they were totally unaware of the scene that took place behind the Corinthian columns between her grandmother and her aunt.

It had started out innocently enough. Bertie had seen, despite the attention that was being paid to herself, that her mother was starting to grow tired. For all her faults, she loved the old woman and worried about her in her advancing years. She approached her and recommended she go home, promising to watch after Lady Sara herself.

Lady Darnton had immediately taken umbrage, believing that her daughter was implying that she was not capable of looking after the girl.

The situation went from bad to worse and through a horrible misunderstanding, each ended up believing the other would remain to chaperone Sara. Bertie returned to the dance floor on the arm of an old "friend" while the duchess repaired to the card room. Less than an hour later, Lady Darnton summoned her carriage and went home with her winnings while Bertie and her escort lingered only minutes more before departing for an undisclosed destination. And so it was that Lady Sara was left on her own, dancing and drinking champagne with the man she was to marry.

Chapter Three

As the night and then the early morning wore on, Sara consumed a great deal of champagne. She had not eaten since the previous day and was unused to the potent beverage and, consequently, became very tipsy. Fortunately, except for the strange glittering of her eyes, there were no visible signs. Her only sensation was a feeling of well-being and an odd numbness around her mouth.

Awick also had drunk much more than he should and, by the time the ball began to break up in the morning hours, his thoughts were muddled. He was, however, so well versed in proper social behavior that he knew instinctively what had to be done. He searched throughout the marble benches in vain for her chaperones. Unable to find them, he at last approached Georgie Tishford and drew her to one side.

"Have you seen either Lady Darnton or Bertie?" he asked in a slightly thickened voice.

She looked at him in surprise. "They left separately some time ago. Did they not tell you?"

It was the viscount's turn to look surprised. "No, they did not. What arrangement was made for returning Lady Sara to her home?"

"I do not know," Georgie replied. "It was all very confused. Maybe the best thing would be for you to drive her home. I know it is not quite the thing, but there is nothing else to be done. I will make sure that you are not seen leaving together. And don't worry. I love the Liviscombes dearly and will make sure there is no talk."

True to her word, Awick soon found himself shuffled out to his carriage. Several minutes later Lady Sara was bundled beside him.

Georgie leaned through the window and whispered, "No one suspects a thing. Now get her home at once."

With that, they headed off into the night. He felt her so soft and close next to him and put his arm around her. She snuggled even closer to him and raised her face to his.

They gazed at each other for a long moment, then he slowly lowered his lips to hers. He kissed her very gently and she felt a tremor pass through her. He kissed her again a little more forcefully, then raised his head again to gaze into her eyes. "I love you, Sara," he said.

"I love you, my Lord," she replied in a voice that trembled slightly.

"Please," he said as he began to kiss her

eyes, nose and cheeks. "You are going to be my wife. My name is Randy."

She giggled as she felt her whole body awakening to his touch. "I love you, Randy."

He very gently opened her lips with his and began to run his tongue inside her mouth. It felt like a small sword probing. Enjoying the sensation, she met his tongue with hers. For all her vicarious knowledge of such things, she had never had any practical experience.

He pulled her up against him and lightly moved his hands across her shoulders. Instinctively, she wrapped her arms around his neck and began to run her fingers through his hair.

He kissed her again, more passionately this time and brought one hand around to fondle her breast. Feeling the nipple stiffen beneath his hand, his kisses became even more intense.

She felt an odd burning sensation within her. She moved her hands exploringly down his back. He was hard and muscular beneath her touch and she found herself wondering what he would be like underneath all these clothes.

Neither could recollect exactly how it came to pass. He willed it or she willed it or perhaps they both did. The next thing either remembered was being together in his townhouse, naked and in bed. They were both sober now and knew full well that the situation had gone too far to back down. And after all, they were engaged—soon to be married—so, in the end, it would be all right.

Lady Sara had never known a man and she was at the outset afraid of his masculinity. As they lay side by side in the huge bed and he gently caressed her breasts, she could feel the reality of him against her. He sensed her fear and immediately tried to calm her. He gently rolled her onto her back, stroking her. Gazing tenderly at her, he ran his fingers lightly over her, caressing the soft undersides of her arms, then her breasts and flat stomach. He continued on, pausing briefly at the soft mound of hair, then down the inside of her legs. Soon she felt a fire deep within her. He started to kiss her, beginning at her toes, then working up.

"Oh, Sara," he moaned, as he ran his tongue around the soft curve of her breasts. "You are so beautiful."

She felt as if she was melting into him. She was curious and wondering, and wanted to please him. Gently, she laid her hands on his erect member, stroking it lightly.

He groaned softly and teased her nipples with his lips. Her body screamed for him—for the release only he could give. She arched up toward him, wanting to be even closer. At last, he entered her, gently at first so as not to hurt. She felt the small pull as virgin flesh tore and then lost herself to the feeling of his body within hers. As he stroked within her, she felt the tension inside building until she thought she could not stand it. Then something exploded and she felt herself slipping away on a tide, clinging to him and moaning softly.

They lay together quietly for a long time, then he raised his body up from hers slightly to look at her. He kissed the closed eyelids. "I do love you, Sara," he murmured. "You truly are beautiful."

Her eyes fluttered open and she smiled up at him. "So are you."

He chuckled at this. "We will have a good life together. Now sleep, my love."

Obediently, she curled up inside his arms, nestling her head against his shoulder. "Good night, Randy," she murmured sleepily. "I love you."

The next thing she felt was his fingers teasing her breasts and his lips kissing her eyelids and nose. She reached up to put her arms around him. Once again, he ran his hands over her yielding flesh. This time, she was not afraid, knowing what to expect and opened herself willingly to him. He played her body like a fine musical instrument and she returned his passion in kind. His body was warm and sinuous and she arched up to meet him longingly. They came together again and once more she felt the yearning deep within her. He moved slowly and sensuously, feeling her passion mounting. And then again came the explosion and she found herself digging her fingernails into his back. Oh, God, she thought, if this is what marriage is all about, I am ready.

Once again, he kissed her gently and told her to go to sleep. "We have all the time in the world," he murmured in her ear.

With that, she fell asleep.

Lord Awick awoke early and lay very still, gazing tenderly at the girl he held cradled in his arms. Her long dark lashes rested delicately on her cheeks, her hair like a black cloud across the pillow. He tenderly swept a strand back from her face. He knew full well they should never have done what they did and that he must be very careful about getting her out of his house and back to her grandmother's.

He also knew the wedding arrangements had better start immediately. People had a way of counting nine months exactly. Of course, he had wanted to marry her from the start and this one night had only served to whet his appetite. For a sheltered girl, she was rapidly developing a very deft way of pleasuring a man.

Beginning to be aroused again, he was just about to kiss her into wakefulness when there came a soft rap on the door. What the devil, he thought to himself. He was sure he had left word that they were not to be disturbed. His first temptation was to ignore the summons but then he thought better of it. His retainers were much too well-trained to disobey his orders unless it was extremely important.

He very carefully unwound his arms from the sleeping Sara, making sure not to wake her, then fumbled for his robe among the bedclothes strewn across the room. At last he opened the door and slipped out, closing it gently behind him.

"Yes, Briggs?" he said, as his valet looked at him uncomfortably.

"I am sorry to disturb you, my Lord, but a messenger has just arrived from Rotham. Your uncle is failing rapidly and the doctor thinks it advisable for you to come at once."

A look of deep concern crossed Awick's face. Since his father had died when he was just a boy, he had been raised by his uncle, whom he dearly loved. "Yes, of course. Have the curricle brought round. I will be on my way within the hour."

"Do you wish me to accompany you, my Lord?"

"No, Briggs, I will travel alone. I want you to pack me enough clothes to last a few weeks, then follow in the carriage. I will expect you at Rotham in a couple of days. And, Briggs?" Awick looked uncharacteristically embarrassed as he paused.

"Yes, my Lord?"

"As you most assuredly know, there is a young lady in my room. And I stress the word 'lady' because she is one, despite appearances."

"Of course, my Lord," the valet replied with just the faintest trace of irony in his voice.

Awick assumed a more haughty tone. "She is, Briggs, my fiancée. We will be married as soon as possible. I had intended to get her discreetly out of here and back to her grandmother. Now this task will fall to you. And believe me, it is one I expect you to take very seriously."

Briggs recognized the hint of menace. "Of course, My Lord. And who is her grandmother?"

"The Dowager Duchess of Darnton," Awick replied calmly.

For once, the very proper valet lost his composure and whistled softly under his breath. "You have Lady Liviscombe in there?"

"That is what I have been telling you," came the impatient reply. "She *is* a lady and I want no gossip about her. Understood?"

"Yes, My Lord."

"Good. I intend to leave her a note telling her where and why I have gone. When you come with my clothes, I want you to bring her and her grandmother with you. We will be married there as soon as she arrives—I will arrange for a special license. I will tell her in the note that she should see you for all arrangements." He thought for a moment. "Anything else?"

"If your uncle should die, my Lord, you will have to go into mourning and it would not be smiled upon by society if you were to marry during that period."

The viscount nodded. "That is why you must get her there as soon as you can. And now I must be off. Make sure you return her safely to her grandmother. I will see you both at Rotham."

With that, he returned to the bedroom, closing the door softly behind him. Sara was still sleeping peacefully in the huge four-poster. He wanted nothing more than to climb in next to her and feel again her soft, tender flesh. Steeling his will, he sat down at the small writing table and penned a note.

My Dearest Love—

I hate to leave you so abruptly, but I have just received word that my uncle is dying and I must reach Rotham Abbey as soon as possible.

I have instructed Briggs, my valet, to see you safely and discreetly home and then to bring you and your grandmother to Rotham at the end of the week. I will obtain a special license and we will be married there as soon as you arrive. Briggs will take care of all traveling arrangements and expenses. I love you so very much, my precious Sara, and will count the moments until you arrive.

Ever,
Randy

He signed the document, then slipped it into an envelope, which he propped on the mantel. He went into the antechamber, where he quickly and quietly changed into suitable traveling clothes.

Returning to the bedchamber, he gazed down at the sleeping Sara. He had the feeling that he ought to awaken her and explain what had happened. A sudden fear washed over him. No, he told himself sternly, you are being a sentimental fool. Everything will be all right. She needed her sleep and she would have his letter and Briggs. He leaned down to kiss her ever so gently and whispered, "I will see you soon, my love." And then he was gone, never realizing that he had forgotten to write her name on the envelope.

That last kiss had been just enough to bring

her to the beginnings of wakefulness. She thought that the sound of the door softly closing was probably Agnes coming with her morning chocolate. She lay still, gathering her wits. She felt wonderful this morning—as if there was something new and magical in her life. Suddenly her eyes flew open and she looked around her. It had not been a dream, she was lying naked in Awick's bed. Glancing quickly about the room, she realized that she was alone.

He has just stepped out for a moment, she thought. She sat up against the pillows and pulled the covers up higher. She thought about the previous night and all the emotions she had felt at their passionate union. Soon she would be the Viscountess of Awick, but more important, she would be Randy's wife.

As the moments stretched on and he did not return, she grew anxious. Where could he possibly have gone? She did not remember him saying anything about leaving early in the morning. She looked around the room. Had he left a letter for her? Leaping out of the huge bed, she ran over to his writing desk. Nothing there but sporting forms and invitations. An unmarked envelope sat on the mantel, evidently not for her.

What was she to do? It was his townhouse and he must return sometime, but what about Grandmama and Bertie? She would have to get home at once. And how was she to leave Awick's house in the early morning hours without calling attention to her disgrace?

She took a few deep breaths to fight down her

rising panic. He probably left word with the servants, she decided at last. She rang the bell pull.

Briggs had waited a long time for the bell to sound from his master's room. He had much to do if he was to close up the townhouse and make arrangements to escort the two ladies to Rotham by the end of the week. At last, he told the housekeeper, Mrs. Strothers, that he would be in the laundry attending to the master's cravats and when the bell sounded from his room he was to be notified immediately. He had not bothered to tell her that the viscount had left the house some time before and the current occupant was the daughter of a duke.

Mrs. Strothers nodded at the valet, vaguely puzzled. Of course she would tell him—it was not *her* place to wait on his Lordship. And why was the master abed so late? He was usually up and about by this time. Shrugging her ample shoulders, she returned to her duties. There was no understanding the gentry.

There soon came a knock on the back door. She called Molly, the little parlor maid, to watch the bell board for a moment, promising to be right back. Molly, at seventeen, was the youngest and newest of Lord Awick's servants. She had only been in his employ for three weeks and had no idea what she was supposed to do if a bell did sound, but at least she knew the layout of the house.

The caller turned out to be Lord Marsh's housekeeper from next door and a great friend of Mr. Strothers. The two returned to Lord

Marsh's kitchen to have a cup of tea and a good gossip. The housekeeper had totally forgotten about Briggs and his message.

And so when Lady Sara at last pulled the bell in Awick's room, it was a frightened Molly who heard it. Oh, Lordie, she thought to herself. What's to do? She glanced around, only to find she was alone. Then she remembered that she had seen Lord Awick leave much earlier that morning. She had been polishing the wall sconces in the front entry hall and had heard Briggs wish him a good trip and promise to join him soon.

She felt relieved. It was probably Briggs up packing the master's belongings. She was a little intimidated by the valet, but that was much better than facing the master—so tall and elegant as he was.

She ran up the stairs and knocked on the door. To her amazement, she heard a small and frightened female voice call "Come in" with an odd mix of hope and fear.

A beautiful young lady was sitting on the edge of the huge four-poster. She was dressed in a shift and her face was very pale. Spread out next to her was a very dashing evening gown.

"Yes, mum?" Molly asked, looking at her curiously.

Lady Sara breathed a small sigh of relief. She did not know much about bachelor establishments but had vaguely thought that a male servant would answer the summons. Somehow the girl's presence was reassuring. "What is your name?" she asked.

"I be called Molly, mum," the maid answered.

"Molly, would you be so good as to come in and close the door? I wish to speak to you."

The little maid looked at her uncertainly. This woman was obviously a member of the upper class—or perhaps a Cyprian considering the circumstances—and Molly could not understand why she would want to talk to her. After all, she was only the parlor maid. The thought went through her mind that she might be mad. But she looked so scared and young, surely no older than herself.

At last, she edged slowly into the room, shutting the door behind her but placing herself directly against it, ready to flee at any moment. "Yes, mum?" she asked again.

All of this was not lost on Lady Sara. She could well imagine what was going through the young maid's mind. Very gently, she said, "You need not be concerned, Molly. I won't harm you. Can you tell me where Lord Awick is? Did he leave any message for me?"

The maid responded to the kindly tone. "No, mum, not that I know of." All of a sudden she liked this lady who was so obviously above her in station but was willing to be nice to her, and walked toward the bed. "What I do know," she said helpfully, "is that the master left the house this mornin' for a trip o' some sort. I heard him and Briggs talkin' in the hall. Ye know, I was cleanin' them sconces like Mrs. Strothers told me and I heard Briggs say he would join him by the end o' the week." She stopped, feeling very pleased with herself for being able to give this fine lady so much information.

Lady Sara bowed her head for a moment, then pulled herself together. "I see. Thank you, Molly. Please do not leave just yet," she said as the maid turned toward the door.

She had been doing some quick thinking as Molly spoke. Awick was gone! The thought filled her with a pain that almost made her sick to her stomach but she rapidly fought it down. There would be time enough later to deal with that. Right now she had more pressing problems than a broken heart.

"Tell me, Molly," she said at last. "How long have you worked for Lord Awick?"

"Just three weeks, mum."

"Then I would guess that you have no idea how to leave this house without being noticed?"

Molly colored, looking uncomfortable.

Lady Sara looked at her intently. "Go ahead, Molly. I swear that I will never betray you."

The maid glanced at her. "Well, mum, it's like this. I just started walkin' out with Ben, the groom here. His days off is Fridays, so last week I slipped out." She stopped uncertainly.

"Why, Molly, how wonderful!" Lady Sara exclaimed. "I hope you and Ben will be very happy!"

"Thank ye, mum," the maid answered, pleased at this reaction to her confession.

"Now tell me, Molly, how you managed to get away without anyone noticing."

Molly smiled at her knowingly. "It were easy, mum. Ben told me." She went on to explain that there was a small door near the kitchen that opened out into the herb garden. From the garden there was a gate out to the mews. From there, it was possible to cross over into the next row of townhouses and just three doors down, there was a tree-arched walkway that led out to the park.

Sara thought. If she could get to the park, she would only be taken for a young lady out for a morning stroll—except for the fact that she had no chaperone and would be dressed in an evening gown—and the same gown she had worn to the Tishford ball, where most of the *ton* had seen her. Oh Lord, she thought. Whatever am I to do? And then a plan occurred to her.

She looked at Molly who was watching her curiously. She was considerably taller than the maid, but their build was about the same. And if she wore a shawl . . .

"Tell me, Molly, do you like this gown?" She indicated the garment spread out on the bed next to her.

"Yes, mum, it's lovely," she replied.

"Would you like to have it?"

"What?" the girl squeaked in surprise. "Why ever would ye do that?"

"Because I wish to have one of yours."

Doubt suddenly assailed her again. The lady was mad. She started to edge toward the door. "I'd best get Mrs. Strothers," she murmured.

"No, please, Molly," Sara begged. "Don't leave. You must help me." She thought wildly for a moment trying to come up with a plausible excuse but nothing occurred to her. She decided she would have to tell her at least some of the truth. She drew a deep breath. "I must admit that I find myself in somewhat embarrassing circumstances. I must return to my family without anyone knowing I have been here. What I wish to do is to dress as a maid and slip quietly away. Can you understand that?"

"Yes, mum, I think so," Molly replied dubiously.

"Good," Lady Sara said, as she showed no more signs of fleeing the room. "And that is why I wish to exchange dresses."

"Oh, mum, don't be such a silly. I'll just bring down my other dress and ye can wear that."

"No, Molly," she replied, touched by the gesture and the generosity of this poor serving girl. "I cannot take advantage of you in that way. I have no money on me and I wish to repay you for the tremendous favor you are doing me. I will return your dress this afternoon, but I want you to have this. Please accept it. You will have to take the hem up some, but I suspect that Ben will be very pleased when he sees you in it."

Her eyes lit up at this. "That he will, mum!" she exclaimed.

Within minutes, the women had exchanged clothes. Except for the length, both looked reasonably well in their new garb. Molly fetched her shawl and helped Sara to drape it across her head and shoulders. Then they worked out the plan for escape.

Molly ran ahead to make sure the coast was clear and soon Lady Sara slipped away from Lord Awick's townhouse. "Please, Molly," she said as she left. "I do not want you to lie, but if you can help it, don't tell anyone about seeing me here. Can you manage that?"

Looking down at the beautiful gown she was now wearing, Molly said fervently, "Oh, yes, mum, not to worry."

As soon as Lady Sara had slipped out the door, she scampered up to her room to change into her other dress, carefully folding the new gown and placing it at the back of her tiny closet. She could hardly wait to see the expression on Ben's face when he saw it. She could take the hem up tonight when she finished her chores.

She was back at the bell board when Mrs. Strothers returned.

"No problems, Molly?" the housekeeper asked.

"No, none," she replied truthfully.

"Good. Then get back to your chores. Time's awastin'."

"Yes'm," Molly replied, relieved at how easy it had been.

Mrs. Strothers was in the kitchen when Briggs entered.

"Has there been no call from his Lordship's chamber?" he asked, a worried look crossing his face.

Mrs. Strothers, suddenly remembering his instructions, swallowed her guilt and looked at him indignantly. "I told you I would let you know if there was." At all costs, she did not want the overbearing valet to know she had spent well over an hour gossiping in Lord

Marsh's kitchen. And anyway, Molly would have told her if there had been a summons.

Ignoring her tone, he shook his head and said, "Odd. Very odd. I had best go up and discover if anything is amiss."

She shrugged her shoulders as he left the room. Honestly, that valet was getting to be as strange as the gentry.

Briggs knocked softly on Lord Awick's door. What if the girl was still asleep? He did not want to awaken her, but he had to get her back to her grandmother—and the sooner the better. He knocked a little louder when there was no response. At last he laid his ear against the door, then, taking a deep breath, slowly pushed it open and looked inside.

His heart sank. She was gone. The bed had been neatly made up and there was no sign that she had ever been there. Oh Lord, he thought to himself. What was he to tell Lord Awick? And what was he to do about Lady Liviscombe? Why had she not rung for him as the master had instructed her to do in the note he left? What a muddle.

His major concern now was getting the two ladies to Rotham. It was not his place to present himself at the household of the Dowager Duchess of Darnton—not without first contacting Lady Liviscombe. Drat the girl! Why had she left so abruptly?

He finally decided that the only thing to do was to get to Rotham Abbey as soon as possible and see what the master wanted him to do next. He returned to the kitchen to explain to

Mrs. Strothers that Lord Awick had been called away suddenly and had left him a note saying he was to follow immediately.

Mrs. Strothers thought this very strange since no message had come that she knew of, then thought guiltily that it might have arrived while she was out. But surely Molly would have mentioned it. Well, anyway, it was no concern of hers—the less said, the better. She sent Molly up to clean the master's room while Briggs went to the attic to retrieve the traveling bags.

It was while she was dusting the mantel that Molly discovered the envelope. She dropped it into her pocket, meaning to give it to Mrs. Strothers or Briggs. But when the valet returned, he immediately told her to go below and get Lord Awick's shirts from the laundry room. She went about her chores, forgetting the envelope.

By drawing the shawl closer about her head and keeping her head bent and her eyes lowered, Sara did indeed look like a serving girl as she made her way, not too quickly, through the park. She kept her soft, white hands hidden in the pockets of the drab black dress. So far so good, she thought. Fortunately, her grandmother did not live far from Awick and soon she saw the welcome facade. Slipping around to the rear, she knocked quietly on the servants' entrance. It was opened by Agnes, whose puffy red eyes and blotched complexion testified to the fact that she had been weeping.

"Yes?" she asked uncertainly. The tall

woman in the ill-fitting gown standing before her with bowed head somehow seemed oddly familiar. As Lady Sara raised her head, Agnes squealed and threw her arms around her.

Suddenly recollecting her station, she dropped her arms and curtsied. "Beg pardon, M'Lady. I shouldn't have done that. I'm just that pleased to see you back safe and all." She was dying of curiosity as to where her mistress had been all night and why she was returning in a servant's costume but knew it was not her place to ask.

"Thank you, Agnes," Lady Sara replied, looking concerned. "But tell me why you have been crying."

"I have just been that worried, M'Lady," Agnes sniffled.

"As you can see, I am home safe and sound, so dry your eyes now. How are my aunt and grandmother?"

"Oh, M'Lady, there was a terrible row last night in the duchess's bedchamber. Them both yellin' and screamin' and throwin' things. It was awful. Finally wore themselves out about dawn and Lady Bertie went stormin' to her room, promisin' to be gone by teatime. I think they're both asleep now."

Lady Sara grimaced as she digested this information. She must get out of this gown and send it back to Molly. Then she would visit Bertie, who would be sympathetic. She was uncertain about her grandmother.

She and Agnes managed to reach her room without encountering any of the other Liviscombe servants. Reviewing the situation, she felt reasonably encouraged. The only people who knew about her escapade, she hoped, were herself, Molly, Agnes, Bertie, Grandmama and—a stab of pain shot through her—Awick. So far, she had kept herself from thinking about his betrayal simply by occupying her mind with other thoughts, namely the salvaging of her reputation. She purposely shut out all thought of him as she prepared to face her family—there would be plenty of time later to consider what had happened.

Agnes helped her change into a golden morning gown banded in green and she gave instructions to have Molly's gown wrapped and returned. She then went to Bertie's room and rapped lightly on the door.

"Come in," her aunt called.

She pushed open the door and entered. Bertie was sitting up in bed sipping a cup of chocolate. She wore a ruffle-covered pink nightgown with a lace mobcap set jauntily on her blond curls. Grinning archly at her niece, she said, "Well, my dear, come in and sit down. I want to hear *all* about it."

Lady Sara crossed over to the bay window and, separating the curtains, looked down at the already busy street. "I will be going to Langton with you today, Bertie," she said in a quiet, sad voice.

"What?" Bertie exclaimed, practically dropping her cup. "But what about Awick and your engagement? What about last night?"

Her voice trembled as she replied, "I do not know. Last evening he asked me to marry him, he made love to me all night—and this morning he was gone."

"Gone? How could he be gone? It was his townhouse, was it not? Where did he go?"

Tears were coursing down her face now as she said, "I do not know. There was no note, no message with the servants, nothing. The parlor maid told me he had left the house early and overheard him tell his valet to join him by the end of the week."

Sobs were now shaking her slender frame and Bertie ran to her, holding her in her arms and rocking her gently as if she were a child. Damn the man, she thought fiercely. To take advantage of a young virgin. She only prayed that Sara was not with child. There were ways to get around that, too, but the procedure was painful and risky. Her next concern was for her niece's reputation. Everyone survived a broken heart, but gossip was fatal. "How did you get home?" she asked anxiously. "Did anyone see you?"

Sara choked back her tears and said in a ragged voice, "I do not believe so. I exchanged gowns with the parlor maid and wrapped a shawl around my head. I walked through the mews out to the park, then came in through the servants' entrance. I did not see anyone and can only hope that no one saw me."

She nodded her relief at Sara's good sense. "Thank God for that, at any rate. Now we must think what to do next." She sat down at her vanity table, staring unseeingly at her reflection. "I have it!" she announced, springing back to her feet. "We will go to Italy! I have not been there since Jeffrey's death and we can open the villa. What do you think?"

Sara looked at her in surprise. "Italy? You have a villa in Italy?"

"Oh, yes," Bertie replied blithely. "I thought you knew. Actually, it belonged to my first husband and I was his sole heir. As I said, I have not been back since his death, but only because I had no one with whom I could travel. My second husband was much too old to endure the rigors of going abroad, so it has just been sitting there empty. What do you say?"

Sara thought about it for a long moment. She loved Langton dearly, but she also knew that for right now, she needed something to absorb her thoughts. "But what about your baron; I thought you were anxious to return to him?"

Bertie waved her hand in a dismissing gesture. "It would have run its course soon anyway. I always prefer to be the one to end an affair. It is so much easier on one's pride." She broke off as she saw the tears welling up in her niece's eyes. "I am sorry, my dear. Believe me, I know exactly what you are going through. What you need is a change. Please say yes."

The girl sniffled and nodded her head. "Italy it will be," she said. "What about Grandmama?"

Bertie shook her head firmly. "Much too old."

"No, I mean, should we not discuss this with her?"

Again she shook her head. "I do not believe that would be wise. She would worry unnecessarily. She is off to Devon anyway, so there is no reason for her to know. We can write her later after we decide how long we wish to stay. For now, it would be best if she just assumed we were only going to Langton."

Sara looked at her dubiously but said no more.

"And speaking of Mama, we had better go tell her you are home."

"Is she going to be fearfully angry?"

"Only at me, dear, and I think she got most of that out last night." She slipped on a frothy pink robe and dainty slippers. "Now soak your eyes and look natural."

Chapter Four

LADY DARNTON WAS SITTING AT HER VANITY
table while her abigail brushed her thinning
gray hair. "Good morning, dears," she greeted
cheerfully for the benefit of the maid. "Wonderful ball, was it not? Georgie's affairs are always
memorable. Peg, would you be a sweetheart
and run down and ask Roberts to send up rolls
and chocolate? We will break our fast in my
sitting room this morning so that we can have a
good coze."

As the maid departed, she looked at Sara
critically. "You have been crying," she said in a
not unkindly tone. "What happened last
night?"

At the hint of sympathy in her grandmother's
voice and eyes, she knew she was going to start
weeping again. She looked to Bertie for help.

Her aunt briefly explained the situation and

said that they planned to leave for Somerset at once.

"Oh, damn!" the old woman exclaimed. She thought rapidly for a moment. "No, you must not run away. We must ascertain exactly how your reputation stands. The major events of the season are over but there are still a few minor events we will attend. And Wednesday will be the last session at Almack's. That will be the ultimate test. If there is any talk, we will find out about it there."

"But, Mama," Bertie objected. "Awick and Sara danced together all evening. Everyone believes them to be engaged. What will we say when they start asking about a wedding date?"

She thought about this for a long moment. "Yes, that is awkward." Again she fell silent, then snapped her fingers. "We will put out the hint that I have decided Sara is too young to marry right away and that we have decided on a long engagement. We will say that Awick was summoned out of town unexpectedly. By next season our two young lovers will have decided they will not suit and will have broken off their engagement. What do you think?"

Bertie looked doubtful. "I do not like it, Mama. We have no way of knowing what Awick is up to. Suppose he has said something to one of his friends? We don't even know where he has gone."

Again, the duchess paused, lost in thought. "It is a risk we will have to take. I will go see his godmother, Emily Warrington, this afternoon and see if she knows anything. I do not know what Awick is doing, but I hope that he is too much of a gentleman to contradict our story." She turned to her daughter. "You may return to Langton if you wish, dear, but I would prefer you to stay. Buy whatever clothes you need. Put them on my account." Her unusual kindness to her daughter was a good indication of her degree of agitation.

Sara, feeling terribly chastened, approached the old lady. "I am so sorry, Grandmama," she murmured.

"Nonsense, gel," Lady Darnton said sympathetically. "Bertie and I failed you and Awick acted the absolute bastard. You have done nothing more than any red-blooded girl would have done. Do not be concerned. We will see you through this." She paused for a moment. "Is there any chance there could be a child?"

Sara colored up but answered levelly, "I don't believe so. I finished my period just two days hence." Her years in the country had put her in good stead to know much about life and she had bred too many animals not to be aware of the cycles of nature.

Both her grandmother and her aunt breathed sighs of relief—their country girl was not so green after all.

They were eating their breakfast and discussing various courses of action when Roberts entered. "Lady Tishford is here to see you, my Lady."

"Very good, Roberts. Send her up."

Georgie burst into the room calling cheerfully, "Good morning, all!" Her eyes went searchingly to Lady Sara.

"Ah, good morning, Georgie," Lady Darnton spoke in the same hearty tone. Roberts closed the door softly behind her. She dropped her voice and said, "What do you think? Did we muddle through?"

Georgie smiled encouragingly. "As far as I can tell, there was not even a suspicion that the two left together." She turned again to Lady Sara. "I see he got you safely home. Thank God for that at any rate."

A blush stole over the girl's cheeks, but she said as calmly as she could, "Yes, I am safely home."

Her grandmother smiled at her approvingly. The fewer people who were in on the story the better. "Thank you, Georgie, for being so quick-witted and for sending that note around explaining that you sent them off together. It arrived just before they did. I do not know how Bertie and I got our signals so badly crossed, but I believe everything will be fine now."

They chatted about other topics, then Georgie took her departure, promising to see them at Almack's on Wednesday and to keep her ears open for any possible gossip.

Later that day, the Dowager Duchess of Darnton paid a call on Emily Warrington. If Emily was surprised by this visit, she was careful not to show it. She asked after the Ladies Alberta and Sara, then waited for her unexpected guest to come to the purpose.

"I believe you did not attend the Tishford ball last night, Mrs. Warrington."

"No, I did not," she said. "I had previously committed to a card party."

"Then you have not heard about the marked attention that Lord Awick paid to my granddaughter. In fact, he asked me for her hand."

Emily clapped her hands. "But this is wonderful! I am so glad he has finally come up to scratch. That naughty boy should have told me. I will send round for him at once."

Lady Darnton looked uncomfortable. "I do not believe you will find him at home. I have reason to believe that he has quit town rather suddenly."

Emily could no longer hide her surprise. "What? Why would he do that?"

"I do not know. That is what I came to discover. You have heard nothing?"

"Not a word." She paused in thought. "Let me send round and see what I can discover. It seems remarkably shabby that he would propose to Lady Sara and then disappear. Would you care for tea while we wait?"

She quickly penned a note for her godson and sent it off with a footman, giving him instructions to wait for a reply.

The ladies were sipping their tea and exchanging pleasantries when the footman returned with the information that Lord Awick had indeed left London and all the housekeeper could tell him was that his valet had been instructed to bring his clothes and follow him. She did not even know his destination.

Emily Warrington was incensed at this piece of knowledge. "Well, I never!" she exclaimed. "What on earth is the matter with the boy? I believed him to have better manners than that!

I can only apologize to you, my Lady. I must say that I am ashamed of him."

Lady Darnton arose to leave. "It is no reflection on you, Mrs. Warrington. I just want no gossip about my granddaughter. As I said, I had suspected as much. The two are believed to be engaged. When the inevitable questions come, I am going to have to put it about that Awick was called away suddenly and that we have agreed to an extended engagement. Then word will come that our young lovers have agreed they will not suit."

Emily thought about this, then nodded. "Yes, that is reasonable. And believe me, I will do everything in my power to track down our miscreant. I think very highly of Lady Sara and I promise I will not allow my wearisome godson to damage her reputation."

The next few days were a terrible strain for Sara. Everywhere she went, people asked about Lord Awick and the wedding. True to her word, Lady Darnton was always there to leap into the fray, explaining Awick's departure. The evening at Almack's proved that Lady Sara's reputation was firmly intact.

The following morning, they closed down the townhouse and departed London—the Dowager Duchess to Devon, Bertie and Sara to Langton. Their farewells were brief.

The duchess hugged her granddaughter and told her not to fret and to try to dismiss the abominable Awick from her thoughts. "He is not worthy of your regard, my love. We will have better success next season—I am sure of it." She then turned to her daughter and hugged her also. "I must say, Bertie, though you have been a mixed blessing for me in the past, you certainly came through this time and I thank you for it. Now please do try to keep out of any further scrapes."

She climbed into her carriage with the assistance of her footman. "I will look for you at Christmas."

"We will be there, Mama," Bertie said, "barring any unforeseen developments."

"Good-bye, Grandmama," Sara said. "We will keep in touch."

The carriage lumbered off and the two younger women climbed into their own vehicle. Lady Sara breathed a sigh of relief as she settled back against the deep blue squabs.

"What was that for?" her aunt asked.

"I am just so glad to be leaving London. This has been a true ordeal."

Bertie looked at the girl worriedly, realizing just how strained she looked. There were deep shadows under her eyes and her complexion was uncommonly pale. "You will feel better once we get to Langton," she promised, "and start making plans for our trip to Italy. The change will be good for you."

Sara nodded absently. She did not believe that anything would help the leaden feeling in her heart, or remove the memories she had of that wonderful night in Awick's arms. She felt as if something had died within her. She shuddered slightly, recalling her grandmother's statement about next season. Another season was the last thing she wanted. Maybe Bertie was right—Italy might very well be the change she needed.

The carriage had just disappeared around the corner when another vehicle drew up in front of the Liviscombe townhouse. Its sole occupant cursed softly when she saw that the shutters were drawn and the knocker off the door. She had come as soon as she had received the letter from her godson saying that he had been summoned to Rotham because his uncle was dying. She had wanted to reassure Lady Darnton that there had been no slight to her granddaughter.

I wonder what I should do now? Emily thought. Awick had said in his letter that he had proposed to Lady Sara and intimated that the wedding would take place as soon as she joined him there. She finally concluded that he must have written to her. At last, she smiled to herself. That is where they have gone—to Rotham Abbey! She suspected she would soon receive their wedding announcement. She was not at all offended that she had not been invited to the wedding. With the dubious health of his uncle, it would not be seemly to have a large affair. At least the two would soon be wed. On that cheerful note, she returned home and gave the matter no further thought.

Lord Awick arrived in Kent to find that, while seriously ill, his uncle was improving. Relieved by this, he set about preparing the house for Sara's arrival. He ordered Rotham cleaned from top to bottom and instructed the housekeeper to lay in whatever provisions were customary for a small wedding breakfast.

He himself obtained the special license so that the ceremony could be performed as soon as his beloved Sara arrived and they would not have to go through the usual posting of the banns.

He was sitting in the library on the day following his arrival, reviewing the estate accounts, when Briggs entered. He leapt to his feet and ran around the desk.

"Briggs!" he exclaimed. "How did you get here so quickly? Where is Lady Sara? Did you show her to her room?"

The valet shifted his weight uncomfortably. "I came alone, my Lord," he said in a muted voice.

"Alone?" Awick asked in surprise. "Did the ladies decide to come on their own? Yes, that would make sense. I am sure Lady Sara would have some shopping to do. When are they to arrive? They will be here soon?"

Briggs looked increasingly shame-faced. "I do not believe they *will* arrive, my Lord," he said at last.

The viscount stared at him blankly. "Not arrive? What do you mean not arrive?"

"My Lord, Lady Liviscombe did not ring and when I went to your room, she was gone."

"Gone? Where did she go?" He sank back down into the leather chair and rubbed his hands over his face. "I do not understand what you are saying, Briggs. Would you please tell me the whole?"

The valet explained what had occurred after the viscount's departure.

"But she had my letter. She must have known." A sudden pain shot through him. She knew and she did not care! That was it! She had decided not to marry him. Why had she simply not told him the truth that night—or at least sent a letter? There was a long, strained silence. When he at last looked back to his valet, there was a set expression on his face. "That will be all, Briggs. Have a bottle of brandy sent to me and then be sure that I am left alone."

"Yes, my Lord," Briggs said and withdrew to carry out his orders. Drat the girl, he thought again.

Lord Awick was in a dreadful tear for the next few weeks. When he was not galloping wildly around his estate, he was locked in his library with a bottle of brandy. The only time he was at all reasonable was when he visited his uncle, which he did punctually twice a day.

When the old man died, Awick announced his intention to go to America. He saw no reason to remain in England. He had good bailiffs to take care of his estates, his young brother Freddie was safely ensconced at Cambridge and, for himself, he needed a change of scene.

It was about the time that Lord Awick was setting sail that the little maid Molly discovered the envelope she had slipped into her apron pocket and then into her night stand. Unable to read, she decided the best course would be to give it to Mrs. Strothers and explain where she had found it.

The housekeeper was also unable to read, but since it had been discovered in the master's room, she decided it ought to be returned to the master. She sent a footman off to Rotham with the little missive with instructions to hand it to the valet.

By the time the footman arrived in Kent, both valet and master had departed. The housekeeper there, also uncertain what to do, at last took it to his Lordship's room and propped it on the mantel where it was to remain untouched and forgotten for years.

Lady Sara and her aunt stayed at Langton for a month, then traveled to Devon to visit the dowager duchess. They explained their intention of removing to Italy and received the elder lady's wholehearted support. She was concerned about her granddaughter, who had lost weight and was looking peaked and haggard. A change was exactly what the girl needed.

By the time the two ladies reached Florence, the worst of Sara's pain had subsided. Now she just felt dead and empty inside. For Bertie's sake, she tried to put on a good front and was careful to keep her own counsel. Her aunt, however, was no fool and was perfectly aware of the girl's hurt. They never discussed it and Bertie did her best to keep her niece amused and her mind occupied.

Despite her emotional problems, Sara was absolutely enchanted with Italy. Fortunately, she had a passable knowledge of the language because of Deborah's excellent instruction and the people were friendly and helpful.

The villa was exquisite—all done in marble and stone in a classically Mediterranean style. The entire central portion of the house con-sisted of a courtyard with the living quarters opening off it on two floors. The courtyard itself featured a mosaic fountain surrounded by lush foliage.

The two ladies rapidly became popular among the aristocratic community. Soon their evenings were filled with social gatherings and their days with short trips about the country-side or tours of the museums and shops. After the rigors of the London season, they enjoyed the slower pace and more relaxed atmosphere.

It was in the early fall that they received a letter from their solicitor giving them the grievous news that the Dowager Duchess of Darnton had suffered a stroke and died shortly thereafter. He recommended that they not re-turn to England since they could not possibly arrive in time for the funeral. In point of fact, his letter did not arrive until long after the ceremony had taken place.

Bertie and Sara were deeply distressed by the news and were only glad that the old woman had not had to endure a great deal of pain. They donned their blacks and went into deep mourning for the requisite one year. Now that they had no reason to return home for Christ-mas, they decided to stay on in Italy for an indefinite period.

Their friends in Italy were a highly eclectic group. There were many French émigrés who had been forced to flee their homeland during the disturbances of the Revolution. A surprising number of Englishmen were also in residence, as well as German, Swiss, Dutch, Portuguese, Spanish and even a few Americans.

As they became more familiar with life on the continent, they began to do more traveling and were enthralled with all they saw and did. They journeyed over much of Europe, with the exception of those areas where battles were raging. But somehow, they were always pleased to return to their Florentine villa, their adopted home, and were at their most relaxed when with their own circle of friends.

They talked from time to time about returning to England, but there never seemed any pressing reason. Sara was in frequent communication with her solicitor and it was evident that her landholdings were being adequately husbanded. She still wrote occasionally to Deborah, who reported that her school was highly successful.

As for Bertie, she was happy anywhere. She made friends readily and, as might be expected, had quickly attracted a string of ardent admirers. She and Georgie Tishford exchanged long and gossipy letters, mostly concerning the latest *on dits* and news of Georgie's daughter, Clare, who was to make her come-out in just a few years. All of the other information the ladies gleaned about their old friends and acquaintances came from the gossip of those wealthy fortunate who were able to vacation abroad.

It was in the seventh year of their residence in Italy that Lady Sara met Frederick Ketcham. Since Bertie had gone off to visit friends, she had decided to go into town to do some shopping. She was walking down one of the narrow, winding streets leading to the main marketing area when she espied a young man holding a guide book and looking around in a rather bewildered fashion.

She knew instinctively from the cut of his clothes that he was British, but she was more struck by the fact that he looked somewhat familiar. He appeared to be about her own age and she wondered if, perhaps, she had met him during her ill-fated season in London.

Since he was obviously in need of help, she approached and asked if she could be of assistance.

At the sound of the English accents, he turned in relief and said, "Thank Heavens! A fellow traveler! My Italian is deplorable and I am hopelessly lost."

Again, she was struck by how familiar he seemed. He was tall and thin, with dark hair that fell in an unruly fashion onto his forehead. She looked at him intently for a moment but the memory eluded her. At last she smiled and said, "Actually, I am not a traveler—I live here. So I suspect all the more that I might be able to give you directions."

He stared at her. "But you're English, aren't you?" he asked.

She laughed. "Yes, I am English. I guess I am what you term an expatriate."

He thought about this for a moment, then

said, "I know many people from England live here, but I always thought they were elderly or ill or . . . or . . ." he stumbled to an awkward halt.

She laughed again. "Or ostracized by society or some sort of passionately fanatic artist," she completed the statement for him. "Don't be alarmed. I am none of those things. If you stay here for any length of time you will discover many of us live here just because we enjoy it. Now, tell me where you are trying to go and I will aid you."

"Awfully good of you," he mumbled, struggling with his embarrassment. "As you have probably guessed, I have only just arrived. My boat was scheduled to dock two days ago, but we had uncommonly bad weather at sea and were delayed. Consequently, my friends were not there to greet me. I asked directions when I arrived, but, as I said, my Italian is so poor that I am sure they did not understand me."

"Where do you wish to go?"

In very slow and halting Italian, he spoke a phrase.

She looked at him blankly for a moment, then said, "I think you just asked me where you could buy twelve lemons." She laughed. "That is probably why you were sent into the shopping district."

He grinned ruefully and pulled a rather crumpled letter out of his pocket.

"Ah," she said. "We are going to be neighbors." She told him the correct pronunciation, which he repeated. "Very good. And now I will show you the way."

"But you were headed the opposite direction, were you not?"

"I was just going shopping."

"I do not mean to inconvenience you," he said. "If you will tell me the way, I am sure I will find it."

Once again, she laughed. "As I said, I live here. I can shop anytime, but it is not often I can help a fellow countryman. Come, I will lead you to your friends." She glanced around curiously. "Do you have no luggage?"

Sheepishly, he replied, "My friends had the forethought to have my bags delivered directly. They apparently thought that I was smarter than my luggage."

She felt a sudden warmth for this engaging young man. She was glad she had been able to assist him in his difficulties.

As she led him back to the residential area, he stopped and swept her an elegant bow. "Excuse my manners, I did not introduce myself. I am Frederick Ketcham, at your service, or rather, at the moment you are at mine." He grinned.

Lady Sara had automatically extended her hand, but she froze at the mention of his name. Awick's brother! She should have known. The viscount had spoken often of his young brother, but she had never had the opportunity to meet him since he had been at Cambridge at the time. Now she understood why he had seemed so familiar.

As he took her hand and kissed it, she tried to put her scattered thoughts in order. "I am Sara

Liviscombe," she said simply. "It is a pleasure to meet you, Mr. Ketcham."

"*You* are Lady Sara?" he asked in disbelief, obviously unaware that he was still holding her hand.

"Yes, I am," she replied. "Why is that so astounding?"

He pulled himself together and realized her hand was still in his. Dropping it abruptly, he said, "I am sorry. I was just not expecting . . . that is, I thought . . . I mean . . ." He at last stumbled to an awkward halt as embarrassed color suffused his cheeks.

She looked at him expectantly for a moment, but when he did not continue, she said, "And exactly what were you expecting, Mr. Ketcham?" in a tone that was colder than she had intended.

His color deepened as he said, "Randy told me about you."

"I see," she said, turning to continue down the narrow, winding street. "In that case, please say no more."

Overcome with remorse at his own bumbling, he ran after her. "Oh please, Lady Sara," he said, "do not be angry with me. I do not know what transpired between you and my brother and, honestly, I do not care. He came to visit me at Cambridge just before he left for America and was in a dreadful fit of the sullens —perfectly blue-deviled. He went on at great length about never trusting women with all their coquettish ways and leading a man on and so forth. And since he always seemed to be referring to things you two had done and said, I had just assumed that you were a—a—"

"A man-hunter?" she asked innocently, a glint of mischief in her eyes. "Did he tell you that I had led him down the garden path?"

His discomposure was complete at this point and he appeared to find the sidewalk totally fascinating. He cleared his throat a couple of times, then finally looked at her beseechingly. "Please forgive me, Lady Sara. I did not mean to offend you."

Ashamed of herself, she relented immediately. "No offense taken, Mr. Ketcham," she said kindly, giving him a dazzling smile.

His countenance lightened at once. "Please call me 'Freddie.' All my friends do."

"Thank you, Freddie, and I would be delighted if you would drop my title. 'Sara' will be perfectly adequate."

They had emerged onto one of the wider streets and she indicated a villa just a block up, painted in a warm pink. "That is number twelve, where your friends live," she said.

"And where is your home?" he asked ingenuously.

"Right down there, the one done in white."

"May I call on you?"

She smiled at him. "Of course. My aunt and I would be delighted to have your company."

He took her hand again and raised it to his lips. "I am truly sorry for what I said earlier, Sara. Please forgive me."

"Already forgiven, Freddie. Do not give it another thought. I look forward to seeing you again."

True to his word, Freddie Ketcham presented himself at the Liviscombe villa the following morning. Sara and Bertie were having breakfast when he was announced.

"Please show him in," Bertie said to the butler as she looked curiously at her niece. "He certainly did not waste any time."

Sara just smiled at her as the young man entered the room. "Bertie, this is Frederick Ketcham, of whom I spoke to you yesterday. Freddie, this is my aunt, Lady Alberta Watson."

Bertie arose and extended her hand. "It is a pleasure, Mr. Ketcham. How do you find Italy?"

"Please call me 'Freddie,' and very well, though I have seen little so far."

"My niece will have to show you around," she said, giving Sara a sly wink. "Will you join us for breakfast?"

As they ate, they spoke of mutual friends and Freddie related the latest London gossip.

Eventually, her curiosity got the better of her and Bertie asked what news he had of Lord Awick.

Freddie looked uncomfortably at Lady Sara, but she had busied herself pouring more coffee. "I received a letter from him shortly before I quit London. He is still in America and seems to like it very well. He is helping his father-in-law tend his estate in Virginia."

"Father-in-law?" Bertie squeaked, as Sara dropped her coffee cup.

He looked at the two women in surprise. "You mean you did not know that Randy had

116

married? It has been some two years now—in fact, they have a baby girl named Elizabeth."

"No, we had not heard," Bertie said, as Sara mopped up the spilled coffee. "But then news is sometimes slow in reaching us. Sara, my love, why do you not take Freddie around to see the sights today? We have nothing planned. Did you have anything scheduled, Freddie?"

He grinned broadly. "Nothing at all. I would be delighted to have such a charming tour guide."

By this time, Sara had regained her composure and looked knowingly at her aunt. Bertie was a born matchmaker. "Thank you, Freddie," she said. "I think you will find Florence to be charming as well."

During the next several weeks that Freddie was in Italy, he and Lady Sara spent a great deal of time together. It was not long before they fell into a comfortable camaraderie. But despite Bertie's best efforts, their relationship developed into that of brother and sister.

With his open countenance and easy manner, Freddie soon became a great favorite with their friends. He was included in all the social functions to which Sara and Bertie were invited. But behind the smiles and chatter, Sara sensed a reserve. They were at a musical one evening when she broached the subject.

"Is there something bothering you, Freddie?" she asked seriously. "You sometimes seem withdrawn."

He looked at her for a moment. "I do not want to burden you with my problems," he replied.

"It is no burden. I thought we were friends. Please tell me."

"Oh, it is hard to explain. I guess it is just that I feel so useless. I am four-and-twenty and a younger son. I have an adequate inheritance but no responsibility. I feel I should be doing something other than attending parties and sporting events."

She was impressed by this. "What would you like to do?"

"Join the military. The war with France is intensifying and I want to take part."

She looked at him sadly. "I hate to think of you in battle, Freddie. The fighting in Portugal is fierce."

He nodded grimly. "That is why I must join. I have written Randy to ask him to buy me my colors since I have not yet come into my own money. I hope to hear from him soon."

They spoke no more as the music started again, but Sara was left with an uneasy feeling.

It was just a week later that Freddie burst into the small parlor where Sara and Bertie were taking tea. He was waving a letter and danced excitedly about the room. "It's from Randy!" he exclaimed. "He has purchased my colors!"

Sara and Bertie exchanged worried glances, but they both knew how important this was to their young friend.

"Why that is wonderful, Freddie," Sara said, in falsely hearty tones. "Do you return to England then?"

"Yes, I sail out tonight." He hugged them

both. "I cannot tell you how much this means to me."

"Take good care of yourself, Freddie," Sara said, as she kissed his cheek. "You will keep in touch?"

"Yes, I promise," he replied. "And now I must be on my way."

Bertie and Freddie exchanged farewells and Sara walked him to the door.

He turned to her and put his hand under her chin to raise her face to his. He leaned down and kissed her lightly on the lips. "You know, Sara, if you were not still in love with my brother, I think I would have tried to win you for my own."

And with that, he was gone, leaving a stunned and thoughtful young woman standing at the door of a Florentine villa.

Chapter Five

London, 1813

AT THE AGE OF NINE-AND-TWENTY, LADY SARA Liviscombe was the despair of all her many friends and acquaintances. After an absolutely dazzling first season during which she had been the toast of the town, she had quit the social scene and later England.

Those with exceptionally long memories recalled that Lord Randolph Ketcham, the Viscount of Awick, had been her constant companion in those days and everyone had expected they would marry. Some even remembered the Tishford ball when the two had danced together all evening—a sure indication that an announcement would be made.

But there had been no announcement and abruptly both had disappeared. Romantics believed that Lady Sara had left due to a broken heart. The gossip-mongers believed there was something more to it, especially since she was accompanied by her scandalous aunt, Lady Alberta Watson.

The season following the joint disappearance had been marked by speculation as to what had actually happened between Awick and Lady Sara. But, as is usually the case, with no new information and neither of the participants present, the matter became a nine-day wonder and was soon replaced by more interesting *on dits*. The tale was revived a few years later when it was learned that Lord Awick had married and seemed fixed in America. About Lady Sara there was no word except that she remained in Italy with her aunt.

It had been just two years before that Bertie had married an Italian Comte and Lady Sara had returned to England. She had gone to her estate in Somerset first and contacted her only other female relative, her mother's sister, Eloise Farley. Lady Sara had decided to return to London to re-open the Liviscombe townhouse, but in order to do so, she needed a female companion. Eloise, having lived on her brother's charity and endured his four obnoxious children for too many years, jumped at the chance.

Despite the ten-year hiatus, the fashionable world had not forgotten Lady Sara and eagerly awaited her return. It was not disappointed. She was still tall and slender, with the same dusky curls, but those who knew her well could detect a hint of sadness in those improbable blue eyes. Her wit and intelligence had matured and her years abroad had taught her a new self-reliance.

But despite the best efforts of her friends to introduce her to all the most eligible men, Lady Sara remained distant and aloof. She seemed to have no interest in making a suitable match. No one ever mentioned Lord Awick to her—in fact, all pointedly avoided mention of him—but those closest to her suspected that he was the reason she remained on the shelf.

As for Lady Sara, she had come to enjoy the seasons in town. She particularly liked the theatre and opera and, at any social event, was able to ferret out the most interesting people.

For the most part, she was well pleased with her life. Her biggest trial was her Aunt Eloise. The two years they had spent together had proved that, though a sweet old thing, she was not overly endowed with mental capacity. While Sara dearly loved her, there were times when she had a very inelegant desire to wring her neck. This was turning out to be one of those days.

The day in question was Aunt Eloise's sixty-fourth birthday, an event that occurred unerringly in the third week of February. The fact that it was her sixty-fourth was known for certain by two people, Lady Sara and Eloise, that lady's parents having had the good grace to die so as not to humiliate her with the truth. Eloise Farley had many virtues, but a strict adherence to the truth—at least as far as her age was concerned—was not among them. Added to the insult of having yet another birthday, the day was cold, windy, damp and overcast. This was enough to send even the most cheerful individuals, of which Eloise could usually be numbered, into the dismals.

The day had begun exactly as every other day in the well-run and efficiently organized Liviscombe household. Sara had arisen early and consumed her breakfast in bed—a repast that consisted of chocolate, toast and the daily newspapers. She had not lost her interest in world affairs since her return from Italy. In fact, now that she was once again immersed in the rather narrow limits of London society, she was even more keenly aware of current international events. Her interest was piqued by the fact that she had visited many of the places that were now prominent in the news. She had fallen into deep thought on the war in the peninsula when she was roused by an uncommon commotion issuing from the breakfast room, located directly below her bedroom.

"But it is my birthday! How could there not have been strawberries and oysters? That was what I requested." On hearing this plaintive cry from her aunt, Sara groaned.

"I'm that sorry, mum," she recognized Cook's voice, "but as I told you, they just didn't have none."

"Well!" Aunt Eloise exclaimed, "we will see about that. Just imagine not having strawberries and oysters!"

Sara, having a horrid vision of oysters covered in strawberry sauce, or worse, strawberries served with cream and oysters, decided it was time to intervene. Foregoing the pleasure of ringing for Agnes, she dragged herself out of bed, pulled a comb through her tousled curls and donned a dressing gown of pink satin laced through with red ribbon trimming. She reluctantly made her way downstairs to enter the zone of combat. Sara was by nature neither cowardly nor fainthearted, but she knew from long experience that the upcoming interview would be as pleasurable as falling off a horse, something she had done once and had promptly resolved not to do again. Assuming her most forbidding expression, she pushed open the door.

"Exactly what is going on here?" she asked the occupants. "Would either of you care to explain why my breakfast room has been turned into a battle field?"

Aunt Eloise, holding a cup of tea in one hand and the crumbled remains of a muffin in the other, had the grace to look guilty. Cook, on the other hand, glowering at Aunt Eloise from her position by the door, had the advantage of long service in her Ladyship's employ and the knowledge that her talents were irreplaceable. She sniffed. "I just told her, M'Lady," said the worthy, "that there weren't no oysters or strawberries, and nothing would do but that she had to fly into a snit."

At these words, Aunt Eloise began to sputter but Sara quelled her with an intentionally haughty stare. Aunt Eloise subsided, and she turned back to Cook.

"Did you check *all* the markets?" she asked, knowing full well that her competent and thorough servants had done everything short of growing the desired delicacies themselves to keep this contretemps from occurring.

"Yes indeed, M'Lady," said Cook in an injured tone. "I sent both the kitchen maid and the footman out this mornin' and they fair scoured London. But them that usually stocks 'em was sold out, and others allowed as how it weren't the season. Though oysters should be had in February." Here she leveled a malevolent glare at Aunt Eloise. "We done our best, M'Lady, but she won't believe it. Just because it *is* her birthday don't mean that things can be had that can't." With that she folded her arms across her ample bosom and all but dug in her heels waiting for the next assault from her opponent.

Aunt Eloise, in the meanwhile, had taken on the look of a deeply wronged sparrow. Small, plump and unworldly, she reminded Sara of a bird that had been accidentally knocked from the nest too soon. There were now two poses that Sara knew from long experience her aunt would adopt—Indignant Anger or Wounded Sensibilities. She irreverently found herself mentally laying odds on which it would be. Unfortunately it was Wounded Sensibilities.

"I do not know what I have done," Aunt Eloise murmured in a voice that was an odd mixture of sorrow and petulance, "to be treated in such a way. It is not as if I ever asked for much or did anything other than try to be a loyal and devoted companion."

Here Sara had to stifle a sigh. She had brought Aunt Eloise into her household as much to give that poor lady a home as to protect her own reputation. It was a little late for that, she thought wryly. The services that the dear old thing rendered could easily have been obtained from a paid companion with the added advantage that such a creature would have been constantly thankful for the pleasant and comfortable life she had been given and the few demands that were ever made on her time. Not that Aunt Eloise was a complainer, it was just that Sara hated to have her peace cut up.

She decided that it was high time to end this little encounter. First, she turned to Cook as this was the combatant whose tantrums could most easily be quieted.

"I am sure that, as always, you have done your utmost to insure the comfort of my aunt and myself. Since you were unable to obtain those items which my aunt requested, would you be so good as to prepare some of those incomparable lobster patties which she so adores and perhaps brandied fruit? Also request that Roberts bring in a bottle of champagne. This is after all a highly auspicious occasion." Cook, mollified by her mistress's reasonable request, made a polite, if somewhat awkward, curtsey and retreated to tell the butler her Ladyship's request.

Sara then turned to Aunt Eloise halfway expecting a flood of tears and recriminations. Actually, her aunt had been somewhat placated by the promise of lobster patties and was not at all averse to a little champagne. Still she felt it necessary to enforce upon her niece the fact that she believed herself to have been badly used. She snuffled.

"It is my birthday, after all, and even though I am turned fifty-nine," she stated with a fine disregard for the truth, "I think I am entitled to a little more consideration. I may just be a poor relation, but I do try—"

At this fortuitous moment, Roberts entered the drawing room bearing a bottle of champagne and two glasses. He set the tray down on the parquet table next to his mistress's chair and bowed. "Will there be anything else, my Lady?"

Sara gave him one of her most enchanting smiles. "No, I think that will be all. Thank you, Roberts."

As the butler bowed himself out, she presented her aunt with a glass of champagne. "I know, dear, and you are everything that one could ask for in a companion. You must not think that you are not a welcome addition to my household." She picked up her own glass. "To a long life of health and happiness."

Aunt Eloise had the grace to incline her head at this toast, and sipped appreciatively at the champagne. "Oh, my dear," she said, "I hope you do not think that I am ungrateful for the kindness that you have shown me. Truly I do not know what would have become of me if you had not taken me in."

Sara held up an elegant hand to silence her. More than tears and complaints, she hated gratitude. "Hush, dearest. I am delighted that you were able to share my home. And now I have a small surprise for you." Rising, she pulled the bell cord and Roberts immediately appeared.

"Yes, my Lady?"

"Would you request that Agnes come to me?" she said.

"Of course, my Lady."

Within moments, Lady Sara's maid entered the room. After a few moments of quiet discussion, Agnes departed and Sara resumed her seat.

"What kind of surprise?" asked Aunt Eloise looking like a child just promised an ice.

"You shall see," Sara replied.

Agnes again appeared at the door and handed Sara a parcel wrapped in brown paper. Having thanked her maid, she presented the parcel to her elderly relation. "Happy Birthday, my dear."

Aunt Eloise impatiently tore off the wrapping and gazed down upon an exquisitely embroidered Norwich shawl. "Oh, Sara," she exclaimed with tears springing to her eyes, "it is lovely, absolutely lovely. Thank you so much."

Lady Sara smiled and refilled the champagne glasses. The two ladies sat for a while sipping their champagne. Sara was enjoying the unaccustomed silence and Aunt Eloise was determining the best way to broach a subject that had been weighing on her mind.

"Sara," she began, "I saw Mrs. Warrington last Tuesday."

This remark seemed innocent enough and Sara looked at her expectantly. She knew full well that her aunt attended Lady Buffield's at-homes every Tuesday and since Mrs. Warrington and Lady Buffield were related by marriage, it was only natural that the two should have crossed paths. She waited to see what item of great portent was coming.

Aunt Eloise took a deep breath and announced in a dramatic tone, "Awick is back!"

Sara raised an eyebrow. "Lord Awick? I had heard that he had decided to settle in America, but why should it come as such a surprise that he would want to visit his home? I am sure that the *ton* is agog to meet his young family."

"You mean you did not hear?" asked Aunt Eloise in a tone of surprise and satisfaction at being the bearer of such momentous news. "His wife died a year ago from a fever she contracted during their travels. He returned immediately and has been spending his time since then on his estate in Scotland. Mrs. Warrington tells me that he wished to remain there for the mourning period, but now that it is over, he has returned to London and re-opened the townhouse."

"And what of his daughter?" Sara asked. "Did he leave her in Kent?"

"No, indeed. Although she is only five, Lord Awick decided he would much rather have her with him than leave her to the dubious ministrations of the servants. I understand he is a devoted father."

With her own experience as a young girl, abandoned to be raised by servants, she totally concurred with this decision. She was filled with a sudden pain, caused equally by the neglect of her father and Awick's mistreatment of her. She had thought she had long since buried all those emotions and was angry at herself for this weakness. "So he has taken on the management of his daughter," she remarked with some asperity. "What do you suppose wrought such a change in his chronically selfish and unfeeling attitude?"

Aunt Eloise looked at her in surprise. She herself, of course, had been immured in her brother's household during her niece's come-out, but even in that country backwater she had heard of the relationship between Awick and Sara and the flattering court he had paid her. She never knew what had happened between them and had not wanted to ask. The few times she had tried to broach the subject, the girl had become aloof and distant and so she had not pursued it.

But Eloise was a hopeless romantic. Somewhere in her weak and befuddled mind she had fixed the thought that the two young lovers were somehow star-crossed and required only a chance to be together again and suddenly all would be well with them.

With this thought uppermost, she asked where Sara had obtained such a poor opinion of his Lordship and why she was so quick to find fault with him.

Her niece shrugged her lovely shoulders. "Surely, dearest, you know that our acquaintance goes back many years and my memories of him are not pleasant ones. Suffice it to say that we did not part on the best of terms. I will grant that he was a devilishly handsome man, but he showed too little regard for the feelings of others. I find it hard to believe that anyone could have changed that much."

At this point Sara began to regret having allowed herself to be drawn into this discussion. Aunt Eloise was a great admirer of Emily Warrington and, consequently, saw herself as a champion of that lady's godson. She now took up the cudgels in his defense.

"I do not know how you can say such a thing," she said indignantly, "about someone who always showed you every consideration and treated you with the utmost politeness and courtesy, from everything I have heard. Besides, after twelve years, it is high time to let bygones be bygones."

Sara almost made a sharp retort but bit her lip and swallowed the words. She recalled as if it were only this morning how she had felt when she awakened in his bed and found him gone. Again, she was surprised and angry and could not help remembering Freddie's parting words of five years earlier. No, she told herself sternly, Freddie had been wrong. There could be no question of love, not after the way Awick had treated her. She was perfectly sure that her feelings for him had long since changed into indifference. She certainly was not about to argue about it with her aunt. Resolutely, she changed the subject. "I hear that Lady Buffield is to become a grandmother," she remarked casually.

For the moment, Aunt Eloise was distracted. With all the enthusiasm of one who had never had children, she exclaimed rapturously, "Oh, yes. Is it not the most exciting thing? Her eldest daughter, you know. After three years they had almost given up hope." She continued on in this vein for several moments, then abruptly recalled the topic that was uppermost in her mind. "But we were speaking of Lord Awick. You two have known each other for so long, and since he is fresh back in town and most likely feeling strange, I have taken the liberty of inviting him and Mrs. Warrington to my birthday dinner tonight. You do not mind, do you, dearest?" she asked, as Sara grew alarmingly still. "It is my celebration, after all," she continued in a somewhat petulant tone. "Since the Tishfords will be coming and that nice Mr. Kline, our numbers will be even." Her niece remained silent. "Oh come, Sara, do say it is all right. It means so much to me you know."

Sara relented. "Of course, Auntie. As you say, it is your celebration and you are free to invite anyone you like."

"Thank you, Sara, you are a love. And now, how about a little more champagne?"

Sara agreed, knowing she would need it to face the evening before her.

Chapter Six

Seated at the dressing table while Agnes fixed her hair, Sara was undecided whether she should throttle her aunt or simply plead a headache and not go down at all. She brooded on these alternatives for a while and at last decided that the first would probably land her in jail and the second would prove to be a victory for Lord Awick since she suspected that he must dislike her as heartily as she disliked him. She thought for a moment. Why on earth had he agreed to dine with them? Then she realized that the answer was obvious. Despite his many shortcomings, he was genuinely fond of his godmother and often allowed her to lead him into situations for which he had no liking. Such as seeing Lady Sara Liviscombe again! With that thought she decided to show Lord Awick just how little she cared for his opinion.

Consequently, she asked Agnes to redo her hair into a more flattering style and to take from the clothes press her favorite ivory silk gown, the one that revealed the creamy whiteness of her shoulders and displayed her slender, graceful figure to full advantage. Clasping a simple diamond pendant around her throat, she felt ready to face the abominable Lord Awick.

In the drawing room, her aunt was seated in one of the floral chintz wing-chairs located on either side of the fireplace. This room had always been one of Sara's favorites, with its heavy wood paneling and ornate mantel nicely balanced by the gay yellow-and-green fabrics of the curtains and furniture. Even the carpet, with its bold yellow pattern, created a feeling of walking through a field of buttercups. Despite her anxiety, Sara smiled as she approached her aunt. In honor of her birthday, that lady had dressed herself in her most becoming puce satin gown and a turban that boasted three ostrich plumes.

"You do not look a day over fifty," Sara remarked as she sat in the wing chair opposite her aunt.

Aunt Eloise gave her a coy look. "Oh come, my dear. Fifty-five perhaps, but fifty?"

Sara laughed. "Really, Auntie, you are incorrigible."

At this moment, the door opened and Roberts entered. In his most formal tone, he announced, "Lord and Lady Tishford and Miss Tishford."

During her two years back in town, Sara had developed a warm friendship with the Tishfords. Their daughter, Clare, had only just arrived from their country estate to make her bow to polite society. Sara was quite curious to see her, especially after all the glowing remarks she had heard from the doting Mama.

As she rose to greet them, she had to admit that Georgie had not exaggerated. Small and pleasingly rounded, with strawberry-blond hair, emerald green eyes and a perfect rosebud mouth, Lady Clare Tishford made a charming picture. Her gown was of flowered sprig muslin, her only jewelry a strand of perfectly matched pearls, befitting a young lady beginning her first season.

Sara and Georgie exchanged a quick hug. "How lovely you look, my dear." Georgie Tishford was a comfortable matron, forever smiling and in agreement with whatever was said to her. Sara noted, however, that she kept a watchful eye on her daughter.

"Thank you," Sara replied. "It must be the candlelight." She next turned to Lord Tishford, tall and trim with the proud bearing and forceful expression of a military man. Indeed, he had left a distinguished career in the army and had gone into politics where he was now equally successful. He clasped Sara's hands and smiled. "As always, my dear, you are positively ravishing."

She never objected to flattery. "Why thank you, sir. But I fear your daughter outshines me completely." She took the girl's hands and said, "It is a pleasure to meet you at last, Clare. I have heard a great deal about your beauty and accomplishments. Are you excited about your coming-out? I am sure you will have no trouble in attracting a great many beaux."

Clare giggled and blushed. Although a beautiful girl, she was still terribly young and all her thoughts were focused on gowns, balls and dreams of dashing young noblemen.

Aunt Eloise greeted her guests and received their best wishes for many happy returns, as well as a footstool worked in needlepoint by Lady Tishford. As she exclaimed over the beauty and practicality of this object, Roberts again appeared at the door to announce the arrival of Mr. John Kline. Upon the entrance of that worthy gentleman, Sara could not refrain from glancing at her aunt. She still found it endearing that a lady of four-and-sixty could blush.

Mr. Kline was an elderly, distinguished-looking gentleman. Of medium height and stocky build, his white hair was thinning and his manner was unfailingly courteous. He had spent many of his youthful years in India and had returned to England, as the saying went, rich as a nabob. At the insistence of his family, he had married a second cousin but the union had not been happy. After her death, he had shown no further desire to re-enter that blissful state and now spent his time looking after his considerable economic interests, putting in appearances at selectively chosen social affairs, and playing piquet at White's. Of late, he had begun to show a marked interest in Eloise Farley. He greeted his hostess then turned to her aunt. He kissed her fingers, then pressed a small box into her hand.

Her blush grew even rosier. "Why, Mr.

Kline!" she exclaimed. "How very thoughtful." She undid the wrapping with trembling fingers.

"Do hurry, Auntie," Sara said. "I do not think any of us can stand the suspense much longer." She glanced at Mr. Kline with an appraising look.

Aunt Eloise at last removed the gray foil wrapping and opened the box. A small gasp escaped her and she raised her eyes to Mr. Kline, only to look down quickly as she saw his intent gaze. "Why, Mr. Kline," she said in a fluttering voice, "really you should not have. It is exquisite, it is . . ." words failed her for a moment. "It is perfect." She lifted the bauble from its box to show her other guests.

It was a butterfly brooch worked in gold filigree with emeralds, sapphires, rubies and diamonds inlaid to represent the markings. All the occupants of the drawing room clustered around to exclaim and admire.

Roberts entered at this moment to announce the last of the guests. "Mrs. Warrington and Lord Awick."

Sara turned to the door, determined to put a good face on this encounter. She had not seen the viscount for twelve years, not since the night they had spent together, and was not sure what to expect. The thought flashed through her mind that he had probably changed— would probably look older and care-worn. She was quickly proved wrong. The figure that greeted her eyes was that of a tall, commanding man with thick black hair tinged at the sides with silver. His bearing was almost regal and his well-cut evening clothes proclaimed the excellence of his physique, lean and muscular with broad shoulders and a narrow waist. His face was strong and handsome, and the blue-gray eyes still had that piercing quality that could be so unsettling as she knew from past experience. His nose was aquiline and there was an arrogant set to his mouth. It was obvious to the most casual observer that he was a proud man, and one very used to having his own way. The years had been good to him, Sara thought, and wondered why his presence after so long should cause a flutter in her heart.

Confused and upset by her own emotions, she turned her attention to the woman who accompanied him. Mrs. Warrington, Awick's godmother, was thin and gaunt. Although she had a reputation for being domineering and forthright, she was a kindly soul with a great deal of charm. Her husband had left her with no children and a sizable fortune, both of which circumstances pleased her immensely. She advanced first to Eloise.

"Happy Birthday, my dear!" she exclaimed, clasping the elderly lady's hands and kissing her cheek. "How good of you to invite us to help celebrate this occasion." Beckoning to the viscount, she said, "I do not believe you have met my godson, Lord Awick. It was awfully sweet of you to include him in your invitation."

Aunt Eloise extended her hand. "I am so glad you could come," she greeted.

Lord Awick bowed over her hand and lightly kissed her fingers. "Thank you, Miss Farley," he replied. "I am honored that you desired my presence for this celebration." His smile lightened his rugged features and made it obvious why he had been so much in demand during his London seasons when he had been a true man about town with a slightly rakish reputation. This, of course, had added a spark of excitement in the hearts of young and impressionable girls and their older and equally impressionable mamas.

He turned to Sara, his face assuming a more forbidding expression. He took her hand and bowed. "Lady Sara," he said, somewhat stiffly. "You have not changed in the years since we last met. I trust you are in good health."

Sara inclined her head and replied, equally stiffly, "Indeed, my Lord, I am blessed with an excellent constitution."

Lord Awick gave a slight smile that did not reach his eyes. "Of course," he murmured and turned to greet the other guests. He had met Lord Tishford often at Brooks's and the two shared many political opinions. He greeted Lady Tishford amicably, then bestowed his attention upon Clare.

"Lady Clare," he said, "what a pleasure to meet you at last. Your father often extols your beauty. I can see he does not exaggerate. Are you excited about your coming-out?"

Clare again giggled and blushed. It seemed this was all she would add to the conversation. Lord Awick extended his hand to Mr. Kline murmuring, "Servant, Sir."

"Awick, my boy. Distressed to hear of your loss. Who would have imagined one of old Kennington's brood would have been sickly.

Not that I ever liked him much, but strong as a horse, as was that woman he married." Noticing the cold look on Awick's face, he stammered slightly. "Oh sorry, you know. Problem with old age—tend to talk before you think." He glanced at Sara hoping she would end his discomfort.

Sara was adept at handling awkward situations. "We were all saddened to learn of your bereavement, my Lord, but I am sure that it is not something on which you wish to dwell." Giving him a gentle smile, she turned to the others. "I believe I heard the dinner bell. Shall we go in?"

As if on cue, Lord Tishford offered his arm to Eloise. Rising gracefully, she allowed him to lead her to the dining room. Lord Awick escorted Lady Tishford and Mr. Kline followed with Mrs. Warrington on his arm. Sara and Clare brought up the rear.

Clare giggled again. "Oh, he is so terribly handsome, even if he is quite old," she said, fluttering her perfect eyelashes.

Sara looked amused. "Old?" she said. "Why he is only eight years older than I." For the first time, she felt her own age keenly. In truth, Lord Awick was almost old enough to be Clare Tishford's father.

Clare looked embarrassed. "Oh, I did not mean to say that you were old, Lady Sara, it is just that . . . well . . ."

Sara took pity on her. "Come, child, no offense was taken. Let us take our seats."

She proceeded to a place at the foot of the long wooden table set with silver and crystal

that twinkled in the candlelight. In honor of
the occasion, she had given her own place at
the head of the table to her aunt and placed Mr.
Kline at that lady's right and Lord Tishford to
the left. Lady Tishford was seated on Mr.
Kline's other side and Mrs. Warrington next to
Lord Tishford. She was seated between Clare
Tishford and Lord Awick.

As they settled themselves, the footman entered with the first course, a chilled cucumber
soup served with buttery rolls hot from the
oven. Course followed course, with particular
attention paid to the lobster patties. The pigeon
pie, veal ragout, baked ham and the numerous
removes and jellies were equally well received.

The conversation soon went from general
topics to more private talks between the dinner
partners. Aunt Eloise turned to Mr. Kline and
murmured, "Your gift is the most lovely thing I
have ever owned."

He replied that the piece was not more lovely
than its new owner.

Lord Tishford asked Mrs. Warrington if she
had heard the latest about Lady Allen. Lady
Tishford engaged Lord Awick in a discussion of
his holdings in Kent and of his daughter who,
at five, was on her first visit to London. Sara
asked Clare how she was enjoying *her* first
taste of London society—the shops, the small
get-togethers that preceded the start of the
season, the bustle of the magical city.

"Oh," breathed Clare, "it is all too, too perfect. Why, yesterday Mama took me to Bond
Street to do some shopping and I saw the most
enchanting bonnet." She described it in com-

plete and absorbing detail. Sara had forgotten what it was like to be so young. Great heavens, she thought, was I ever so wrapped up in appearances that all my thoughts were focused on my apparel?

As she stifled a sigh and politely hid a yawn, she encountered Lord Awick's gaze upon her, a look of wicked amusement in his eye. She stiffened. How dare he laugh at her! Putting on her best smile, she returned her attention to Clare, and tried to follow the spate of words with a look of interest.

Finally, Aunt Eloise arose and suggested the ladies retire to the drawing room so that the men could enjoy their brandy and cigars. The other ladies followed her from the room.

Sara seated herself on a brocade sofa and soon Mrs. Warrington joined her. "What a lovely dinner, my dear," she began, "and it was so nice of you to include Awick in your invitation. I know he has been looking forward to seeing you again."

As this was said with a perfectly sober expression, Sara wondered if she had heard correctly or if Mrs. Warrington was becoming addled in her advancing years. As her mind wandered, the lady beside her continued speaking. "—But it was such a long time ago and we must allow bygones to be bygones."

Sara understood this enigmatic statement perfectly well, even though she had only heard the last part of it. She found it hard to believe that anyone still remembered such ancient history. There were now actually days on end when she herself did not think about it. Unknowingly she sighed.

Mrs. Warrington, a shrewd and perceptive lady, noted Sara's sigh as well as her wistful expression. This was exactly what she had wished to discover. She was perfectly aware that her godson had seemed to be as averse to seeing Lady Sara again as she was to seeing him. She had found it amazing that he had even accepted the invitation. She knew Awick would never have agreed to do something he found distasteful just to please her. He had too much pride.

Her curiosity was thoroughly aroused by this time, but she knew that further conversation on this topic would be fruitless. She did not want to open that particular door yet, merely turn the knob.

She glanced across to where Eloise sat with Georgie and Clare. "Come, my dear," she said, "I believe it is time I presented your aunt with my little gift." So saying, she crossed to the other party and handed Eloise a package from her capacious handbag.

Aunt Eloise happily tore off the wrapping, exposing a delicately worked silver net reticule. "Oh, Emily, thank you so much. It is lovely!" she exclaimed. "Did you make it?"

Mrs. Warrington smiled. "One has to do something to fill the time. I hope you will have occasion to put it to use." This was said archly: Mr. Kline had just entered and was heading toward Miss Farley. Seating himself beside her on the loveseat, he exclaimed over the gift's fine craftsmanship, much to the satisfaction of the ladies.

Lord Tishford joined his wife, and Sara was surprised to find Lord Awick by her side. She raised her eyes to his and smiled uncertainly. She was still wondering why Mrs. Warrington had said that he had been looking forward to seeing her. He had seemed so distant when he had greeted her. She decided that cool politeness would be the best course.

"I'm pleased that you could join us this evening," she said. "I hope it did not interfere with any other plans you might have had. I realize that the notice was short."

Lord Awick looked at her questioningly. "What obligation could I have possibly had that would take precedence over such a charming celebration?"

Sara blushed, fearing she had sounded too inquisitive about his personal life. After all these years, a single glance from those piercing blue-gray eyes made her feel like a silly schoolgirl. She quickly gathered her scattered wits. "I am sure, my Lord, that how you choose to spend your time is totally your own affair. I meant only that my aunt is honored by your presence here this evening." She bit her lip. She had not meant to sound so cold.

His expression darkened. "Indeed it is always a pleasure to see Miss Farley," he replied in a distant voice. "And now if you will excuse me." He bowed and crossed the room to join Lady Tishford and her daughter and engaged them in a lively conversation.

Sara wondered what on earth he found to

talk about that would hold Clare's interest. Of course, he was renowned for his charm and had, at one time, well deserved his reputation as a rake. She shrugged and found Mr. Kline taking a chair beside her.

"Your aunt is a lovely woman," he said, glancing at the lady in question with a look that was decidedly affectionate. "Hard to believe that she is fifty-nine. Hope she doesn't think me too old for her."

Sara almost laughed. "My aunt believes one is only as old as one feels. I take it, sir, that you are very fond of her?" She wanted to ask him if his intentions were honorable but did not quite know how to say it without sounding presumptuous.

"Yes indeed. Very fond." He seemed unwilling to continue.

"That was a lovely brooch that you gave her. I know she will wear it with the slightest excuse."

Mr. Kline chuckled. "I plan to provide her with many opportunities. It is, I am afraid, a poor reflection of her own beauty."

Sara looked across at Aunt Eloise. While she was the first to admit her relative's many good qualities, she would not have listed beauty among them. Still, she had spent too much time in polite circles not to know when to hold her tongue. Also she had a real love for her aunt and hoped that this match would come about, as much for her own sake as her aunt's. She recalled the morning's contretemps. "Indeed, sir, she is a remarkable woman."

This was all the encouragement Mr. Kline

needed. He embarked on recitation of Eloise Farley's many virtues. Sara settled herself deeper into the sofa, donning a look of intense interest.

Lord Tishford had engaged his wife and Aunt Eloise in a discussion of the Bonapartist activity on the peninsula. With an insider's knowledge of the events and their significance, he had captured the ladies' attention, especially when he recounted the adventures of the Duke of Wellington.

Lord Awick was in close conversation with Clare Tishford, while Mrs. Warrington seemed perfectly content to sit listening to their inanities. Sara did not realize that Mrs. Warrington was finding it increasingly difficult to stay awake and that Lord Awick was beginning to fear that the smile he wore was fixed indelibly on his face.

It was with a feeling of distinct relief that Sara, Mrs. Warrington and Lord Awick turned to the door as Roberts, with the assistance of the under-housemaid, entered with the tea tray. "My Lady," he said. He advanced to his mistress and placed refreshments on the table in front of her.

Sara poured, unconsciously adding a slice of lemon and one lump of sugar to Lord Awick's cup. He accepted it from her, looking slightly amused. Sara, suddenly self-conscious about having remembered how he preferred his tea after a lapse of twelve years, looked down and busied herself with the task of serving the rest of the company.

The viscount, however, was not content to let

the matter go. Bending over her he murmured, "I am flattered, but then old habits are hard to break."

Sara, very aware of his nearness, put on her best dismissing manner. "You would be amazed, my Lord, how very many can be broken with no trouble at all." She smiled up at him, hoping he would take the hint.

He did not. "Indeed, how is it then that you recalled exactly how I like my tea?"

"One tends to remember inconsequential details as one ages. Do you not find that to be true?" she asked sweetly, still trying to hide her own embarrassment.

Awick stared at her for a moment, and again his expression grew cold. He said sardonically, "Oh, yes, my dear, the most inconsequential details such as broken promises and lies. But then that is the price of age and wisdom." He turned abruptly and rejoined Clare.

Sara stared at his retreating back. Exactly what had he meant by that? "Broken promises and lies," indeed. How dare he! After all it was he who—

Aunt Eloise broke into her reverie at this point. "My dear, I trust you will not mind, but Mr. Kline has invited me to share his box at the theatre tomorrow evening and hopes that you, Lord Dydlefield and the Tishfords will consent to make up our party. Mrs. Warrington and Lord Awick have pleaded previous engagements."

Lord Dydlefield, a foppish bachelor with a deep belief in his own consequence and a strong inclination to believe that his mother should be the final arbiter of all decisions concerning his life, had been paying Sara marked attention for the past several weeks. Since the case did not yet seem desperate, Lady Dydlefield had decided not to take any overt action. She knew her son very well, and had no doubt that Lady Sara herself would give that gentleman a disgust of her with her forthright and independent ways. Lady Dydlefield had no objection to her son marrying, but she wanted a girl who could be ruled as easily as he. Sara was not that girl. Still she was certain of the outcome of this little affair and so was prepared to let nature take its course, especially when it coincided with her own designs.

Sara was much more aware of that lady's motives than anyone guessed and rather enjoyed playing the game, particularly since she knew that Lord Dydlefield's affections were in no way seriously engaged. He was interested in her in much the same way that he was interested in his extensive art collection—as something to draw out and exhibit. She told Aunt Eloise she would be delighted. The theatre was a passion of hers. She loved watching people become what they were not or pretend not to be what they were. Sara did not know why this should so appeal to her. Perhaps it had to do with her painful relationships with men—like her father and Lord Awick.

At this moment she heard Clare giggle and looked over to see the girl smiling up at Awick, charming dimples appearing in her cheeks. Again Sara wondered what he could possibly be saying to hold the chit's attention.

Shortly thereafter the party began to break up. The Tishfords were the first to leave, again wishing Eloise their very best and complimenting their hostess on her superb dinner. Mrs. Warrington kissed Eloise on the cheek as she departed and warmly shook hands with Sara. Lord Awick bowed, expressed his thanks and said he looked forward to seeing them again soon. Aunt Eloise looked delighted, Lady Sara skeptical.

Mr. Kline looked determined to stay all night but eventually, bowing low over Miss Farley's hand, he said, "Until tomorrow then." Accepting his hat and cane from the footman, he departed.

As the door swung shut behind him, Aunt Eloise turned to her niece. "Oh, my love, was it not wonderful? Such a delightful evening. I do not know when I have enjoyed myself more. And did you see how taken Lord Awick was with young Clare? Of course he is somewhat older than she but I am convinced that a man of experience is just what she needs. Would it not be glorious if we brought them together?"

Sara's mind was full of uncharitable thoughts about the kind of experience Lord Awick had and Clare Tishford's ability to feel love for anything beyond her wardrobe. Consequently, she was relieved to notice her elderly relation yawning hugely.

"Yes, it was a lovely party," she said, "but now it is time to retire. We must be fresh if we are to accompany Mr. Kline to the theatre tomorrow."

She arose and kissed her aunt on the cheek.

"Sleep well, dearest, and please don't pin that brooch to your nightgown."

As Eloise blushed, Sara laughed and escaped to her bedroom. It had been a long day. She snuggled between sheets still warm from the heating brick, and thought back over her discussions with Awick. Odd that he could still affect her after all that had happened between them. At any rate, it was long since over and she resolutely decided not to give him or their relationship any further thought. And, with that admirable intention, she fell asleep, dreaming of black hair streaked with silver and blue-gray eyes that alternately smiled and mocked.

Chapter Seven

"LOVELY DAY, M'LADY" AGNES REMARKED, opening the drapes and pulling back the curtains on her mistress's ornate four-poster. Sara blinked in the sunlight. "I slept later than I intended."

"It's these late hours you've been keeping," said her abigail, handing her mistress her dressing gown. "The maid will be up directly with your chocolate and newspapers."

Sara sat down on the window seat to enjoy the scene outside. Even though her townhouse was located in the heart of London, the garden was uncommonly large and her bedroom looked out over it. With the trees again in full leaf and the spring flowers in bloom, the sight was mellow and restful. It was going to be unusually warm for early April; only the tiniest of fluffy white clouds fringed the horizon.

There was a knock at the door and the maid

entered with the breakfast tray. Sara smiled her thanks and began to read through the papers. As was her custom, she turned first to the news from the peninsula. As the campaign in Spain escalated, more and more of the British regiments were being called into active service. The reports varied daily as to what was actually happening but the overall tenor was ominous. Reading through these reports, she was struck by the mention of a familiar name. Captain Frederick Ketcham, officer in the Seventh Dragoons, younger brother of Lord Randolph Ketcham, Viscount Awick, had been posted home following an injury taken in battle. Sara had read enough of these notices to know that by the time they appeared in the paper, the soldier had usually arrived. She smiled to herself. She had always enjoyed Freddie with his open, cheerful countenance and ready humor. She only hoped his injury had not been a serious one.

She rang for Agnes and was soon dressed in a pale-green walking dress, her dark curls smoothed back from her forehead with a few tendrils allowed free to caress her cheeks. She descended to the morning room to catch up on the household accounts. She met Aunt Eloise in the main hall.

"Oh there you are, my dear. I wanted to let you know that I have invited Mr. Kline to tea this afternoon. You don't mind, do you?" As this was said in a tone reminiscent of a child asking a special treat, Sara was forced to smile.

"Of course I don't mind, Auntie. Your friends

are always welcome in this house." She put just the slightest emphasis on the word "friends."

Aunt Eloise blushed. "Yes, yes," she said, "it's just that I wanted you to know in case you have other plans. I mean, I don't wish to intrude on your time."

Sara laughed. "What you are trying to tell me, dear Aunt, is that you would prefer to entertain Mr. Kline by yourself." Casting her eyes upward, she folded her hands together and said primly, "You know, of course, that it would be most improper to allow a lady to be alone with a gentleman to whom she is not engaged." She held up one hand. "I have the perfect solution. I will ask Agnes to join you to insure that we uphold the proprieties." She laughed again at the absurd look that crossed her aunt's face. "Don't worry, love, if you promise to behave, I will make sure you are left alone. Anyway, I was planning on taking a walk through the park and visiting the lending library this afternoon."

Aunt Eloise raised up on her tiptoes to give her niece a kiss on the cheek. "Thank you, my dear. I was sure you would understand. Are you going out alone?"

"No, I am to be accompanied by Clare Tishford."

"Clare Tishford?" her aunt repeated, looking startled. "But I did not think that you and she had much to talk about."

"Oh, there is plenty of talk, just nothing of significance. Actually, it's a favor to Georgie.

As you know, tonight they are holding their annual ball and with all of the last minute details to be attended to, she asked if I would get Clare out from underfoot. I offered to play chaperone for the day and truly I do not mind. Clare is a beautiful girl and, though terribly young and naive, many of her observations are refreshing."

Aunt Eloise still looked a trifle dubious. "Well, if you think so, my dear." She patted Lady Sara's arm and wandered off down the hall.

After a tedious morning spent catching up on some belated correspondence and going through the household accounts, a task she hated but felt obligated to do, she was more than ready to escape into the warm spring day. Just as she was finishing a light luncheon, Clare was announced.

She entered the room in a breathless rush, looking an absolute picture in a dimity gown with a wide green sash that exactly matched her eyes. Her heart-shaped face was framed by a chip bonnet tied below her ear with green ribbon.

"Oh, Sara," she began. "Wait till you hear! Last night at the Avonsworth ball, I danced with two marquises and an earl! It was so exciting, even though the earl did tread on my feet a couple of times. I danced every dance and Mama said I was a success. And tonight is our ball! You are coming, are you not? What are you wearing? Mama wants me to wear my new jonquil with the blond lace—"

Sara listened to this rush of words and found herself envying the younger girl her enthusiasm and delight. She presumed that she herself had been that young once, though never quite so giddy. She had learned all too soon, however, that people were not always what they seemed and much of the glitter had faded. Why did she think of that one episode so often recently?

When Clare paused for breath, Sara grabbed her bonnet so the two could be off to enjoy the pleasure of seeing and being seen by the fashionable members of the *ton* who thronged the park.

They were soon under way, attracting the attention of many gentlemen. They made a charming pair—the one tall, dark and slender, the other all petite blond effervescence. They admired the elegant curricles and high perch phaetons, and laughed over the antics of the dandies and pinks in their garish attire.

They stopped often to greet friends and acquaintances. Lady Jersey, passing by in her barouche, waved to Lady Sara, then abruptly called to her coachman to halt. She beckoned to the girl. "Good afternoon, my dear. Nice to see you again. Who is your lovely friend? Is this the Tishford chit?"

As Sara performed the introduction, Clare blushed and made her curtsey, saying in a demure voice that she was delighted to meet her Ladyship. Lady Jersey looked her over carefully. Being one of the patronesses of Almack's, her assessment of the girls who appeared every year on the marriage mart was of vital importance.

"Well, well, very pretty," she said at last and turned to Lady Sara. "Is she under your tutelage?"

"Not really. The Tishfords are old friends and since their ball is tonight, Georgie asked me to stand *in loco parentis.*"

Lady Jersey smiled. "I will send her a voucher to the assemblies on one condition—that you accompany her. It has been much too long since you graced our rooms and it is so nice to have someone to talk to."

As Lady Jersey was known to her friends as "Silence" because of her inability ever to achieve that golden state, Lady Sara knew that she wanted someone to talk at rather than to. She smiled ruefully and said that she would be delighted to renew her old acquaintances. Recalling how dull an evening at Almack's could be, she decided that at least Lady Tishford would be pleased that her daughter was to enter those hallowed portals and she decided that it was worth the price. Smothering a groan, she said she would be delighted.

As Lady Jersey drove off, Sara and Clare found two gentlemen in uniform bearing down upon them. The younger one, a tall, slender youth, was pale and somewhat drawn and leaned heavily on a cane. Despite this, he was an attractive man with dark hair falling on to his forehead and a cheerful countenance.

Upon seeing him, Sara rushed forward to throw her arms around his neck and kiss him on the cheek. "Freddie!" she exclaimed. "How wonderful it is to see you! I just read this morning that you had been billeted home. Is it your leg? Were you badly wounded?"

Captain Frederick Ketcham, for indeed it was Awick's young brother, returned her hug as best he could while holding on to his cane and laughed at the spate of words. "Why, Sara, my love," he said, "never tell me that you were concerned. You know I lead a charmed life."

She frowned. "But, Freddie, you have grown so thin." She looked worriedly at his haggard countenance. "Are you sure you are all right? Would you like to sit down?"

The young officer smiled down at her, noting her concern. "No, love, truly. I did take a bullet in the leg and they had the devil of a time removing it. But beyond a twinge now and then, I don't feel a thing."

"Nonsense," said his companion, a short, stocky man with red hair and bushy mutton-chop whiskers. "Poor boy took a fever and damned near died—begging your pardon, my Lady," he flushed.

Freddie laughed. "No need to apologize, Tom. Sara will not mind a little rough talking. Not at all missish, you know." Recalling his manners, he performed the introduction. "Sara, I would like to make known to you Captain Thomas Ashnell of the Seventh Dragoons. Tom, this is Lady Sara Liviscombe, undoubtedly the loveliest lady in all of London."

Sara laughed as she acknowledged the introduction. "I thought you said it was your leg that was wounded, Freddie, not your eyesight."

"His eyesight was not affected in the least, nor his judgment," said Captain Ashnell gallantly, sweeping her a bow.

"Thank you, sir," she replied, "and allow me to introduce Lady Clare Tishford, the daughter of my dear friends. Clare, I would like you to meet Captain Ashnell and Captain Ketcham."

Captain Ashnell swept her a bow and kissed her hand, then Clare turned to Freddie. There was a long pause while the two gazed at each other.

"This is Captain Ketcham," Sara prompted as the two did nothing more than stare.

At this urging, Freddie at last lifted the girl's hand and kissed it. "What an honor it is," he said, "to meet such a beautiful young lady."

Clare blushed and looked down, murmuring.

Sara watched this with considerable interest. This could prove to be a fascinating encounter. She turned to Captain Ashnell. "Were you billeted home, too, sir? Not an injury, I hope."

The captain smiled. "No, indeed, but I thank you for your concern. I had some documents to deliver to the Home Office and was requested to see Freddie safely home on my way. Brave lad, you know. Shows more hair than wit sometimes when it comes to his own safety, but what a man to have beside you in a battle."

Freddie, pulling himself out of his contemplation of Clare's beauty, heard the last part of the speech. "You will have to learn, Sara, that Tom tends to exaggerate."

"Nonsense," Captain Ashnell said again.

"The boy saved my life. That is how he got the bullet in his leg."

Clare was obviously agog to learn about the bravery of this young, dashing soldier and Captain Ashnell was not loath to recount the story of their adventures.

Freddie looked uncomfortable and Sara took pity on him. "Tell me the truth," she said. "Are you sure you are all right?"

He looked sheepish. "Yes, truly I am, though I must admit that at times it hurts like the very devil. Randy did not want me to come out today, but I have been moping around the house and he finally agreed it would be better to have me go out than to sit and sulk. He has been a perfect nurse, but you know Randy—" He stopped, recalling exactly how well his companion *did* know his brother.

Sara ignored the slight pain she felt at this, and simply remarked that fresh air would do him a world of good as long as he did not try to push himself too hard.

Freddie, relieved, said that they had just been ready to turn back toward home when she had accosted him so abruptly. She laughed and turned to Captain Ashnell. "I believe, sir, that it is time you escorted our young hero home. We do not want him overly tired or he shall start moping around again."

As they made their farewells, she noticed that Clare was gazing soulfully at Freddie. Sara quickly improvised, "We are having a small dinner on Thursday night. Would you both be joining us? Nothing formal—a few close friends and, of course, the Tishfords."

She gave Clare a meaningful glance. The young lady looked surprised for a moment then, taking the hint, nodded significantly.

"Delighted," said Captain Ashnell. "It would be a pleasure to see you charming young ladies again."

Freddie grinned at Clare. "Couldn't keep me away," he said.

"Excellent." Sara took Clare's arm and steered her off. "Until Thursday then." The younger girl peeked over her shoulder at Captain Ketcham, still standing in the middle of the path staring after her while Captain Ashnell pulled on his arm. Clare blushed. "Oh, Sara, how wonderful he is, so handsome and brave and—and—"

Sara turned to her. "Isn't Captain Ashnell a little old for you, my dear? I am not sure he is exactly what your Mama had in mind but if you feel strongly . . ."

"Not Captain Ashnell," Clare exclaimed impatiently. "Captain Ketcham! Did you not notice how beautiful his smile is and how—" She noticed the teasing look on her companion's face. "Oh, that is too bad of you. You knew who I meant all along." She paused for a moment as a thought struck her. "Ketcham? Is that not Lord Awick's family name?"

Lady Sara explained that Captain Ketcham was Awick's younger brother.

"Oh, I see. So that is how you come to know him so well." It was obvious that despite her tender years, Clare had been exposed to plenty of gossip.

Sara was for a moment uncertain how to

answer this ingenuous statement, then settled on honesty. She took a deep breath. "I do not know what you may have heard about my connection to the family, but I met Freddie in Italy just before he went into the military. As far as his brother is concerned . . ."

It was at this interesting point in her revelations that she was interrupted. "My dear Lady Sara." It was Lord Dydlefield sporting a flowered brocade waistcoat, a jacket of blue superfine and unmentionables of pale yellow satin. He was, as always, impeccable.

Sara extended her hand in greeting. "How do you do, Lord Dydlefield. You remember Lady Clare Tishford, I believe?"

He bowed deeply. "Who could forget such a lovely young lady? And where are you two bound? May I offer my services as escort?"

"If you do not mind visiting the lending library, you may indeed," said Sara.

"Nothing would give me greater pleasure," he replied, offering an arm to each of the ladies. As they made their way out of the park, Lord Dydlefield kept up a running commentary on the people they passed. As his remarks were both scandalous and amusing, the ladies spent a very agreeable half hour.

Upon approaching the doors of the library, Lord Dydlefield said he would await their return and turned to greet some friends who were passing by.

Clare and Sara entered the elegant old building and began to browse among the shelves. It was obvious that Clare's interest did not lie in the tomes that faced her. "Did you mean it?"

161

she asked in an overly loud voice. Sara placed a finger on her lips and she continued more quietly, "Will you have a dinner on Thursday and will you invite me?"

"Of course I shall," her companion answered. "Did I not say so?"

Clare blushed. "Yes, of course you did but it seems too good to be true to get to see Captain Ketcham again so soon."

Lady Sara shushed her. "Come now, Clare. You refine too much upon it. Don't expose your feelings to the world—that is the way to heartbreak."

Recalling what she had heard about Sara's own romantic past, Clare lowered her head and whispered, "Of course you are right. I am sorry, Sara. Mama says that sometimes I *am* a trifle impulsive."

Sara felt a perfect brute for having scolded such an innocent creature but she merely said, "Come, Clare, let us forget about it. You and Freddie will dine with us on Thursday and in the meantime let us see if we can find that new book, *Pride and Prejudice*. I have heard it is excellent."

Upon leaving the library, they were rejoined by Lord Dydlefield who offered to escort them home. Arriving at the Liviscombe residence, Sara invited her companions in for tea, then recalling that Aunt Eloise was engaged in a tête-à-tête with Mr. Kline in the drawing room, led them into the front parlor requesting Roberts to bring in the tea tray.

Within moments he reappeared, bearing the teapots, cups and saucers, and a tray of cakes and tiny sandwiches. Sara poured and listened as Lord Dydlefield and Clare discussed the latest fashions and gossip.

Feigning interest in this conversation, she found her thoughts returning to Freddie and his praise of his brother's care during his illness. The picture of Awick playing nursemaid was an amusing one. Of course he had always been fond of his younger brother, but still.

Clare's voice broke into her thoughts. "Would it not be absolutely famous? Do say we can go. I have always wanted to go to Vauxhall and I am sure Mama would raise no objection if she knew you were with me. We have nothing else planned for Friday, I am sure."

"We will have to ask your Mama, of course," Sara said, "but if she grants her permission, I will be delighted to accompany you."

Lord Dydlefield rose to take his leave, promising to send round the next day to complete the details for the proposed outing. Sara rang for her carriage, and the two girls exchanged farewells. Sara retired to the library with her new book.

Two hours later, there was a knock on the door, followed by the entrance of Aunt Eloise. "Why, my dear Sara, what are you still doing down here? It is almost time for dinner and you are not even dressed. Surely you have not forgotten the ball tonight? It is sure to be a dreadful squeeze but it should be most entertaining."

Sara started guiltily and glanced at the clock on the mantelpiece. It was much later than she had thought. She had not even noticed the shadows lengthening across the room. Reluctantly setting aside her book, she stood up.

"Don't worry, Auntie. It will only take me a moment to dress, and you know I would not dream of missing tonight's entertainment. I understand that Mr. Kline will be there. Perhaps he'll ask you for a waltz."

Aunt Eloise tittered. "You know perfectly well that a lady of my years should never take to the dance floor. However, he might indulge me in a game of whist and there is always supper."

Sara laughed and hurried up to her room to dress for dinner.

Chapter Eight

As AUNT ELOISE HAD PREDICTED THE TISHFORD
ball was a dreadful squeeze which was, of
course, exactly what Lady Tishford desired. In
other words, it was a success. In the magnificent ballroom pink ribbons had been swathed
from the ceiling to the walls to imitate a circus
tent. A fountain flowing champagne had been
set at one end of the long room and flowers
bloomed everywhere in a gay profusion of
color. The light from thousands of candles
flickered on the elegant company.

The ladies, in silks and satins of every conceivable color and enough glittering jewels to
finance an army, wore headpieces ranging
from tiaras to towering creations that sported
fruit bowls, flower arrangements and even tiny
ships. The gentlemen were no less elegant and
in many cases just as colorful in their velvet

evening attire, with lacy cravats and cuffs and jeweled fobs, stickpins and shoe buckles.

Aunt Eloise had chosen a gown of deep lilac for the occasion and her favorite plumed turban. Sara wore a blue mesh silk over a cream underdress with the flounce hemmed in Brussels lace. The bodice was cut low and showed her white shoulders and slender figure to perfection. She had completed her toilette with her mother's diamond and sapphire necklace and ear-drops, and a gold fillet that was wound through her curls. Aunt Eloise thought that she had never seen her niece look lovelier, but her compliments were brushed aside. "Honestly, Auntie," she laughed, "at nine-and-twenty-one is no longer a beauty, if ever she had been one."

The musicians were just tuning up for the first dance as the ladies entered the ballroom. They were immediately surrounded by friends and acquaintances. Mr. Kline was one of the first to reach them and it was clear that he had been waiting for Eloise to arrive. "My dear Miss Farley," he greeted her, clasping her hands. "How enchanting you look this evening."

Aunt Eloise blushed and smiled. "Why thank you, Mr. Kline, you are quite elegant yourself." Indeed he was in his black evening dress and foamy white cravat tied simply with one large ruby set in the folds.

As her niece had predicted, he asked for the privilege of escorting her in the first dance. She demurred, "Oh no, not at my age. I would look a perfect fool among all those children."

"Perfect you might look, my dear, but never a fool," Mr. Kline replied. He took her hand and drew her toward the dance floor. "It's time we showed these children how it should be done."

Sara, looking amused, gave her aunt a little push. "Go along, do." She nodded to the rows of chairs placed around the edge of the ballroom where the mamas and chaperones were sitting. "Maybe others will take your lead and join in the fun."

As Lord and Lady Tishford took their places in the first set to begin the dancing, Aunt Eloise was swept onto the floor, still murmuring objections. Then the music began and she felt a thrill that she had not known for years. She had forgotten how much she loved to dance. And to think she could still remember the steps. Her pleasure was complete when she discovered that Mr. Kline was a fine dancer.

Sara joined a set on the arm of Lord Dydlefield, who was lavishing compliments on her. Usually, this kind of attention amused her but tonight she found it irritating. She changed the subject. "Georgie has outdone herself tonight. And Clare is looking better than ever—that gown is exquisite."

Lord Dydlefield glanced toward Clare, who was dancing with a tall, thin, red-haired boy whose face was rapt with adoration. "Yes, she is indeed beautiful but still very young. That is Multon's youngest, is it not? Takes after his mother's family, I fear. That unfortunate red hair."

As they separated and came together in the figures of the dance, the conversation continued on these lines. "Now there is a surprise," he remarked at one point. "Wonder what Awick is doing here? Thought this kind of entertainment was a little tame for him, but then I hear he is hanging out for a wife. Needs a mother for that brat of his, you know. Cannot imagine why else he would marry again."

Sara felt breathless for a moment. Awick here? She had not seen him since her aunt's birthday celebration in February. It took some effort not to look at him. What did she care anyway? He had every right to attend the Tishford ball and she suspected that Lady Tishford was pleased with his presence. Ever since he had inherited the title and fortune, he had been much sought after. At least he will not seek me out, thought Sara, so there will be no necessity for me to even speak to him. She felt unaccountably depressed.

As the dance ended, Lord Dydlefield led her off the floor. He took her hand and kissed it, sweeping an elegant bow. "Thank you, my dear," he said. "It was, as always, a pleasure."

As he moved off, Mr. Kline and Aunt Eloise arrived at her side. The lady was flushed and a little breathless from the exertions of the dance, but her eyes were glowing. "That was marvelous," she beamed. "Makes me feel like a young girl again."

Sara chuckled and turned to Mr. Kline. "I am glad you convinced her, sir. I have not seen her so radiant in years."

He took her aunt's hand. "No reason we should grow old before our time. I must admit I cannot remember enjoying myself so much."

Since the two seemed willing to sit down and enjoy a glass of punch, Sara allowed herself to be drawn onto the dance floor again. As the evening progressed, she found herself claimed for every dance and finally begged her latest partner to allow her to sit down and rest a while. As he departed to fetch her a glass of champagne, she was joined by Clare Tishford.

"Such a lovely evening it is," said the girl. "Did you see that Captain Ketcham is here? He is wearing his regimentals and looks ever so handsome. He cannot dance yet, of course, but we have been sitting out and having the most lovely chats. He has gone to get some punch and I told him to join me here."

The two young men soon returned bearing the champagne and punch. Sara's partner presented the refreshment then bowed over her hand and left to claim another young lady for the set that was forming. Freddie joined the two girls on the sofa and regaled them with humorous tales of life on the peninsula. The three were soon laughing immoderately.

Sara was the first to become aware of the approach of Lord Awick. She noted the look of concern that crossed his face as he gazed at his young brother. "Not overdoing it, are you, Freddie?"

Freddie looked up at the tall figure in front of him. "Don't worry, Randy, I'm having a wonderful time." He winked at Sara. "I promise to return home the moment I feel the least bit weary. You're becoming quite the mother hen, you know." He smiled warmly as his brother flushed. "Thank you for your concern, Randy, but truly I'm feeling fine—especially when I have such charming company."

Lord Awick looked searchingly at his face, then seemed to relax. "Indeed you are looking better. And you are right about the company." He bowed over Clare's hand, then took Sara's in a light clasp and raised it to his lips. Grinning mischievously, he said, "Your aunt is having quite an evening—first dancing with Mr. Kline and now engaging him in what appears to be a very private conversation. Do you think it proper, her carrying on in such a fashion?"

Sara laughed up at him, recalling her own lectures to Aunt Eloise. "To tell the truth, my Lord, I have warned her against damaging her reputation. Heaven knows, I have tried to restrain her, but she will not heed my strictures. I may have to take sterner measures. Perhaps it's time to ask Mr. Kline about his prospects and whether his intentions are honorable. I hate to think of my poor, defenseless aunt being led down the garden path."

Awick joined in her laughter. "You are looking lovely tonight, Lady Sara. Blue was always your best color."

Startled by the compliment, she felt the color rise in her cheeks. "Thank you, my Lord." She glanced down at her hands folded demurely in her lap.

"May I have the pleasure of escorting you to supper?" asked Awick. "I think our companions will not miss us." He looked to where Freddie and Clare sat, their heads close together, talking quietly.

Sara placed her hand on Awick's extended

arm. "I believe you are right, my Lord. I doubt they will notice we have gone."

They made their way to the supper room where a lavish collation had been laid out—creams and jellies, aspics, every conceivable kind of fruit, oyster pies and lobster patties, hams and roasts, nuts and sweetmeats. Awick, piling two plates with these delicacies, joined her at a small table. They sipped champagne and nibbled at the food for a few moments.

"I think Freddie is looking better this evening," said Sara. "When I saw him in the park this afternoon, he looked rather haggard."

Lord Awick looked surprised. "He did not mention he had met you. All he could talk about was the Tishford chit. I should have realized that you had made the introduction."

Sara felt her temper flare. "There is absolutely nothing wrong with the Tishford family," she declared. "They have been our friends for years. It is an old family of impeccable lineage and the girl is well mannered."

"I intended no insult to the girl or her family," he replied calmly. "I only meant that, since you know both Freddie and Lady Clare, it was not surprising that you should have been the one to introduce them."

Sara felt foolish. Why could this man anger her so easily? "Yes, my Lord, of course," she said meekly.

They sat in silence for a while, then Awick said, "Mr. Kline has been paying much attention to your aunt. Is something in the wind?"

Sara sighed. "I do hope so. I have never

171

known her to be so attracted to a man before. My only concern is that he not toy with her affections. I know that sounds a ridiculous thing to say about a man of his years, but I cannot help worrying about her. It has been going on for months now and there is still no sign of an offer."

"He has been very content without a wife. To take one on would prove a drastic change."

Again Sara bristled. "Are you suggesting that my aunt is an encumbrance? Are comfort and marriage not compatible?"

"I do not believe my feelings on the subject are your concern," he replied coldly.

A voice came from behind them. "Ah, there you are, my dears." Mrs. Warrington was bearing down on them with Lord Tishford close behind. "This room is so crowded there is simply not another chair to be found." She smiled sweetly at this blatant untruth. Most of the other diners had returned to the dance floor; the room was half empty.

"Are you not finding this delightful?" she said, settling into a chair. "I *do* love garish entertainment. I would not miss one of Georgie's balls. Each is more outlandish than the last. Can you believe a circus tent? And she must have acquired every bloom in London. I hear that she used over five thousand roses alone." She kept up in this vein for quite some time and soon the tension between Sara and Lord Awick eased.

They were next joined by Aunt Eloise and Mr. Kline. It was not long before they were all

laughing comfortably as they exchanged anec-
dotes. Chuckling at some outrageous story of
Lord Tishford's, Sara glanced around the room
and spied Clare and Freddie. They were seated
at a table opposite and were staring into each
other's eyes looking for all the world as if no
one else were in the room. She frowned slightly, wondering if it was a good idea to allow two
such very young and impressionable children
to be alone like this.

Echoing her thoughts, Awick whispered,
"Don't worry. They are just in love with love. I
intend to make sure they know what they are
about lest they make a foolish mistake. However, I believe Clare has already done Freddie a
great deal of good."

Sara smiled in gratitude. "Your concerns
match my own, my Lord. And I am sure you are
right. We both know how misleading first love
can be."

Awick stared at her for a moment. "Yes, do
we not?"

At this point, Aunt Eloise asked her to join a
party picnicking in Waltham Abbey the following Tuesday. The setting was rumored to be
idyllic and it would make a pleasant change
from the social whirl. Sara said she would be
delighted and the arrangements were made.

They soon adjourned, Aunt Eloise and Mr.
Kline to the card room for a game of whist, and
the others to the ballroom. Lord Tishford went
to seek his wife.

Lord Awick spotted his brother standing with
Clare Tishford and leaning heavily on his cane.

"I believe it is time I took our young hero home. The best place for him now is in his own bed. If you will excuse me, ladies?"

Sara said that she appreciated his concern and only hoped that Freddie would improve rapidly.

Mrs. Warrington kissed his cheek. "Do not linger here, my dear. He is just as headstrong as you were at his age and likely to make the same mistakes. Watch out for him."

Lord Awick bowed, made his farewells, then gathered up his young brother, and departed.

Mrs. Warrington turned to Sara. "He is certainly taking his responsibilities seriously. I'm glad to see he is finally settling down. And he is so good with Beth. Have you met her yet? An adorable child but becoming a bit wild, I fear. Of course, not having a mother's care it is only to be expected."

For the first time, Sara wondered about Lord Awick's first child. Would she look like him? Was she a happy child or did she miss the mother she had lost so early?

Mrs. Warrington observed the expressions flitting over the girl's open countenance and smiled to herself. The knob had been turned and the door was pushed ever so slightly open. She began to formulate a plan.

Chapter Nine

THE DAY DAWNED SULLEN AND OVERCAST. Sara, uncommonly depressed, lay in bed, reading the newspapers. The evening at Almack's had been tedious. Aunt Eloise had gone to a card party given by Mrs. Kennelworth, and Sara had been left to chaperone Clare. The girl danced every dance and was widely praised for her beauty and excellent manners, but Sara, positioned with the other chaperones, was forced to endure their endless gossip and chatter.

Drinking orgeat, the strongest beverage allowed within those sacred walls, and nibbling on stale cakes, Sara had a most unladylike desire to do something outrageous. She passed the time conjuring up wild fancies, from saying something horribly rude to the biddy seated next to her, to exposing her bosom and waltzing across the floor.

At last Clare admitted she was ready to return home. Gathering up their cloaks, the two had departed.

Sara yawned and stretched. At least she had nothing planned for the day and could probably steal a few hours to continue her new book. Then she remembered she had invited Freddie, Captain Ashnell and the Tishfords to dinner this evening. An unladylike epithet crossed her mind, and she decided she had better arrange a suitable menu with Cook. When she and Aunt Eloise dined alone, they tended to be rather lax in their requirements. But a dinner party! She rapidly counted up and realized that it would be a party of seven! She decided she had better get off an invitation to Mr. Kline right away to make their numbers even. She rang for Agnes.

"Yes, my Lady?"

"Oh, Agnes, I find that I have much to do today. Help me with my gown, if you would."

Soon Sara was dressed in a pale-blue round gown, her hair hidden beneath a lace mob cap. Her first order of business was to send a note around to Mr. Kline. She then rang for Roberts to send Cook to her in the library. When she appeared, Sara explained her dilemma. "Do you suppose that you can prepare something on such short notice?"

"Of course, M'Lady. You just be telling me what kind of dishes them folks would like and I can get 'em prepared."

Sara smiled gratefully. "Truly, Cook, you are a wonder."

The two prepared an elegant menu and Cook

descended to the kitchen to begin her preparations.

Sara glanced out the window. It was starting to rain. Oh bother, she thought. Well, maybe it was just as well. She had no reason to go out and now could continue her reading. She rang for Roberts. "Have a fire made up for me, please. And let me know if a note comes from Mr. Kline."

She was soon ensconced in the big over-stuffed leather armchair facing the cheerfully glowing fire. Knowing she was alone, she propped her feet up on the ottoman and proceeded to lose herself in her novel. She was startled by a knock on the door.

"A note from Mr. Kline, my Lady," Roberts said, extending the silver salver. She took the note and read:

Dear Lady Sara,

Nothing would please me more than to attend your dinner this evening. I am flattered by your invitation and look forward to seeing you and your delightful aunt.

Yr. Obdt. Srvt.
John Kline

Sara, with a small satisfied smile, refolded the note. "Thank you, Roberts. This is what I had hoped for. That will be all."

Less than an hour later, Roberts again knocked at the door. "I beg your pardon, my Lady, but Lord Dydlefield has called. I took the liberty of showing him into the back parlor."

Sighing resignedly, Sara again set down her book. "Tell him I will be there in a moment."

As she entered, Lord Dydlefield was looking out at the back garden. Hearing her approach, he turned. "Ah, Lady Sara. I am sorry to call at this unreasonably early hour, but I wished to make certain that you and Lady Clare would be able to attend Vauxhall tomorrow evening. I have reserved a box, and I understand that there is to be a fireworks display, which I am sure the young lady will enjoy."

Sara smiled. "Yes, my Lord, we both look forward to the expedition. Who is to make up our little party?"

"Only yourselves and my mother and me. I did not wish to alarm Lady Clare with a gathering of unfamiliar faces."

Sara stifled a chuckle at the thought of Clare, with her enthusiasm for all the sights and sounds of life, being alarmed by unfamiliar faces. She would in all likelihood be less alarmed than Lord Dydlefield's mother. However, she merely said, "Your thoughtfulness is commendable, my Lord. At what time may we expect you?"

Having worked out the details, Lord Dydlefield made his departure. Lady Sara returned to the library and again picked up her book.

There came another knock at the door. "Yes, what is it?" Sara asked, again setting down her book. Aunt Eloise fluttered into the room. "Good morning, my love. Did you sleep well? Is it true that Mr. Kline is joining us for dinner tonight? You really should have told me, you know. I don't have a thing to wear."

Sara smiled, thinking of the wardrobe presses lining her aunt's rooms, containing more clothes than that lady could wear in a year. She managed to look rueful. "I apologize for the short notice, but surely you can conjure up *something*." She handed her aunt Mr. Kline's note. "This may help you decide how you would like to appear tonight."

Aunt Eloise, recognizing Mr. Kline's writing, could hardly wait to read the note in private. "Of course, my dear. Perhaps the emerald-green satin. Mr. Kline has not seen it before. Or is it too dressy? I could wear the brown taffeta . . ." she continued as she fluttered back out the door, the note clasped firmly to her breast.

Sara laughed indulgently and again picked up her book. She threw it down on the table beside her when the next knock came. She wished she had locked the door and denied herself to all callers.

Roberts entered. "Mrs. Warrington, my Lady, and . . . a young friend. They asked to join you here."

Mrs. Warrington appeared at the door. "Good morning, my dear. I hope you don't mind the intrusion. We were on our way to the park to feed the ducks, but it started to rain so we stopped to seek shelter."

Feeding the ducks in the park sounded like a peculiar pastime for a woman of Mrs. Warrington's years until Sara noticed her companion.

Clinging to the elderly lady's hand was a very small child, with a halo of white-blond hair and huge green eyes.

At Mrs. Warrington's urging, the child took a step forward. "Lady Sara," Mrs. Warrington said in her most formal manner, "may I present Lady Elizabeth Ketcham? Beth, please make your curtsey to Lady Sara Liviscombe."

The child, looking pleased at this adult way of going about things, took another step forward. Sara took the tiny outstretched hand. "I am delighted to make your acquaintance, Lady Elizabeth. I have heard much about you."

"Oh, please," the girl giggled, "call me Beth. Papa says my title is longer than I am. Are we going to be friends, Lady Sara? I don't have many friends in town 'cept for Aunt Emily." Again she grasped Mrs. Warrington's hand.

Sara smiled. "Of course we're going to be friends, Beth, but I must insist you not use my title either. 'Sara' will do nicely."

Beth grinned at this mark of distinction and began to tell her new friend about the pony her papa had given her.

Sara found the girl enchanting. Her resemblance to her father was slight—only the determined thrust of her little chin and the straight, almost aquiline nose hinted at her father or uncle. She speculated that she must take after her mother.

As if reading her thoughts, Mrs. Warrington said, "The very image of Randy's mother, you know. The coloring is identical."

Sara was surprised. She had never met the

late Lady Awick but had assumed her to be as dark as her two sons.

Beth was anxious to be outside and since the rain had stopped for the moment, Sara gathered up her cloak and bonnet and the three ladies set out for the park. Beth walked in the middle clasping one hand of each of her companions.

It being early still and the sky threatening, the only people enjoying the park were nannies with their charges and a paid companion walking her mistress's lapdog.

At the duck pond Mrs. Warrington produced a large bag of bread crumbs. Beth grabbed a tiny handful and timidly dropped them in the water. Soon the ducks, spotting this action, paddled over.

Beth laughed as they snatched up the crumbs. Sara took a handful from the bag and scattered them on the grass. The ducks were not afraid to climb onto the shore to continue their feast. Soon the ladies were all laughing delightedly, watching as the creatures squabbled over a particularly large crumb and at the little pecks they traded when one, rushing after a morsel, fell against another.

"Don't get too close, my love," Mrs. Warrington said, pulling Beth back from the edge of the pond where she was trying to coax some ducklings closer.

At this moment a brilliant streak of lightning lit the sky, followed instantly by a deafening crack of thunder. The startled ducks hurried back into the pond, one knocking against Beth, who toppled into the water. Sara, seeing what was about to happen, made a leap for the girl but was already too late. At Beth's cry of fear, she jumped into the pond and caught the frightened child to her. Since the water was only waist deep, there was no real danger and she carried Beth to the edge, handing her over to Mrs. Warrington. She hauled herself out and examined her ruined gown. She smiled ruefully. "I guess that's what comes of feeding ducks on a stormy day. Next time I think we will take tea in front of a cozy fire."

Mrs. Warrington exclaimed, "Oh, Lady Sara, you were so brave—diving in after her that way."

Sara held up one dripping hand. "Since the water is no more than three feet deep, I don't believe there was either much danger or much bravery. But we had best get home and into some dry clothes."

As they turned to make their way out of the park, Beth wrapped in Mrs. Warrington's cloak, large rain drops began to fall. Lady Sara smiled. "It looks like we are all going to be soaked together."

At this moment, a carriage pulled up beside them and a deep voice inquired sardonically, "What on earth has happened here? Have you decided to give my daughter swimming lessons, Lady Sara?"

She flushed angrily. It was bad enough that she looked absolutely wretched, but for him to insinuate that the misfortune had somehow been her fault! She was much too angry to notice the look of anxiety that had crossed his face. Mrs. Warrington had noted it. Better and better, she thought.

"Well, Randy, do you mean to keep us standing out here in the rain? It may not affect my companions, who can't get much wetter, but I have given up my cloak and at my advanced age I must be careful about taking chills."

At this, Lord Awick swung open the door, jumped down and took his daughter from Mrs. Warrington. He then handed both the ladies into the carriage and climbed in behind them. He settled Beth on his lap, pulling the borrowed cloak closer around her, then asked what happened in the park. It was Beth who answered him. "Oh, Papa, I was so scared. There was a terrible roar and something hit me and I fell into the water."

Awick looked at Mrs. Warrington. "Were you shot at?"

That lady laughed. "No, Randy, I think it safe to say that the duck pond is generally free from that kind of incident. Actually there was a flash of lightning and a rather loud thunder roll and one of the ducks we had been feeding knocked against Beth sending her into the water."

"But then Sara jumped in and saved me," the child piped in again looking adoringly at her new friend.

Lord Awick followed his daughter's gaze. "'Sara?'" he inquired. "Is that not a rather informal address for such new acquaintances?"

Sara smiled at Beth. "Oh, no, my Lord. We decided that our titles were terribly cumbersome and have agreed to drop them."

"Oh, yes, Papa. Sara and I are friends, you know. Can she come and see me? I want to show her my pony and we could go to the 'Change and see the lions and to that shop you said had all the strange things."

Awick laughed. "Really, child, you can't impose on Lady Sara. I am sure she has plenty of other obligations."

"Not at all," Sara replied. "I would be delighted to take Beth to the Exeter Exchange and the Pantheon Bazaar. In fact, I will set aside next Wednesday if that will be convenient."

Beth clapped her hands and squealed delightedly. "Oh, Papa, may I, may I?"

He placed his hands on her shoulders in an attempt to stop her bouncing up and down on his lap and said ruefully, "I would be a great villain if I disallowed such an adventure. I will give my permission on one condition."

"What?" both asked at once.

"That I be permitted to act as your escort. And I think you might enjoy an ice at Gunters, and perhaps a visit to the Tower of London."

At this point, the carriage pulled up in front of the Liviscombe townhouse. Awick made to assist her but Sara jumped down. "Just get Beth home and into some dry clothes. We don't want her sick for our expedition." She kissed the girl on her damp cheek, and bade farewell to her companions. "Till Wednesday, then."

She ran lightly up the steps as Roberts opened the door for her.

The carriage rumbled off. "Oh, Papa," Beth sighed. "Isn't she the most beautiful lady in the entire world? And she is my friend. I wish she could come and live with us, then everything would be perfect."

Mrs. Warrington glanced at her godson to see how he had received this suggestion and was pleased to see an arrested expression cross his face. Yes, indeed, she thought. Better and better and better. Leave it to a child to recognize the obvious. She knew she had an ally in the Ketcham household.

Sara's impromptu dinner party that evening turned out to be highly enjoyable. Cook had come through and prepared a delicious meal featuring turtle soup, a succulent roast beef, fish in a delicate cream sauce, and a selection of meringues and glacés. Captain Ashnell, Mr. Kline and Lord Tishford engaged in spirited discussions of economics, politics and the Peninsular War. Lady Tishford and Aunt Eloise had a wonderful time discussing the foibles and follies of their many mutual acquaintances. Sara joined in both these discussions while making sure her guests were receiving all that they desired. Freddie and Clare spent most of the evening staring at each other and exchanging intimate smiles. Sara, recalling Lord Awick's words about being in love with love, let them be. After all, first love was never lasting.

The ladies rose to retire but the gentlemen claimed that they had no desire to lose the company of such a charming group. They all made their way into the front parlor where Sara asked Clare to play for them on the pianoforte. Clare's playing was not brilliant, but she had a light touch and her voice was sweet and clear. Freddie offered to turn the pages for her.

Mr. Kline took a seat beside Aunt Eloise and the two were soon laughing merrily. Captain Ashnell joined Lady Sara. "What a delightful evening," he said. "I am sorry I will have to be leaving soon."

"Oh, must you rush off?" Sara asked. "You can stay for tea, surely."

"Of course, Lady Sara, I did not mean tonight. I am being sent back to Portugal on Saturday. My mission here is completed and duty calls."

"Oh," Sara said, "I had hoped you would be staying longer. We shall all hate to see you go. I know Freddie in particular will miss you."

Captain Ashnell glanced to where Captain Ketcham was leaning over Lady Clare. "Somehow, I think he will manage to survive. In fact, if I am not mistaken, I have already been forgotten."

Sara joined in the amusement. "Indeed, I would be surprised if they realized there was anyone else left in the room."

After the tea was served, the party decided to try a hand of whist. Two tables were set up and stakes were placed at a penny a point. The rest of the evening passed with a great deal of raillery and hilarity. Aunt Eloise came up the winner and announced she was going to take up gambling as a means to secure her old age. As the company laughed, Mr. Kline whispered something in her ear that caused her to blush furiously.

The party soon broke up and Sara and Eloise were left alone.

"Am I to wish you happy, Aunt?"

Aunt Eloise gave a little mysterious smile. "All in good time, my dear. You might say that John and I have an understanding but there are items that need resolution. Do not worry, though, you will be the first to know and I believe it is all in a fair way to being settled." She arose and kissed her niece. "Good night, dearest, and sleep well. Just be sure you are not seeing only what you want to see." On this enigmatic statement, Aunt Eloise retired.

Sara went into the library and stared a long time into the fire. What had her aunt meant by that? She recalled her misadventure at the duck pond and the trip home and was again surprised by Awick's desire to accompany Beth and her on their proposed outing. Was he only concerned about trusting his daughter to her care? If that were so, he could have sent a footman along. Surely he had no desire to pursue their re-acquaintance. His manner toward her had changed. He was even civil to her now, if still distant. And how did she feel about him? They could never go back to where they had been—there could be no trust, but could both put behind them what had happened so long ago?

As the fire burned low, Sara shivered and sat

up. It was time she was in bed. Tomorrow night they were promised to Lord Dydlefield for the excursion to Vauxhall. She was not looking forward to an evening spent in the company of that gentleman's mother, but she had accepted and there was no help for it. She looked forward to Wednesday's expedition. Beth was such a dear child. It would be fun to see the world through five-year-old eyes. She was soon asleep.

Chapter Ten

THE RAINS OF THE PREVIOUS DAY HAD CLEARED the sky and left the city clean and sparkling. Sara arose early and decided to do a little puttering around in her garden. At home in Somerset, and also at the villa in Florence, she had always loved tending the flowers and vegetables. It was something she missed when she was in London. Donning an old, faded gown and her jean half-boots, she pulled a battered bonnet off the rack in the back hall and made her way outside. The air was crisp and fresh, and there seemed to be birds everywhere adding their melodic songs to the quiet. She was soon absorbed in her task, pulling weeds, trimming, cutting off dead blooms.

She lost all sense of time and the morning flew by. She was so intent on her work that she jumped when Roberts spoke behind her. "Captain Ketcham, my Lady. Will you receive him in the drawing room?"

She looked down at the dirt all over her dress and could feel her hair escaping the confines of the old bonnet. "Oh dear," she said, "I must tidy up first. Tell him I will be with him shortly."

"Oh come, Sara. You do not need to stand on ceremony with me." Freddie walked into the garden with only the barest sign of a limp. "I have seen you look much worse than that. Remember that time in Italy when I tried to teach you to ride and you fell off the horse and landed right in a mud puddle?"

"It is just like you to remind me, Freddie," she smiled ruefully and held out her hands. Noticing how dirty they were, she immediately tucked them behind her. He laughed.

"You do look a sight, my dear, but I promise not to breathe a word. Come, sit down here and talk to me. I need some advice."

His expression had grown serious, and Sara joined him on the bench, a look of concern in her eyes. "Of course, Freddie. You know I will do what I can. Is there anything wrong?"

"Not 'wrong' exactly. It is just that I am considering making a change in my life and I'm not sure how to explain it to Randy. He thinks I'm still a child, but I'm nine-and-twenty and it's time I made my own decisions."

"But, Freddie, you have been doing just that. After all, you have been in the army for five years and from what I have heard you have been making many important decisions."

"That was different, Sara. There are things

you are expected to do so you do them. I am talking about setting up my course in life." He paused. "I have been thinking about this for some time and I do not believe my decision is hasty or impulsive, though I know that is what Randy is going to say." He looked at the girl beside him. "Sara, I want to sell out my commission. I have the competence from my mother, but it will not be enough to maintain a wife. I have spoken to Lord Buffield and he is looking for a secretary. He thinks he can get me a position in the Home Office." He took a breath. "And then I intend to ask Clare Tishford to do me the honor of becoming my wife."

Sara listened to this confession with mixed feelings. She was impressed with Freddie's desire to do something useful, rather than set up the wastrel life of so many other younger sons. She was concerned, however, about the choice of Clare Tishford as a wife. She was so terribly young and seemed so empty-headed.

Freddie, as if reading her mind, said, "Oh, I know Clare is young, but she will learn her way around. She has such a sweet disposition and would make a comfortable wife. And she is not nearly as bubble-headed as you might think. She learns quickly and is able to think things through."

He paused again. "What do you think, Sara? Will you help us?"

Sara stared in front of her for a moment. "Have you discussed this with Clare? Is she willing to become the wife of Lord Buffield's secretary?"

He grinned. "She said that, if she could

marry me, she would be willing to follow the drum. Of course, I would never allow that." He looked at her beseechingly. "Oh, Sara, we are in love. I cannot tell you what Clare means to me and I know she feels the same!"

She laughed slightly. "But tell me, my dear, what do you think I can possibly do to help you? You must know that your brother would never listen to me and it is obvious that Clare does not need any convincing."

Freddie lifted a hand. "You are right, of course, my love. Actually, I just wanted to know that I had your support. Am I wrong?"

Sara admitted this was the best program Freddie had so far presented to her, far outweighing his schemes to raise race horses, set up a gaming hall or embark on an active pirate trade in the West Indies, ventures he had proposed from time to time.

"You know I will support you, Freddie, but what do you need? You have never come to me before just to gain my approval. Come now, cut line. There is something else."

Freddie looked sheepish. "Well, if you must know, there *is* a slight favor."

Sara grinned. "Just name it, Freddie."

Freddie took a deep breath. "I fear Lord Tishford will not approve the match. I am, after all, a younger son and Clare is his only child. He wants only the best for her but that is what I want too." He clasped her hands in his and gazed at her intently. "You know the Tishfords very well. Would you put in a word in my behalf? It would make me the happiest man in all of Christendom to have such a beautiful lady as my wife. It will only take a word from you and I know that everything would come right. I cannot tell you how my happiness depends on it."

A sarcastic voice interrupted them. "What an affecting scene. I am sure I should not have intruded at such a moment but when Roberts said you were in the garden I believed it safe to announce myself. May I wish you happy? I am sure, Lady Sara, that you will enjoy following the drum. Since you are of an age, I feel confident you will come to an amicable agreement. Let me know when I can make the announcement. At last, Lady Sara is to marry a Ketcham." He bowed crisply and stalked out, leaving the two still clasping each other's hands and looking like children caught raiding the cookie jar.

"Randy!" Freddie exclaimed rising from his seat.

"Awick!" Sara exclaimed simultaneously, also jumping up.

But Lord Awick had already disappeared and they heard the front door slam shut.

Freddie turned to Sara. "Oh, sweetheart, I'm sorry. If that isn't the devil's own luck that he would choose such a moment to enter. I will talk to him, I promise. I never meant to make trouble for you."

Sara looked at him, a hint of anger in her eyes. "I am not surprised at your brother's totally unreasonable behavior," she said. "It is consistent with everything that has gone before. And, please, do not say anything at all to him. Let him believe what he chooses! I suspect when he discovers that it is Clare Tishford and not me who has caught your fancy, he will welcome the girl with open arms. I do not think there could be anything more distasteful to him than to have our families joined."

At this statement Freddie looked more cheerful. "Yes, you are probably right," he said, unaware of the sudden pain that Sara experienced. "Perhaps it is best to let him believe that it is we who are engaged, at least for the time being. I had best be going now." He took her hands again. "Sara, I cannot tell you how much this means to me. I know Clare will thank you, too. You shall be the godmother of our first child!" With that he kissed her on the cheek and left.

Sara sank back onto the bench. Oh, God, what a muddle! Things between her and Awick were just getting ironed out—and now this. It was always the same. He wanted to think the worst of her and seemed to be looking for reasons. Fine, he had found one and he might as well revel in it. It would serve him right. She had a strong desire to cry.

Lord Dydlefield arrived promptly that evening but, for once, Sara was not ready. She had spent the afternoon wandering disconsolately from one room to another, her depression increasing by the moment. When the dinner bell had finally sounded, she had requested that a tray be brought to her room. Since Aunt Eloise had departed somewhat earlier to enjoy a dinner with Mr. Kline, followed by a trip to the Drury Lane theatre, she had not felt any need to dress only to sit in solitary splendor at the dinner table. When the tray arrived she found it difficult to swallow any of the succulent morsels displayed before her. She did, however, imbibe freely of the carafe of wine that was sent up.

Eventually, she allowed Agnes to dress her but no matter what efforts that superior attendant made, Sara was not happy with her appearance. This gown was too flashy, that one was too dull, her hair looked dowdy then it looked insipid, on and on until Sara realized that she was acting like a spoiled child and Agnes was at her wits' end. When Lord Dydlefield was announced, Lady Sara was still sitting in front of her mirror wearing only her petticoat. She could not plead illness she decided. She turned to her abigail, who was fluttering around her, trying to determine what she had done to so displease her mistress.

Drawing a deep breath and gathering her scattered wits, Sara said, "I believe, Agnes, that I will wear the green striped dimity over the yellow underdress. The emeralds will do well and I think I will wear my hair loose with no adornment."

Since this was the first costume that Agnes had proposed, she only sighed and began again to dress her mistress.

Within a matter of minutes, Sara was dressed and gazing critically into the pier glass. She was not pleased with her appearance but could not decide exactly what was wrong—perhaps the melancholy look in her luminous blue eyes. Well, best to get it over with. Gathering up her gloves and reticule, she bade Agnes good night and told the girl not to wait up for her. "I will be late and there is no need for both of us to miss our sleep."

With that, she hastened down the stairs to greet Lord Dydlefield. He stepped forward and kissed her hand. "Charming, my dear, as always. Mother is in the carriage and is looking forward to seeing you."

Roberts opened the door and the two descended the steps to Lord Dydlefield's carriage. He handed her up, then took the seat opposite the two ladies. Mrs. Dydlefield inclined her head toward Sara. "Nice of you to join us, Lady Sara. I'm sorry to see you looking so worn. Have you been ill?"

Sara replied that she had never felt better.

"Oh," remarked Lady Dydlefield, "it is probably just advancing years then. Age does creep up on one, you know. One can hardly be expected to look as fresh as one did in one's youth."

Sara bit back a rejoinder. She was, after all, the guest of the Dydlefields.

The next stop was the Tishfords'. Lord Dydlefield again sprang down and rapped on the door of the stately townhouse. Within moments Clare joined the two ladies in the carriage.

Having made her acknowledgments, she launched into a breathless statement. "Oh, I am so excited. I have wanted to attend Vauxhall forever. Mama says it's ever so lovely and there is to be a fireworks display! Can you imagine anything nicer? I know it's going to be absolutely unforgettable." She was more correct than she knew but not quite for the reasons she had imagined.

At the renowned pleasure gardens, thousands of outdoor lanterns glittered against the night sky. There was the murmur of conversation around them, pierced now and then by a girl's high-pitched laughter. They joined the crowd strolling along the various paths and found themselves caught up in the spirit of gaiety that surrounded them. Lord Dydlefield led them into the central area where there was a dance floor set round with individual boxes. He had procured one of these and they were soon seated. They were just opposite the dance floor and had an excellent view of the occupants of the other boxes and of the ladies and gentlemen who thronged the better lit of the walkways. The evening's entertainment included a soprano of some repute singing a bawdy tune that Clare did not understand but had Mrs. Dydlefield bordering on a guffaw.

At the conclusion, they were served the exceptionally thin slices of ham for which Vauxhall was famous and several bowls of rack punch. Lady Dydlefield seemed never at a loss for words. "Can you imagine wearing purple with that impossibly red hair?" A moment later, "I will never understand how a man with that physique would dare present himself in public wearing *yellow* unmentionables!" And finally, "This place becomes more vulgar every time I attend. I wonder that any truly fashionable persons would consider attending."

Sara had had enough. Turning to Mrs. Dydlefield she said in a silky undertone, "It is becoming obvious that no 'fashionable' people do attend." Lady Dydlefield sputtered as Sara looked away. As she did she saw Lord Awick, Captain Ketcham and Captain Ashnell seating themselves in one of the adjacent boxes.

Clare, who had not heard the earlier acrimonious exchange whispered to Sara, "Oh look! There is Captain Ketcham! He said he would be here tonight but I had almost given up hope. He looks so handsome! Do you think he has seen us? Should I wave?"

She was saved from any untoward behavior as Freddie spotted her. He smiled and lifted a o indicate he would join her as soon as mpanions were situated.

Clare, contented, settled back into her seat.

Lord Dydlefield, on the other hand, had not missed the confrontation between his mother and Lady Sara.

"Really, my dear, I thought you had better manners. She is, after all, an old lady and deserves to be treated with respect. I never thought that you would lower yourself to such a common level."

Lady Sara, who had felt badly about snapping at his mother, now felt her anger rising again. "I would not have found it necessary to speak on a common level as you put it if I had not found myself conversing with a 'common' person."

At that moment she was relieved to see Freddie Ketcham approach their box. He made a stiff bow to Lady Dydlefield, then turned to Lord Dydlefield murmuring "Servant." Next, he took Sara's hand and kissed her fingers. "Hello, sweetheart." He gave a small grimace and whispered, "Why do you let yourself be seen in the company of that fop and his dragon of a mother? Thought by now you would have developed better taste." As this statement exactly matched Sara's own thoughts, she laughed ruefully. At last he turned to Clare Tishford. Gathering both her hands into his own, he declared, "You look more beautiful every time I see you. I was so afraid that somehow you would be prevented from coming tonight. Is it everything you had heard?"

She gazed at him earnestly. "Oh Captain Ketcham, it is now. I had looked forward to seeing you here." She stopped as if suddenly aware there were other people around them. "It is a lovely place and the Dydlefields are all that one could wish for as hosts," she said primly.

Freddie and Sara both laughed at this modest display. He held out his hand, "Come, Lady Clare, I hear a waltz striking up and even though I might yet be terribly awkward on the dance floor, I would like to give it a try. And"—he smiled at her—"if it proves too much for me, we could retire to one of those little alcoves and carry on a private conversation." He looked to Sara. "Am I being indiscreet? Will you trust your charge into my care?"

She gazed sternly into the faces of the two young people for a moment, then relented. "All I ask, Freddie, is that you allow no one else to approach her. The gardens do attract some unsavory people. I know she will come to no harm as long as she is with you."

The two smiled gratefully at her and took themselves off to join the glittering crowd on the dance floor. Lord and Lady Dydlefield had turned to greet some acquaintances, and Lady Sara jumped when she heard herself addressed.

"Lose your suitor again, Lady Sara?" a voice murmured in her ear. "With your experience, I would have thought you might have learned the trick of keeping them. But maybe you only let them go when you wish to be rid of them. Has it ever occurred to you that perhaps some of the poor fools actually have feelings? Or do you just revel in the victory over their misguided hearts?"

Sara was positively speechless with rage. How dare he! She took several deep breaths and counted to ten five times. At last she turned to her persecutor. "You wrong me, Lord Awick. At least I have the kindness to break it off before anyone's feelings are too deeply involved. I would never dream of leading someone along to the last moment only to deliver a heart-shattering blow."

Awick flushed angrily. "Oh would you not indeed? Then exactly how do you explain—"

"Ahem, excuse me, Awick," Captain Ashnell interrupted. "Don't mean to intrude but thought Lady Sara might like to dance before the fireworks display. Don't mind, do you, old chap?"

Both Sara and Awick realized that the captain had been trying to save them from an embarrassing scene. People were already turning to stare as their voices rose. They both smiled graciously at his suggestion and she allowed him to lead her onto the dance floor as Awick turned to speak to Lord and Lady Dydlefield. When the music ended, Captain Ketcham, Clare, Sara and Captain Ashnell returned to the Dydlefield box.

Lady Dydlefield's wounded sensibilities had been soothed by the assiduous attentions that Awick had been paying her. Really, thought Sara, he could be charming when he tried. Why in the world did he find it so difficult to be charming to her?

Awick asked his brother how he had fared on the dance floor. "Did the leg give you much pain?"

Freddie glanced at Clare. "With such a lovely partner, I hardly even noticed it." Suddenly remembering who he was supposedly about to become engaged to, he turned to Sara. "I do think I will rest for a while, however."

Sara, taking the hint, asked Lord Dydlefield if he would mind if Captain Ketcham joined their party. Lord Dydlefield, apparently willing to overlook the earlier contretemps, waved to a chair. "Of course, Captain, do be seated. Maybe you can coax Lady Sara into a more amiable mood."

Awick scowled at this and, spotting some friends entering a box at the end of the row, made a curt bow and left.

Captain Ashnell requested the favor of a

dance with Clare and the two made their way back to the dance floor.

"Randy is in the devil's own temper," said Freddie. "Even heard him yell at his valet—not like him, you know. Do you think he is that upset about what he overheard in your garden this morning? Should I tell him it was all a misunderstanding?"

Thinking over what had just passed between them, Sara felt her anger mounting again. "No, not yet. He was being unreasonable, jumping to conclusions. I have no intention of explaining my actions to him." And, she thought, I hope he is just as miserable as I am. Glancing down the row at the box to which Awick had gone, she saw him bending over the most beautiful woman she had ever seen. A tall, statuesque blonde, wearing a gown that left nothing to the imagination, she was laughing at something he had said and the look that they exchanged was embarrassingly intimate. He certainly did not look miserable, she thought bitterly.

Trying not to sound overly interested, she asked Freddie who that lovely lady was with whom Awick was conversing.

Freddie followed her glance, and then colored. "That is no lady, my dear. It is a Mrs. Willoughby—married a rich old man who had the good sense to die before she had cuckolded him too often." Realizing the impropriety of this statement, he blushed.

Sara laughed at his confusion. "Oh, come, my dear. You know there is no point in being missish with me. What is she to Lord Awick?" she could not stop herself from asking.

But Freddie refused to be drawn. "One hears things, of course, but I don't know the truth of it. I believe that they are old friends. Ah, here come Clare and Tom. I think it must be nearly time for the fireworks display."

The party rose and joined the crowds who were making their way to the area where the display was to be held. Captain Ashnell took Lady Dydlefield by the arm and led the way. Sara followed with Lord Dydlefield while Freddie and Clare walked slowly behind.

"I hope you are feeling a little more the thing?" Lord Dydlefield said.

Sara knew she had been terribly rude. "Yes, thank you, sir, and I must apologize for my shocking manners. I have been suffering a headache all afternoon—but that is no excuse for poor behavior." This was not precisely the truth but she felt she had to say something to ease the unpleasantness.

Lord Dydlefield looked concerned. "I understand perfectly, my dear. Mother is subject to the most horrid headaches and, while usually the kindest person in the world, they do cause her to be less than amiable. Do not give it another thought. I forgive you completely and I know Mother will too."

Sara was amused by this speech. She had never known Lady Dydlefield to be anything approaching kind, but she decided that she had caused enough problems for one evening and merely thanked her companion for his forbearance.

They soon arrived at the display grounds and enjoyed an agreeable half hour watching the fireworks. All around them ladies were shrieking and exclaiming at the deafening roar as the guns were shot off and the spectacular colors lit the sky. At the conclusion, they returned to their boxes and Captain Ashnell and Captain Ketcham made their farewells to the Dydlefield party. Sara glanced over to where Mrs. Willoughby had been sitting, but the box was empty.

Lord Dydlefield ordered another bowl of rack punch then turned to his mother.

"Lady Sara has been telling me that she too is prone to headaches. In fact, she has had one today."

Sara took the hint graciously. "Indeed, Lady Dydlefield, a headache does cause me to be irritable, and I am sure that accounts for my earlier bad manners. I do pray that you will forgive me?"

Since Lady Dydlefield liked nothing better than to have someone else appear in the wrong, she accepted this and proceeded to detail in great length just how severe her headaches were and the many remedies she had tried, all of course to no avail. One of the best methods she had for guaranteeing her son's obedience was her imaginary ill health.

The hour was growing late, the punch was flowing freely, and the revelry was beginning to get raucous. Lord Dydlefield decided it was time to escort the ladies home, especially since he could see that Lady Clare was becoming inordinately interested in some of the goings-on. They waved farewell to Freddie and Captain Ashnell, and made their way to the carriage. There was still no sign of Lord Awick.

By the time Sara arrived home, her headache had become real. She felt exhausted but her mind kept reviewing the interview she had had with Awick. How dare he insinuate that she had been in the wrong! She had tried to forget that horrible chain of events which had occurred so many years before but now she found herself recalling it as if it had occurred yesterday.

Once again, she felt the aching loneliness that had been her constant companion for years. Her mind whirled in confusion. Why was he blaming her? He was the one who had abandoned her. What had he meant?

At last, she fell into an uneasy sleep and dreamed that she and Awick were in a carriage race, constantly pursuing each other but never reaching the finish line.

Chapter Eleven

CAPTAIN ASHNELL ARRIVED EARLY THE FOL-
lowing morning to bid farewell to the ladies of
the Liviscombe household. He was shown into
the front parlor where Aunt Eloise was working on a piece of embroidery and Sara was
writing a letter to Bertie.

"Good morning, Miss Farley, Lady Sara," he
greeted them. "I am sorry to be calling at such
an early hour, but we leave at noon and I
wanted to say good-bye."

The ladies expressed their regret at his departure, and hoped that next time he was sent
to London he would pay them a visit. Sara rang
for tea and the three chatted for a few minutes.

Roberts entered to announce Captain Ketcham. "Ah, there you are, Tom. I figured this
would be your last stop." He turned to greet the
ladies. "I hate to see Tom go, you know. He has
been a good friend to me."

Tom looked at his young friend. "So you do not intend to rejoin us. Have you decided to sell out then?"

Freddie nodded. "Yes, Tom, I have. I spoke to Randy last night and he agrees that a position with Lord Buffield would be good for me. He said I was welcome to stay with him as long as I wanted, but I went round to Mount Street this morning and found some lodgings for rent. With the income from my secretarial position I shall be able to afford them, so I will move in next week."

Sara and Aunt Eloise expressed their agreement with this plan, and they all talked of Freddie's plans and hopes for the future.

At last Captain Ashnell arose. "It is time I got on my way. Are you going to see me off, Freddie?"

"Of course, Tom. That is why I was trying to find you."

The ladies bade them good-bye and wished Captain Ashnell a safe trip and a speedy return. Freddie said that he would see them on Tuesday for the trip to Waltham Abbey.

The ladies settled back down to their occupations.

"I am pleased that Freddie is making such an effort to establish himself," said Aunt Eloise. "He is such a dear boy. I think Clare will make him a good wife. She is a biddable girl and will be a credit to him as a hostess should he advance in the Home Office."

Sara agreed. "I had my doubts, but I think you are right. She seems truly fond of Freddie, and I believe that she has matured recently.

Freddie told me he was concerned about how the Tishfords would feel about the match, but I don't believe there is much cause for worry, as long as he can prove himself reliable and well able to care for Clare. They are not the sort to hang out for a title or a fortune."

They shared a light luncheon, then decided to take a turn through the park. The day was cool but clear and the park was congested with the fashionable crowd. They had stopped to talk to Lady Buffield and her eldest daughter when Sara's eye was caught by an elegant equipage drawn by a pair of neatly matched grays. She was not surprised to see Lord Awick at the reins wearing a tan driving coat and brown buckskins. His Hessian boots gleamed in the sunlight. Seated next to him was the beautiful woman she had seen with him the previous evening at Vauxhall. She wore a deep green gown and dashing bonnet with one plume curling over her cheek. She carried a parasol that she kept twirling in her hand. As Sara watched, she saw Awick turn and murmur to her and Mrs. Willoughby smiled up at him. Again it was a look of such intimacy that she felt herself color and quickly looked away. She tried to follow the conversation of her companions but was relieved when the parties separated. They were soon joined by Mrs. Warrington and Lady Tishford. They exchanged greetings.

"Where is Clare, Lady Tishford?" Aunt Eloise asked as the two ladies began to walk together down the crowded path. "Never tell me she would pass up a chance to be outside on such a pleasant day."

Georgie laughed. "No indeed. In fact she just rode by with Captain Ketcham a few moments ago. He stopped by after lunch feeling sad about the departure of his friend and said nothing would cheer him up like a ride with a pretty girl. He is becoming quite marked in his attentions lately but so far he has not spoken to Lord Tishford. I believe he is trying to prove himself in our eyes. Quite sweet really. I am beginning to think very highly of him. Not the rake his brother was, you know."

Sara overheard this remark and could not help glancing to where Awick and Mrs. Willoughby were driving, apparently lost in a private conversation. She said under her breath, "*Was* indeed. Old habits *do* die hard."

Mrs. Warrington heard this and sighed. Drat the man! she thought. Why in the world was he flaunting his ex-mistress in this way? She knew full well he had not taken up with her again so what reason did he have for this? She decided that yet another problem had arisen in the troubled relationship of her godson and her friend. She determined to find out what had gone amiss this time.

"I see Randy is escorting that Willoughby woman again," she said to Lady Sara. "I am surprised that Kenton allows it."

"Kenton?" repeated Sara. "Lord Kenton? What does he have to say to it?"

"Why, didn't you know, dear? She is under his protection now. Randy gave her her *congé* years ago, back when you and he . . ." She stopped awkwardly.

"No, I did not know," said Sara thoughtfully, ignoring the reference. "But he was dancing attendance on her last night at Vauxhall."

"Yes, Freddie told me about that. Did you not see Lord Kenton there? He was escorting her you know."

Casting her mind back Sara realized that there had been other people in the box. Perhaps she had leapt to conclusions, but if that were so why was he driving her out today?

"Tell me, Lady Sara, do you agree with Freddie's decision to sell out? Randy stopped by this morning and told me that he has decided to take a position with Lord Buffield, and that he is contemplating matrimony. Is it the Tishford chit?"

Sara laughed. "It is, but I must admit you have a great deal more perception than Lord Awick. He has taken it into his thick head that it is me Freddie intends to offer for."

Mrs. Warrington looked surprised at this disclosure. "You, my dear? But how can that be? You treat him just like a brother."

Sara explained the scene that had occurred in the garden the previous afternoon. Mrs. Warrington shook her head. "Well, if that isn't just like him," she said at last. "Honestly, my dear, I do not know how you ever put up with him. Of all the sap-skulled, dim-witted—"

Unaccountably, Sara leapt to his Lordship's defense. "No, Mrs. Warrington. It was as much my fault as his. I should have explained then and there, or at least made an effort to do so later. It was just that he made me so angry, and then it was too late. And last night he accused me of leading men on. That was the outside of enough. It wasn't me who made a formal declaration of marriage and then disappeared without a word."

Mrs. Warrington was fascinated by this statement. She had always wondered what had separated the two so many years before. She tried to recall the events that had led up to the rupture but it was so long ago she could not quite remember. There was something tickling her mind—something she knew she must recall.

She looked at Sara. "Disappeared, my dear? I must admit that with the advancing years, my memory does not always serve me well."

Sara did not seem aware of her companion. She had sunk into thought. Abruptly she asked, "Why did Awick go to America?"

"To America?" she asked in some surprise. "I am not perfectly sure. It was after his uncle died . . ." She stopped as, suddenly, it all came back to her—Randy's uncle falling ill and his abrupt departure for Kent, the visit of the dowager duchess and her questions as to where Awick had gone, her own trip to the Liviscombes', only to find that they had closed down the townhouse. She even recalled thinking he must have left her a note of some sort.

"His uncle?" Sara questioned.

"Yes, the old man had been taken ill and Randy was summoned to his bedside at Rotham Abbey. Your grandmother visited me just before she quit London and said she had heard he had left town. I knew nothing about it and later when I learned he had been called away, I came to tell you but the townhouse was closed. I assumed he had been in touch with you."

Sara only shook her head and Mrs. Warrington thought for a moment. So Randy had not left word and Sara felt that she had been abandoned. And now he believed that she was in love with his young brother. What a rare muddle these two had made of things. This was going to take more effort than she had supposed. She wanted nothing more than to get home and try to think it through. "Come, dear, let us catch up with your aunt and Lady Tishford. I am growing tired and would like to return home."

Sara looked concerned. "Oh I am sorry, Mrs. Warrington. I did not mean to ramble on so."

The ladies said farewell, and Aunt Eloise and Sara turned for home.

"The expedition to Waltham Abbey on Tuesday is all arranged," said Aunt Eloise. "The Tishfords have invited Mr. Kline, Freddie and Lord Awick. I hear it is a long drive but the Abbey is supposed to be lovely. I do hope the weather holds."

The day in question dawned clear and warm. Because of the length of the journey, the party had agreed to make an early start. The Liviscombe ladies were ready and waiting when the rest of the party arrived. Sara had chosen a gown of Indian muslin and wore a shawl of lace shot through with silver thread. Her bonnet was a lacy confection that perfectly framed her face. Aunt Eloise had picked purple satin and a turban of the same color. The Tishfords had brought their carriage, Lord Awick his phaeton and Captain Ketcham and Clare had elected to ride. Clare looked lovely in a riding habit of deep green. As the party set off, the Tishfords shared their vehicle with Mr. Kline and Aunt Eloise, and Sara joined Lord Awick. She had given a great deal of thought to what Mrs. Warrington had told her, and could not help wondering if she had misjudged Lord Awick. She wanted to say something but did not know how to begin. The silence between them began to grow uncomfortable.

"Lovely day for an—"

"Couldn't have had nicer—" they began simultaneously, then both laughed.

"That should dispose of the weather," said Awick, smiling at the girl beside him. "I am surprised you did not wish to ride with Freddie."

"After my one unfortunate experience on horseback," she smiled ruefully, "I do not believe I wish to embarrass myself in front of a crowd."

"What was that?" he asked curiously. "Surely, having been raised in the country, you learned to ride?"

She looked a trifle embarrassed. "If you must know, I have always been frightened of horses. I cannot explain why. Anyway, when Freddie was in Italy, he decided it was high time I overcame my fear. He hired the most gentle, docile mount he could find and bundled me up onto its back. It moved along slowly and placidly, then proceeded to deposit me very inelegantly in a mud puddle. Freddie, of course, found the whole episode uproariously amusing. I did not share his enjoyment."

"And you mean you have never been up since?" He forced himself not to laugh at the thought of Sara sitting in a mud puddle.

"Indeed, that is exactly what I mean. That beast was absolutely delighted with my comeuppance. I could see it in his eyes. I am thoroughly convinced that one should be perched behind a horse, not on top."

"I'm afraid that you and Freddie are not going to see eye to eye on that point," he said. "It's all I can do to keep him off a horse long enough to sit down to dinner."

She had a sudden urge to tell him the truth about her relationship to his brother but some perverse devil in her made her remark, "I can assure you that, after he is married, he is welcome to spend all the time he desires on horseback. I would never seek to curb his enjoyment."

Lord Awick gazed at her for a moment, then abruptly turned his attention back to his grays. "I presume it was you who convinced Freddie to sell out. But I must admit I was not pleased to think of him in battle on the peninsula. The situation there is growing grim." They then fell into a discussion of the latest reports that had come through and this lasted until they reached their destination.

Waltham Abbey was a lovely place, as Aunt Eloise had said, and the view was enchanting.

The Tishfords had sent the servants on ahead to set up the picnic for them. There was cold chicken, pigeon pie, fruits and cheeses and thick slices of bread, all to be washed down with champagne, wine and lemonade. The group sat on the lush green lawn and ate until they were replete. The older members of the party decided to relax where they were and just enjoy the fresh air and sunshine, while the younger people took a stroll. They wandered the flower-strewn paths, enjoying the sights and smells. Conversation remained general and pleasant. As the afternoon wore on, a breeze came up, and the four returned to the main clearing where Lord Tishford and Mr. Kline napped, while Aunt Eloise and Georgie gossiped. As they returned, it was Lady Tishford who exclaimed, "Why Captain Ketcham, you're limping again. Are you in pain?"

Freddie looked embarrassed. "Only a little, Lady Tishford. It's just the exercise I have had today. Nothing to be concerned about."

Lord Awick looked anxious. "Oh, Freddie, forgive me. I should have known better. Why did you not say something?"

"Hush, brother," he replied. "If I had been in severe pain, I would have told you. Let us not worry the ladies."

Lord Awick looked at him for a long moment. "Still, I forbid your riding back. I will ride Pegasus and escort Lady Clare. You may drive Sara home in the phaeton."

"Really, Randy, may I?" he exclaimed, bubbling with excitement.

Lord Awick thought this was caused by the anticipation of spending so much time alone with Sara. He had no idea that his younger brother had been positively bursting to drive the grays. "Of course, you may. Just be sure you are careful with my horses. Their mouths are sensitive and they tend to be skittish. You will need your wits about you to make sure you do not come to grief. And, of course, you will enjoy the company of Lady Sara."

With the promise of this treat, Freddie was ready to start back at once. As the wind was becoming increasingly chill, the other members of the party agreed that it was time to return home.

The Tishford carriage moved to the fore and set a restrained but steady pace. Clare and Lord Awick rode along beside. Soon Clare challenged him to a race to the top of the next knoll and the two set off. Freddie kept the grays to a slow trot, getting used to the feel of their mouths and not allowing them to spring. He was a competent driver, having been taught by his brother, but he was also conscientious and cautious, not wishing to harm the excellent team.

Thus it was that Freddie and Sara soon fell behind the other members of the party. As they went along, Freddie began to feel more comfortable with the horses and was able to divert his attention long enough to strike up a conversation with his companion. "I think the Tishfords are beginning to accept me, don't you, Sara? Lord Tishford asked about my new position today and seemed quite friendly. I think I will soon be able to approach him for Clare's hand."

"You are right, Freddie. Lady Tishford is full of praise for you, and I believe they are impressed with the course you have chosen." She paused. "It will be pleasant to not have to pretend to your brother that we are promised to each other. While I love you dearly, it is a bit awkward."

He smiled ruefully. "Don't I know it? I have almost given the game away on countless occasions. In fact I was thinking that I would tell him tonight. I am moving into my lodgings tomorrow, and we had intended to have dinner alone this evening. It would be a good opportunity to tell him all the plans I have made for my future. Then I can address Lord Tishford. I start work for Lord Buffield on Thursday. If things work out, Clare and I could be married this fall. Oh, Sara, I am so happy. I am beginning to believe that everything is going to be fine. Clare is such a—"

Exactly what Freddie thought Clare was would never be known. At that moment, a rabbit dashed in front of the skittish grays. They reared up, to pawing. Freddie, who had not been paying close attention, was caught by surprise. He drew back on the reins to get the team under control, but they had already seized the bits between their teeth and set off at a thundering pace. They took a turn much too quickly and the occupants of the phaeton felt a sickening jolt as the off-wheel collided with a stone. There was the sound of splintering wood as the wheel came off the axle. Sara felt a rush of air as she was thrown from the vehicle. She landed some way away with a harsh thud, and knew no more.

She came to, wondering where she was and why there was such a crushing pain in her left side and arm. She must have slept wrong. But it hurt so badly. She then became aware that it was not the canopy of her four-poster bed she was looking at but a late afternoon sky. Consciousness slowly returned to her and she recalled the accident. Freddie! she thought in alarm, and raised herself up. She immediately sank back down. Her head was swimming and the pain in her side was awful. She had better take this slowly. She lay still for a moment until the world had stopped spinning, then cautiously started to raise herself up again. That was better. She found she could sit up although the pain in her side and arm was close to making her nauseated. She looked around for Freddie. He was lying still, his face drawn and pale. She got to her knees, and then at last stood up. She made her way to his side and awkwardly knelt down placing her ear against his chest. He was breathing shallowly, but his pulse was good. She felt his arms and legs, detecting no broken bones. She glanced at the road. The horses were still standing in front of the wrecked phaeton. They did not seem to have taken any harm. At that moment Freddie stirred and groaned. He opened his eyes to see her gazing down anxiously at him. "What happened?" he asked.

"There was an accident," she said as calmly as she could. "Are you all right, Freddie?"

"Yes, I think so," he said, cautiously testing his arms and legs. "I think I must have hit my head, since I have developed a splitting headache. Are the grays all right? Randy would never forgive me if anything—"

"Yes, they are fine. Don't worry about that. What we had better worry about is what we are going to do next. The phaeton has lost a wheel and I am afraid we are miles from anywhere. We can only hope that someone will come along. Can you stand? We should try to make our way back to the road. Perhaps we can flag someone down."

Freddie sat up, then noticed the expression of pain on her face. "You're hurt!" he said.

"No, no," she said. "It is nothing to worry about." But as she attempted to rise again, she staggered, clutching her side. Her left arm dangled uselessly.

"Oh God, Sara," Freddie said alarmed. "Your arm is broken and, if I'm not mistaken, you have crushed some ribs. Here, my dear, put your right arm around my neck." He carefully lifted her up. "If it wasn't for this damned leg of mine, I would carry you. But look, we will go very slowly and you just tell me when you want to stop."

Haltingly, they made their way back up to the road. Freddie lowered her down then sat beside her, considering their possible courses of action. "I could take one of the grays and ride for help," he said, then dismissed the idea. He dared not leave her alone on a public road, injured. There was no sign of a vehicle approaching. He thought for a moment. "There is a public house a couple of miles down the road. If I help you, do you think you can make it?"

Sara was convinced she could not go a quarter of that distance but she also knew that they had no choice. Gathering up her strength she said, "Let us try it. We cannot very well sit here all night."

Freddie grinned at her. "You are a real Trojan, Sara," he said. "Randy was right, you *could* have followed the drum."

He helped her to her feet again and the two set off with Freddie leading the grays. They stopped every few yards for Sara to take a rest. The journey became a nightmare, as every footstep jarred her pain-wracked body. The only thing that kept her going was the thought that soon Lord Awick would have noticed their absence and sent someone looking for them. She tried to hold his image in front of her eyes but her mind kept blurring and eventually all she could concentrate on was the painful task of setting one foot in front of the other.

Chapter Twelve

LORD AWICK WAS IN A TOWERING RAGE. "WHAT do you mean he has not returned yet? Dammit, man, it is dusk already. He should have been home two hours ago."

Briggs, his valet, looked down uncomfortably. "I am sorry, my Lord. Maybe he stopped off at the Liviscombe's when he delivered Lady Sara home."

"He would not stay for two hours!" Awick paced the room for a few moments. "Surely the young fool would not have made off with her. No, why should he? There could be no possible objection to their match." He paced again. "There must have been an accident. But why have we not heard anything?"

He turned again to his butler. "Ring for my curricle. I will stop by the Liviscombe townhouse and see if there has been any word of the truants. If not I will travel back along the road to Waltham Abbey."

Several minutes later his curricle was at the front door. Donning his many-caped driving coat and curly-brimmed beaver, he ran down the steps and climbed up to grab the reins. Giving his horses the office to start he rattled off down the square, driving a little faster than safety dictated. He arrived at Lady Sara's house and, tossing the reins to a groom, he mounted the stairs. Within moments, Roberts opened the door.

"Lord Awick, I am glad to see you, sir. Do you have any word of Lady Sara?" he so far forgot himself as to ask.

"No, not a word," said Awick. "Where is Miss Farley?"

"She is in the drawing room with Mr. Kline, and very near hysterics. I am sure you will know what to do for the best, my Lord."

"I hope so," said Awick heading for the door to the drawing room. "I will announce myself."

He entered to find Aunt Eloise stretched out on a sofa weeping, with Mr. Kline hovering around her and pushing a vinaigrette under her nose, saying tears would do no good. He was sure there was a sensible explanation, and Lady Sara would be home any moment safe and sound.

Both looked up expectantly as the door opened. When they saw it was Awick, Aunt Eloise's weeping increased and Mr. Kline rushed forward to greet him.

"You have no word, my Lord?"

"No, none," said Awick. He advanced to

Aunt Eloise. "She said nothing to you, ma'am? You have no reason to believe she might have done anything precipitate?"

Aunt Eloise looked at him in confusion. "Precipitate?" she repeated, momentarily too startled to weep. "What on earth do you mean?"

"Elope, for example."

"Elope?" said the lady, half-rising up from the sofa. "Who on earth would she elope with? Why she is not even in love with anyone."

"She's not?" said Awick, staring at her. "But what about Freddie?"

"Freddie?" repeated Aunt Eloise staring at him as if he had lost his senses. "But Freddie is going to marry Clare Tishford. Why in the world would Sara elope with Freddie? She is not in love with Freddie."

Mr. Kline came forward at this point. "Treats him like a young brother, you know. What ever gave you such an idea?"

Lord Awick found himself at a loss for words. "She did . . . they did . . . I mean, dash it, I had assumed that . . . oh blast it all!" He began pacing. "But if they have not eloped, where in the blazes are they?"

Mr. Kline, again administering the vinaigrette to Aunt Eloise's nose, said, "That does seem to be the question. They must have met with an accident. Those grays did seem temperamental. We ought to set out on the road back to Waltham Abbey. There is not much traffic there after dark and if they have come to grief, they will have a hard time finding assistance."

Lord Awick finally pulled himself together.

"You are right, sir. I will set off at once." As Mr. Kline indicated that he wanted to accompany him, Awick held up a hand. "I think it best if you stay here with Miss Farley. I believe she needs your help more than I do." He turned back to the old lady. "Don't worry, Miss Farley. I will restore your niece safely to you. We will be back before you know it."

So saying he headed for the door. Mr. Kline joined him. "You're sure you don't need my help?"

Lord Awick thanked him. "No, sir, I have a light vehicle and a good team. I should be able to cover the ground rapidly. If anything is wrong, I promise to send word instantly. Keep Miss Farley calm and, if you can, get her to take some brandy."

He waved farewell and departed. Mr. Kline returned to Aunt Eloise's side. She had grown alarmingly pale and was now sobbing uncontrollably. He rang for the butler. "A bottle of brandy, please, Roberts."

"Of course, sir," said that worthy and returned within moments bearing a decanter and two glasses.

Mr. Kline poured some of the amber liquid into a glass and, supporting Aunt Eloise on one arm, he held it to her lips. "Drink up, my love, it will make you feel better." She swallowed some of the fiery liquid and choked slightly but a little color appeared in her cheeks. He gave her some more, and her sobs subsided somewhat.

"Oh, John, she will be all right, won't she? I am just glad that Awick has gone after her.

He will not let anything happen to her, I know."

Sara wondered how many years they had been trudging down this road. She could almost believe that it had been all of her life. Was there ever a time when she had not known this burning agony in her side or the excruciating pain of her feet hitting the road? She kept slipping in and out of consciousness. But on they went. As time passed, she noticed a weight on her right side and realized it was Freddie. He still had her arm draped around his neck and was trying to help her along but he himself had begun to limp badly, and was now starting to lean on her. She suggested they rest for a while. They had come to a large tree and Freddie tied the reins to a branch. Then they collapsed against the trunk.

Freddie immediately dozed off. Sara was in too much pain. She kept listening for the sound of hooves or voices, and looking for the sign of lights. She could detect none in the gathering dusk and finally gave herself up to wondering if it was possible they would die out here. She knew her own injuries were bad, and she was beginning to worry about Freddie. He had not been strong since his injury in the peninsula, and now it was obvious that his leg was giving him a great deal of pain. They had no food or water, and the night was turning bitterly cold.

She at last pulled herself together. They could die out here like frightened rabbits or they could try to help themselves. They had to reach civilization soon. She turned to Freddie.

"Wake up, now, Freddie. We have got to keep going. It is growing cold. We should reach the inn soon. Let us try a little bit further."

Freddie groaned. "Oh, Sara, it hurts so much. I am sorry." He dragged himself to his feet with the help of the tree trunk, then collapsed back against it.

Sara had an idea. "Tell you what, Freddie. Do you think you could mount one of the grays if I helped you?"

He considered it for a moment. "Yes I think I could. That is a good idea, love. What about you? Could you ride?"

Sara laughed shakily. "I cannot ride when I am in perfect health, let alone now. But with you mounted on one and leading the other, we ought to be able to at least travel on."

She struggled with the reins of one of the horses and returned to his side. Freddie found a large rock nearby to use to mount. Gathering the reins of the other horse in his hand, he instructed Sara to hold on to his leg with her right hand and to tell him the moment she felt she had to rest.

And so the little cavalcade again started down the road. Sara was beyond pain now. She felt almost euphoric—as if she were floating above her own body watching this scene as a dispassionate observer.

Again the time stretched endlessly before her. There was nothing beyond this road, beyond placing foot after foot. No beginning, no end, just this road going on forever.

Lord Awick dared not urge his team too fast. As he left the city, he knew he must observe everything around him. If there had been an accident, the phaeton could be in one of the ditches lining the road, and the occupants thrown on one of the fields. He tried to stop himself from these gruesome imaginings but he kept thinking of Sara lying still in a field, her face pale and beautiful in death. Oh, no, she could not be dead. He had lost her once already. He could not possibly lose her again.

His team moved forward steadily and he looked this way and that, searching for some telltale motion. By now the wind was blowing gustily and he frequently saw the movement of shadows. Every time, his heart leapt into his throat, and every time it turned out to be the shadow of a tree or bush. He kept on going.

He was several miles outside of London when he saw a horseman approaching him. No, it was not a horseman. There were two horses, one with a strange-looking figure on its back and something clinging to its side. With a horrible premonition, he urged his team forward. Within moments, he was able to make out the pathetic little group. Freddie was slumped on the back of the gray, holding onto the reins as if his life depended on it. Sara had one hand grasped around Freddie's knee. Her left arm hung at her side. She seemed unconscious.

Lord Awick sprang down from his coach and

ran toward them. "My God!" he exclaimed. "What happened?"

Freddie looked at him and blinked several times. "What, Randy, you here?"

At this Sara also roused herself. "Ah, Lord Awick, a pleasure I am sure. May I ring for tea?" With that she lost consciousness and fell onto the road. Awick sprang forward. "She is injured!" he exclaimed.

"Oh yes," said Freddie calmly. "Badly, I think. But she is a brave girl, Randy. You know you could do worse." And with that Freddie himself slipped from his precarious perch on the gray.

Lord Awick caught him and hauled him to his curricle where he placed him as comfortably as he could in the back seat. He tied the grays to the back, then lifted Sara carefully in his arms trying not to touch her left side. It was obvious that her ribs had been broken as well as her arm. He wrapped his own cape around her as he set her carefully on the seat, then climbing up beside her, he gathered up the reins and placed his free arm carefully around her, trying to protect her as best he could from the jolting of the curricle.

He could hear Freddie sleeping soundly in the back seat. He was sure his young brother had sustained no lasting injury. He had probably bothered his leg again with his exertions but beyond being exhausted he seemed all right. It was Sara who worried him. She kept fading in and out of consciousness, obviously in terrible pain. Despite his attempts to protect her, she moaned with every bump.

As they rode along, Awick decided that the best thing to do would be to take them to his own townhouse since he lived closer than the Liviscombes to the main road. He could then send round for the doctor and alert Aunt Eloise that he had Sara in his charge. Now it was Awick who began to think the journey was endless but by this time his companions were both unconscious.

He paced back and forth in the library thinking ruefully that he had done a lot of pacing this day. He stopped by a sidetable and poured himself a glass of brandy from the cut-crystal decanter. He resumed his pacing.

There was a tap at the door. The doctor entered looking serious, but not grave.

"Well?" said Awick impatiently.

"Your brother has taken a nasty rap on the head and has suffered a mild concussion. He is badly bruised and has sustained several small cuts and abrasions. He should remain in bed for a week, on a light diet. I have left a sleeping draught in his room but he should not need it more than a night or two. He will be stiff and sore for several days."

"And Lady Sara?"

"She is a courageous young woman. To have walked any distance in her condition— amazing." He shook his head admiringly. "Her injuries are serious but should all heal without any lasting effect. She sustained three broken ribs, a break to the ulna in her left arm and also a slight concussion. I have bound her ribs and set the arm. She too has multiple bruises, cuts and abrasions. There will be a great deal of pain for several days I fear. Keep her as quiet as possible and if I were you I would not try to move her for three to four weeks. I have given her a sedative but she will probably wake up during the night. If she does, give her this in a glass of water." He handed Awick a packet of white powder. "I will come by in the morning to see how they do."

The two men shook hands. "Thank you, Doctor."

Awick made his way upstairs. He glanced into his brother's room and saw he was sleeping, his breathing regular. He then went on to the room he had had prepared for Lady Sara. Entering quietly he walked to the huge four-poster bed that seemed to dominate the room. She looked so small and frail lying there, dressed in a voluminous nightgown of his housekeeper's. Her hair was spread in a dark cloud about her frighteningly white face. The splinted arm rested across her breast. He touched her forehead and smoothed back her hair. Bending over her he placed a gentle kiss on her lips. "Sleep well, my love. I will be here if you need me."

He returned to the library and summoned Mrs. Strothers, his housekeeper. "Have one of the maids sit with Lady Liviscombe. She should sleep for several hours but I do not want her to be alone. I am going out but should be back within the hour."

"Very good, my lord," she replied and hastened below stairs to do his bidding, and to compare notes with the butler on the uncommon interest the master was showing in Lady Liviscombe. From the way he was carrying on, you would have thought she was at death's door, not suffering a few broken bones. It was beginning to look like something was in the wind.

Upon their arrival at his townhouse, Lord Awick had immediately sent a message off to Aunt Eloise to allay her fears. Not wanting to alarm her, he had simply said he had found the truants, brought them back to his house, and summoned the doctor since it appeared that Sara had broken her arm and perhaps a rib or two and he did not wish her to travel any farther than absolutely necessary. He had promised to come by as soon as the doctor had given his report.

Consequently, Awick set out for the Liviscombe residence. He found the household much calmer than when he had left. Roberts showed him into the drawing room where he found Aunt Eloise on the sofa, dozing lightly, and Mr. Kline gazing out the window at the darkened street.

He turned at the sound of the door opening, then rushed forward when he saw the viscount. "Ah Awick, my boy!" he exclaimed, grasping his lordship's hand and shaking it heartily. "I cannot tell you how much I appreciate what you have done. The poor love"— nodding at Aunt Eloise's recumbent form— "was beside herself, as you saw. Just knowing you had gone after Lady Sara had a wonderfully calming effect on her. She kept saying that she knew you would not fail to find her. I gave her some brandy, as you instructed. When we received your note, saying Lady Sara was alive and safe, I convinced her to take some laudanum. She dozed off a couple of minutes ago."

At the sound of voices, Eloise stirred and then sat up. "Oh, Awick!" she cried. "Bless you. How is my dear niece? What did the doctor say? Where is she? Did you bring her home?"

Awick went to the sofa and knelt down beside her grasping her hands in his. "Hush now, Miss Farley. Everything is fine. She does indeed have a broken arm and a couple of broken ribs. But beyond that and being a little banged up, the doctor says she is going to be fine. She is still at my house, and right now is asleep, with a maid watching over her. The doctor recommended she not be moved for a while, to prevent any further damage to her ribs."

"Oh, thank God," said Aunt Eloise, beginning to weep. "Oh Awick, what would we ever have done without you?" She was silent for a moment. "But how is Freddie? I was so wrapped up in my own problems that I never even thought—"

"Freddie is fine," said Awick smiling reassuringly. "He suffered a mild concussion but a few days in bed will see him right as rain." He broke into a grin. "You will be pleased to know that the grays also came through well—in fact they sustained no injury at all. The only casualty out of the whole mishap was my phaeton and I am afraid it is damaged beyond repair. A small price to pay though, all in all."

He arose. "And now I must return. I believe my work as nurse is just beginning."

"Oh, dear," Aunt Eloise said, struggling to stand, "let me return with you and help."

He laughed and pushed her gently back down onto the sofa. "Not tonight, Miss Farley. Right now you need your sleep. You have had a trying day." He held up one hand as she seemed ready to protest. "No arguments now. I have given my orders." He turned to Mr. Kline. "And I expect that you, sir, will make sure they are carried out."

Mr. Kline held out his hand. "I believe you're in charge here, my Lord. I'll see your instructions are followed to the letter."

"Good, I will hold you to that." Awick turned back to Aunt Eloise. "You may come and visit us tomorrow morning, but I do not want any long faces around the sick bed. So get some rest and do not worry. Everything is going to be all right." With that he took his leave.

"Oh John," said Aunt Eloise as the door closed behind him. "Do you think it will work out this time? He seems genuinely concerned."

Mr. Kline nodded. "Yes, my dear, I think it just might work out."

When Lord Awick arrived home, he went immediately to Lady Sara's room.

"You may go now," he told the maid who was sitting in a chair by the fireplace. "I will look after Lady Liviscombe."

The maid curtsied, murmured, "Yes, M'Lord," and left quietly.

Again he approached the bed and gazed down at her still form. My God, she is beautiful, he thought. He fancied there was a little more color in her cheeks. He checked her pulse and found it faint but steady. He pulled a chair to the side of the bed and took her good hand in his. He then settled back to watch and wait. He heard the clock in the main hall striking off the hours. Occasionally there was a sound in the street of some late reveller making his way home. He heard the watch passing by declaring that all was right with the world.

It was just after two o'clock that Sara stirred. He sat up and gazed into her face, still clutching her right hand.

Her eyelids fluttered. "Randy?" she whispered.

"I am here, my love," he said huskily.

"Randy?" she said again. "I had such a terrible dream. I dreamt that you and Papa—" she stopped.

"What happened to me and Papa?" he asked gently.

"You and Papa died, and left me alone and . . . and . . . Oh, Randy, I could not bear it!" she sat up suddenly and then fell back, her face ravaged by pain. "Oh God," she moaned. "Oh, it hurts, it hurts."

"Hush, darling, I'm here now." He took the packet of white powder and dumped it into a glass. Filling it with water from the pitcher set on the washstand, he lifted her head. "Drink this, it will help ease the pain."

She swallowed, choked, and then finally drained the glass. He set her back down upon the pillow. She swallowed convulsively a few times and then subsided.

Several moments passed.

"Randy?"

"Yes, love?"

"Tell Papa I'm sorry. I know he wanted a son. Tell him I tried. Tell him I never meant to . . . make . . . him . . . unhappy."

Lord Awick sat by her side, clutching her hand. He knew she would never remember what had passed between them this night. She was bordering on delirium. The pain, the trial she had endured, and the laudanum had taken their toll. But he also knew she had cried out for him in her suffering. That was all that mattered. She had known instinctively that she could turn to him.

He sat for a long time beside her bed, contemplating what she had said. He realized he knew very little about her. Had the old duke resented her so much? Had he really made her regret that she had not been born a boy? The poor child!

Dawn was paling the night sky. At last he rose. The fire had gone out hours before and his legs were stiff and cramped. Sara still slept. Leaning over her, he wondered how he could ever make it up to her. Well, he decided, one thing at a time. First he had to convince her to trust him, and then he had to prove to her that not everyone she loved would abandon her. Oh my sweet darling, he thought, if only you could realize that you have always been the greatest love of my life. Still she slept. He wondered for the millionth time why she had run away so many years ago. Had it been him? Had he hurt her? Maybe this time he could convince her to stay.

He heaved a great sigh. At least she was here now, and he could take care of her. He strode to the end of the room and tugged the bell cord. Within moments the little maid again appeared at the door.

"Yes, M'Lord?"

"Please sit here with my Lady for a while. I am going to freshen up. If she awakens, summon me at once."

The little maid seated herself in the chair recently vacated by her master and stared anxiously at the beautiful lady lying in the bed.

It was only moments later that Lady Sara again regained consciousness. This time she looked around the unfamiliar room and could not seem to place her surroundings. She then saw the maid sitting nervously beside her. She tried to recall what had happened but to no avail.

Finally she said, "Who are you?"

"I am Molly, M'Lady. Don't you remember me?" the little maid replied.

"Molly?" asked Sara. "But what are you doing here?"

"I live here, M'Lady," said the little maid. "Ye be at Lord Awick's. Ye took a terrible spill, ye did, and . . ." At the mention of Lord Awick she recalled his instruction that she was to summon His Lordship the moment M'Lady awoke. She hastened to the cord and gave it a firm tug.

She returned to Sara's side. "Just ye be easy now. Nothing fer ye to worry about. Lord Awick hisself is looking out for ye."

The door opened and Lord Awick strode into the room. He dismissed the maid with a smile and turned to Sara.

He was dressed in buckskin breeches and his lace shirt was unbuttoned. There was a stubble of beard on his chin, and his hair looked as if he had been running his hands through it. There were dark shadows under his eyes, and lines of worry etched around his mouth.

She stared at him for a moment and then memory came flooding back. "Oh, God, it's not Freddie is it? Has something happened? He seemed all right."

He rushed to her side and grasped her hand. "No, no, calm yourself. Freddie is fine. He has suffered a lump on the head but nothing serious." He gazed searchingly at her face. "Were you so concerned about him?"

"Oh, yes," said Sara lying back against the pillows. "He is such a dear boy. If I had ever had a brother, I would have wanted him to be just like Freddie."

The tension in Awick's eyes eased. "Yes, he is a good boy." He paused. "How do you feel?"

She gazed up at him and gave a shaky smile. "The only words I can think to describe it are not accepted in polite conversation."

He laughed delightedly. "In that case, you must be feeling better." He grew serious. "Is the pain awfully bad? The doctor left a draught . . ."

"No, not right now. But could I have a glass of water? I'm dreadfully thirsty."

He poured some water from the pitcher. Lifting her head against his arm he held the glass to her lips. She drank slowly, then said, "Thank you, my Lord. And now I think I would like to rest."

Seconds later she was asleep. Awick stood by the bed for a long time, staring down at her. If only he could talk to her and make things right. . . .

Chapter Thirteen

THE NEXT TIME SARA AWOKE IT WAS TO FIND Aunt Eloise at her side. "How are you feeling, dear?" that lady asked. "I have requested Lord Awick's cook to prepare some beef broth for you. Would you like to sit up?"

Sara nodded and smiled. "Yes, I think so, Aunt. Thank you."

Aunt Eloise rang the bell cord then settled back down by her neice.

"What time is it?" Sara asked. "Have I been asleep long?"

"Not long," said her aunt, complacently. "A little under two days."

"Two days! Surely you are joking."

"No, not at all. It is now Thursday afternoon. In fact it is almost teatime. Lord Awick tells me you have been a model patient. There has been a steady stream of people coming by to inquire after you, and we have received so many flowers that I have started sending them around to the hospital. You have had one very persistent visitor, and I am not sure how long I can hold this friend off. In fact, I received specific instructions that the moment you felt strong enough I was to beg an interview."

"Who in the world do you mean?" asked Sara.

"Let me give you a hint. You recently missed an engagement you had and this particular friend is clamoring to know why."

At that moment, the door opened a crack and a tiny blonde head appeared in the opening. A whisper came. "Is she awake?"

Sara smiled. "Yes, Beth. I am awake. Please come in. I owe you an apology. I missed our trip to the 'Change,' didn't I? Do you suppose we could set another date? I promise not to disappoint you again."

The child walked solemnly to the side of the bed and timidly touched Lady Sara's right hand.

"What's wrong, Beth?" Sara asked.

"Papa said you were very sick and that I could only come in if I promised not to disturb you," she whispered.

"Oh, Beth, my love, you're not disturbing me. Aunt Eloise, please help her up so she can sit on the edge of the bed." The child was soon settled, her tiny hand in Sara's.

"There now, tell me everything you have been doing. How is your pony?"

Beth was soon chatting happily. Aunt Eloise was delighted and Sara only had to caution her once about bouncing on the bed.

The door opened again to admit Lord Awick.

He looked sternly at his daughter. "Not tiring my patient, are you, Brat?" he asked.

Beth looked at him and blushed guiltily. She turned to Sara. "Am I tiring you? Papa said I could not come back if I made you uncomfortable." She looked so woebegone that all of the adults were forced to laugh, although the action made Sara wince in pain.

"No, you are not tiring me, dear, but I must insist you not make me laugh. If you promise me that, you can come back any time you like."

"But for now," said Awick lifting her off the bed, "you had better let Lady Sara rest. Why don't you go down and see if Perkins will take you out on your pony? And then it will be time for tea. You may join Miss Farley and me today."

"Thank you, Papa," she said. She took Sara's hand again and kissed her on the cheek. "I'm glad you're better, Sara, and I am awfully glad you are here. I will come visit you every day." And with this promise she left the room.

The broth was brought up and again Awick helped her hold the cup.

"I am feeling much better," she said. "I understand I have you to thank for the care I have received."

"It has been my pleasure, Lady Sara. But now I am going to take your aunt away and you are going to go back to sleep."

She nodded. "Yes, I would like that, thank you."

Aunt Eloise kissed her cheek. "I will come visit you every day too," she promised.

As she left, Awick said, "It seems that this is

the accepted sick room practice." He bent over and kissed her cheek. "I will come visit you every day, too. If not more often." He smiled warmly at her, then followed Miss Farley out the door, closing it gently behind him.

Sara lay staring up at the rich canopy. She lifted her hand to her still burning cheek. It was not the broth that had caused the sudden flush of warmth. She thought for a long time. There was something she wanted to remember, something about Awick. But her mind was fuzzy and finally she fell asleep.

The days settled into a pattern. Aunt Eloise called every morning and sat with her niece, reading aloud the newspapers, then the mail, telling her who had inquired after her the previous day, and finally giving an account of her own activities. Mr. Kline seemed to figure ever more frequently in these doings. Eloise left when the luncheon tray was brought in.

Beth came every afternoon. Often she would bring her lessons and Sara would listen as she worked them out. Sometimes they would just sit and talk. Beth was a curious child and had an endless supply of questions. She stayed until tea time.

Lord Awick arrived after tea and sat with her until dinner, then returned and stayed until she fell asleep. It was a comfortable time. They talked about many things, though sometimes they sat in a companionable silence with no words necessary at all. When Sara felt well enough to sit up, they would play chess. Awick insisted, however, that she get plenty of rest so he always left at an early hour.

One morning, just a week after the accident, there was a knock at her door. She was surprised and looked at Aunt Eloise. "Who can that be? I thought Lord Awick was allowing no visitors except for you and Beth."

Aunt Eloise shook her head. "I cannot imagine, my dear. Of course there is one way to find out." So saying she rose to open the door. "Why Freddie, my boy! So the tyrant has let you up at last, has he? Come in, come in."

"Hello, Aunt Eloise. How is my brother's other prisoner? Not allowed out of bed either, I will bet."

"Indeed you would win," said Sara from her bed. "But in my case at least I am afraid he is in the right of it."

Freddie walked over to her and bent down to give her a light kiss. He wore a dressing gown, but was freshly shaven. "How are you, love? Randy tells me you were knocked about. Well, at least you're not the color of that pillowslip, as I feared."

Sara smiled. "Truly, Freddie, I am feeling much better. The doctor says that I should be able to get up in a few days. How are you feeling? I notice your limp is not too bad."

"No, I think a few days in bed helped that too. I am feeling fine, but getting bored with being cooped up."

After that, Freddie became a regular visitor, too, often coming in the afternoon with Beth. The three soon devised all sorts of games to play and the time passed quickly.

After another week, the doctor allowed Sara to get up for the first time. Awick helped her sit up on the edge of the bed, then lowered her feet to the floor. He placed an arm around her and slowly helped her rise. She felt light-headed and dizzy for a moment, but it passed as she leaned against him. He then assisted her to a chair he had placed by the window. He wrapped a blanket around her legs and drew the curtains. It was a lovely day, the sky clear and soft blue.

"Would you open the window, please?" she asked. "It seems so long since I breathed fresh air."

"As long as you will tell me if you get too cool."

There was a slight breeze but the day was warm. She sat silent for a while. "Where is Beth?" she asked. "She is usually here by this time."

"I sent her out for a ride with Perkins. I told her she could come in later for a brief visit. I did not want you overtaxed on your first day up."

She smiled at him gratefully. "It is pleasant just sitting here quietly with—" she stopped herself.

"With—?" he prodded gently.

She looked down to hide her confusion. "Oh, I was just going to say with the sun shining and . . . and—" she stopped again searching her mind for a safer subject. "How is Mrs. Warrington? I have not heard you mention her for several days."

Recognizing her tactics, he smiled. "Did I not tell you? Her niece in Somerset was delivered of a baby girl two weeks ago and she went off to attend her. I hear that mother and baby are doing fine but my poor godmother is beginning to miss the pleasures of town. She never did enjoy rusticating. I expect her back any day."

They were silent again. "Oh, by the way, did Freddie tell you he has decided to move into his lodgings in Mount Street tomorrow? He says he is feeling well enough to assume his duties now and the doctor has given his permission. The boy has been chafing at the bit, you know—anxious to get himself established."

Sara smiled. "Aunt Eloise tells me Lord Buffield was very understanding about the delay."

"'Understanding' is hardly the word. Even offered to start paying him from the day he was supposed to report. Freddie refused of course."

Again there was silence. "Lady Sara," began Awick. There was so much he wanted to talk to her about but realized it was too soon. She had to get her strength back first. He did not want to take advantage of her weakness.

"Yes?" she asked when he did not continue.

"Oh, I just thought you might like some tea or wine. May I ring?"

"Yes, a glass of wine would be nice. We can toast my first venture out of bed."

The tray holding a decanter, two glasses, and a plate of small cakes was soon brought in. Awick filled the glasses and handed one to her. "To your speedy recovery," he said. They sipped their wine.

She asked him about an article that Aunt Eloise had read to her from the newspapers that morning and they kept the conversation in general channels until Awick convinced her to return to her bed. "That is enough for one day. Beth will be here soon and I am sure you will have plenty of excitement then."

He helped her back into bed and was just tucking the covers in around her when Beth erupted into the room. "Hallo, Papa! Hallo, Sara! I had the most exciting ride! Perkins let me trot today and he says I have got a good seat." She noticed the chair placed by the open window. "Did you get up today? Are you going to come downstairs soon?"

"In a few days, maybe," her father said. "We will have to see how Lady Sara feels."

Suddenly, Beth had a horrible thought and her face crumpled. "That doesn't mean you're going away, does it?"

Sara smiled at her. "I have to go home sometime, you know."

"But why?" the child asked. "Why can't you just stay here forever? I love having you here, and Papa won't mind." She turned to her father. "Would you, Papa?"

"I think, Beth, we should discuss this later. Lady Sara will be with us for a while yet, and when she decides she wants to go home, I don't want you to make her feel bad. Understood?"

"Yes, Papa," she said in a small voice. Then she perked up again. "But she's not going away yet."

She soon settled down into her usual chatter, and the matter was dropped.

Later that evening, however, after the household was asleep, Lord Awick sat in his library sipping a glass of brandy and recalling the discussion. He had been bothered for several days now by the impropriety of having Sara, an unmarried lady, staying in his house, a bachelor establishment. He had realized shortly after the accident that he should have brought in Aunt Eloise or some other female to play chaperone. And with Sara up and about the impropriety would worsen. In the petty and gossipy minds of many of the sticklers of the *ton*, Sara would be compromised and therefore ruined. Granted she had many friends who would never believe the tattle, but tattle there would definitely be and she would probably be denied entrance to the more exclusive establishments. He doubted if this would bother her, but the chance word, the curious stare, the slighting reference might. The entire situation was ironic. She had miraculously avoided being ostracized after he had truly compromised her and now her reputation was endangered by the happenstance of an accident.

She had run from him the last time he had proposed to her but this time she had no choice if she wished to continue living comfortably among the fashionable world. Marriage was the perfect answer. Her reputation would be saved, Beth would be ecstatic and he would be the happiest man on earth. He often got this far in his thinking, then stopped. How could he convince Sara? She had said yes so many years ago, only to disappear. Why had she left without a word? Had anything changed since then? She seemed warm and friendly now and she obviously adored Beth. Well, he finally decided, all I can do is ask her. At the worst, she will turn me down, and at best— a smile spread across his face and he sank deeper into his leather arm chair.

Four days later, Sara went downstairs for the first time since the accident. Lord Awick wanted to carry her but she insisted on walking. This was accomplished with a footman on one side and Awick on the other. They escorted her into the morning room, and settled her on a chaise longue.

"What a lovely room, Lord Awick," Sara complimented. And indeed it was. It had been remodeled by his mother when she was brought here as a bride. The effect she had created was that of walking into a garden. The thick deep-green carpet, the floral brocade fabrics, the light blue wall-covering all seemed an echo of a well-tended flower garden on a sunny day. Sara was enchanted.

"I'm glad you like it, my dear," Awick said. "It was my mother's favorite room. She redid a great deal of the house but she always maintained that this was her very best effort."

When Aunt Eloise was announced, he excused himself. "My godmother has returned to town and has requested my attendance. Do you feel strong enough to have her pay a visit? I know she will ask."

"That would be delightful," replied Sara. "It's time I caught up on the events of the outside world."

He laughed. "With Miss Farley reading the papers to you every day, you probably know more of the outside world than any of us, but I will tell Emily that you will receive her tomorrow."

After he left, Aunt Eloise gazed at her niece for a while, a worried expression on her face. "My dear," she began, "there is something we need to discuss."

Sara looked at her in surprise. "Yes, Aunt? Why such a somber tone? There is nothing wrong, is there?"

"Yes, Sara, I am afraid there is. There is gossip about you staying here alone with Lord Awick."

Sara laughed at this. "Oh come, Aunt, hardly alone. We are surrounded by servants, not to mention Beth and Freddie."

"None is a proper chaperone."

"With three crushed ribs and a broken arm, exactly what do the tattle-mongers imagine can have happened? The situation is hardly romantic."

"My love, you know gossip does not need a basis in fact. And the fact remains that you have been staying in Lord Awick's house." She paused. "I blame myself, you know. I should have come here the first night. But I had been so hysterical that John gave me laudanum, and after Lord Awick came to tell us you were safe, I was so relieved, and with one thing and another . . . Well, it was not until the following day that I even thought about the impropriety. And by then it was too late. I talked to Awick about it."

Sara interrupted at this point, looking dismayed. "You spoke to Awick about this?"

"Of course, my dear. You must realize that I had to. There can only be one honorable way out."

"Oh no," her niece groaned. "You are not going to tell me that you told Awick to—"

"Yes, exactly," said Aunt Eloise, pleased with the girl's quick comprehension. "He will have to marry you."

"And what did he say?" she asked weakly.

"He said that he had come to the same conclusion and that he thought it would serve very well. He needs a mother for little Beth, you know, and you two seem to rub along together very well. I think it is a perfect solution."

"Well, I do not," said Sara vehemently. "I will not marry a man simply to still the tongues of the gossips."

"But Beth—"

"Or because a man needs someone to look after his child. That is what nurses are for."

Aunt Eloise was taken aback by Sara's anger. "I thought you *liked* Lord Awick."

"I do like Lord Awick, but I have yet to hear a good reason why I should marry him."

"And what do you consider a good reason?"

"What about love? Should that not enter into the matter somewhere?"

"Why, I am sure it should, dear, but that is often something that develops after marriage."

"I know, Aunt Eloise, but it is simply not enough for me. How could you have broached the matter to Lord Awick! I do not want him to marry me out of pity."

"Oh no, dear, it is nothing like that. He spoke very highly of you and I am sure that the two of you can come to a compatible agreement."

"No," said Sara, emphatically. "It will not

do. Let us say no more about it, please. The subject upsets me."

"Yes, dear." Aunt Eloise looked contrite.

"Now tell me about yourself and what you have been doing."

They were soon talking amiably about their many friends and acquaintances.

Lord Awick's butler entered and said that a small luncheon had been prepared. Soon a footman appeared to set up a table by Sara's longue. A tray held thick slices of bread, cheese, and sweet butter, a cold meat pie and a bowl of cherries and peaches. The butler produced a bottle of claret and left the ladies to their repast.

When they were finished, Sara asked Aunt Eloise to ring for the butler. "I will return to my bed now," she said. "I'm feeling tired again."

With the assistance of the butler and a footman, Sara was soon installed in her bed once more. Aunt Eloise said that she had some shopping to do before joining Lady Buffield for tea.

"Get some rest now, dear. I do hope you'll consider Lord Awick's generous offer, but if you decide against it, we can still go back to being comfortable again. John will understand."

"John?" said Sara. "What does John Kline say to the matter?"

"Why, did I not tell you?" Aunt Eloise blushed. "He has asked me to marry him. But, of course, I could not possibly leave you alone."

"Oh, Auntie! Why did you not tell me? I am so happy for you! Of course you shall marry him. There can be no question about it. I have been thinking seriously about returning to Langton. I am tiring of town life, and would enjoy going home. Let us discuss it no further. You will marry John Kline, and we will worry about everything else as it comes along."

At this speech, Aunt Eloise positively glowed. "Thank you, dear. As you say, I am sure it will all work out somehow."

She kissed her niece. "I will see you tomorrow."

For once, Sara found it impossible to sleep. She lay on her bed remembering what her aunt had said. How could she face Lord Awick? What could she possibly say? At last she drifted off, her mind in a turmoil.

She was awakened by the opening of the door. It was Lord Awick. He strode to the side of the bed and gazed down at her a moment.

"Are you awake, Sara?" she heard him ask.

She struggled for a moment, then pulled herself up. "Yes, my Lord, I am."

He drew a chair up beside her bed. "I think we need to talk for a moment," he said. He took a deep breath, steeling himself. "Lady Sara," he began, "there are problems that have arisen due to my precipitate action in bringing you into my home." He paused, unsure of himself, then plunged on. "I must ask that you do me the honor of becoming my wife."

Sara stared at him for a moment and felt the color rise in her cheeks. She looked down and sat for a while, unmoving. "You see, do you not, my dear, it is the only alternative? I can offer you all you wish. And Beth loves you, as you know," he continued. He took her hand. "Will you, Sara?"

Still she sat, quiet and motionless. "I believe, my Lord, that we had this conversation once before. While I am highly sensible of the honor that you are doing me, I believe I will have to decline your very generous offer."

"But, Sara, the situation has changed."

"Has it, my Lord?" she looked at him at last, her face drawn and pale. "I do not believe so." No, she thought, it has not changed. He did not love me then and he does not now.

"Of course, it has. In the eyes of the world I have compromised you. The only way we can save your reputation is for you to marry me."

"In the first place, my Lord, my reputation does not mean enough to me to force us into an untenable alliance. In the second place, you are not called upon to make any such sacrifice."

"But, Sara, it is no sacrifice. I wish very much to have you as my wife."

"No, please, my Lord, let us not continue this discussion. I am sure that there will be some unpleasantness, but I have a great many friends who will not believe the gossip. I shall not become a social outcast, on that you may depend."

He stared at her, wondering how to convince her. Had he been mistaken after all. Was she so opposed to marrying him that she would sooner face a life of disgrace? He found it hard to accept, but she looked so cold and distant.

"Is that your final word, then?" he asked.

She lowered her head again. "Yes, my Lord, it is."

"Very well, then." He arose and walked slowly to the door, willing her to stop him, to call him back.

"My Lord?" she said in a stifled voice.

He turned eagerly. "Yes, Sara?"

"Would you arrange to have my carriage brought round in the morning? I think it best if I return to my home."

His heart sank. "I will make my own available to you, whenever you are ready."

He turned back to the door, and so did not see the tears splashing onto her clasped hands.

Chapter Fourteen

SARA SPENT A WRETCHED NIGHT. HER MIND kept repeating the interview over and over. While she thought highly of his desire to help her out of a painful situation, she felt humiliated every time she thought about needing his assistance. Maybe she should have accepted him. She was fond of Beth and though it would not have been the marriage she had dreamed of— no, she would not marry where there was no love.

And what *about* love? Awick liked her, at the moment he felt sorry for her, but did he love her? Sometimes recently she had turned to find his gaze upon her, a warm look in his eyes. He had certainly been good to her while she was injured. She thought back over the interview yet again. No, the only mention of love had been in connection with Beth. She sighed. The love was all on her side. She had loved him twelve years before and she loved him still. It was no surprise that she had never married—she had compared all of her suitors to Awick and all had come up lacking. Ah well, she had been on her own for years now, nothing had really changed. On this depressing thought, she at last fell asleep.

She awoke at the sound of a faint tapping on her door. She sat up and called, "Come in."

The door was pushed open and Beth stuck her head in. "Are you awake, Sara? I have to talk to you."

"Of course, child. Come in."

Beth walked over to the bed and climbed up on it at Lady Sara's invitation. Once she was settled, Sara asked, "Now, what is it you wished to talk to me about?"

Beth looked at her for a moment, then said in a small, earnest voice, "Papa says that we are going to Kent next week. Have I done something to displease him?"

Sara's first reaction to the news of Lord Awick's leaving was one of keen disappointment. But why should she expect anything else? She had already told him she would be moving from his townhouse to her own, and after all the season *was* winding down. Many families had already left town for the summer, some to the fashionable watering holes of Bath and Brighton, some to their family estates to begin the round of house parties that would continue throughout the rest of the year. She had no reason to expect him to stay. In fact did she want him to? Would not the pain be worse if she had to see him at every occasion? Then she recalled Beth's question. "Displease him, dear? Why would you imagine that?"

"Because whenever I have been naughty, he says that if I do not behave, he is going to send me to Kent."

Sara smiled. "No, I am sure that is not the reason. Did he not explain to you why he wants to go home?"

Little Beth shook her head, her eyes fixed on Sara.

"Most people who have estates, like your papa, only come to town in the spring. Summer in London is not very pleasant. The weather here is impossible—hot and stifling. Most of the fashionable people either remove to a summer resort or to their country homes. It's only natural that your papa would decide to take you back to Kent. And it will be lovely, dear. You will be able to ride your pony around the estates, and there will probably be house parties."

Beth began to look more cheerful. "I had not thought of that. Yes, it will be fun. Papa says there is a lake and he can take us rowing and maybe Papa will take us fishing and—"

Sara interrupted at this point. "Beth, my love, you don't completely understand. Your papa is taking *you* to Kent. I must return to my own home."

"Surely you are coming with us. Papa did not say you were leaving. Of course you are going to come. It is the only place for you."

"No, child, I'm sorry, but I must go home now."

Beth looked bewildered. "But your home is with us now."

"I have my own home and obligations and now I must go back."

The child sat and thought about this. "Oh you mean because of your aunt. But she is going to marry Mr. Kline."

"How in the world did you know that?" Sara could not help laughing.

"Oh, I hear lots of things," the child replied. "Sara, you must come. I love you—you're my best friend."

Sara put her arms around the girl. "I love you, too, Beth, but you must understand that it is just not possible. Even when Aunt Eloise marries, I cannot continue to remain here. Now please," she said as Beth started to interrupt her. "There are things that I just do not wish to talk about. You will have a good time in Kent and I promise that we will meet often. I have been thinking about returning to my own home in Somerset and when I do, I promise that I will invite you to come and stay with me. It is a wonderful place and we can do ever so many things."

Beth hung her head and began to cry. "But, Sara, I don't want you to leave. I will miss you dreadfully."

"I will miss you, sweetheart, but it just has to be this way. Now dry your eyes. You are a big girl now and must realize that we cannot always have everything we want. Please, Beth," she said as the child's tears continued unabated, "this is hard on me too. Don't make it

258

harder. Just promise to take good care of your papa and yourself."

Beth, realizing the importance of this responsibility, straightened up, wiping her eyes. "I'm sorry to make you unhappy, Sara, and I will do my best."

She kissed Sara then clambered off the bed. "Please say you will invite me soon."

"I will, love, I promise." Sara found tears in her own eyes. "Run along now, I am sure Nurse is looking for you. And Beth, no matter what you may hear, remember that I love you and that I wish you only happiness."

Beth looked at her in surprise. "Of course everything will be all right. I have you and Papa." She turned around when she got to the door. "And you will come to see me in Kent. I will just tell Papa that he has to invite you to come to stay—forever."

And then the child was gone.

Sara rang for the little maid, Molly, who helped her dress and gathered up the belongings Aunt Eloise had brought for her. Fortunately, she had also sent one of Sara's older, loose-fitting gowns. This being the first time she had dressed since the accident, she found her bandaged ribs awkward and her arm a decided nuisance.

After a great amount of pushing and pulling on Molly's part and considerable pain on Sara's, she was ready. Molly ran off for the footman and asked the butler to have the carriage brought around. Sara looked around the bedroom one last time. Until yesterday, she had loved staying in this house. She longed to make one more visit to the morning room, but she decided against it. What if Awick caught her out? She sighed. She had had her chance to make this place her own. The decision had been hers and she had made it. Now she would have to live with it and regrets would be to no avail.

The footman arrived and assisted her down the stairs. Molly followed behind with her satchel. When they reached the main hall, the butler told her the carriage was ready. "Lord Awick, my Lady, said to make his apologies for not being here to see you off himself. He was called out early this morning."

Sara felt a keen disappointment. She had hoped to see him once more, and thank him for all he had done for her. "Please tell him I was sorry to miss him, and extend my thanks for his hospitality."

Then, bidding farewell to the servants in the hall and expressing her gratitude for their care and assistance, she allowed the footman to escort her down the stairs and help her into the waiting carriage. Once she was settled as comfortably as she could be, he raised the steps, closed the door and gave the coachman the office to start. As they pulled away, Sara looked back and gave a slight wave. The curtains moved in one of the upstairs windows and she could see Beth waving to her. She felt tears well up in her eyes.

Despite the excellence of Lord Awick's carriage and the short distance that she had to travel, Sara found herself stiff and sore by the time she arrived home. Her ribs were hurting and her arm ached. No wonder the doctor had cautioned her against returning home too soon.

Roberts opened the front door at the sound of the carriage halting and, upon seeing the occupant, so far forgot himself as to rush down the stairs and open the carriage door himself. "My Lady!" he exclaimed. "What on earth are you doing out of bed and traveling!"

She smiled rather wanly at him. "That, my dear Roberts, is a question I have been asking myself for the past several minutes. Do you suppose you could help me into the house?"

"Of course, my Lady," he said recalling his dignity. He summoned one of the footmen and between them they soon had her safely installed in the library.

"May I get you anything, my Lady? A cup of tea or a glass of wine?"

"Wine would be lovely, thank you, Roberts, and you might inform Aunt Eloise that the prodigal has returned."

Moments later Aunt Eloise flew into the room, almost colliding with Roberts as he brought in a tray with the wine decanter and glasses.

"What are you doing here?" she exclaimed, seating herself in the chair opposite Lady Sara's and pouring the wine.

"I rather thought I lived here," replied her niece. "Have things changed that drastically during my absence?"

"You know perfectly well that is not what I meant," Aunt Eloise said, offended. "The doctor has not given you permission to return home until the bandages come off, and that will not be for another week. What has happened to send you home like this?"

"I missed you, Auntie."

"Ha! You saw more of me at Lord Awick's than you ever did around here. Come now, I want the truth."

Sara sighed. "Oh, Aunt Eloise, I just could not stay any longer. I had imposed on Lord Awick long enough. And now that I am able to be up, I thought I would recover faster in my own home."

Aunt Eloise looked at her searchingly for a moment. She knew there was much more to the matter than her niece was admitting but decided not to push her. "I am sure you are right, dear. Drink your wine. It will put some color in your cheeks."

Sara dutifully drained her glass, and sank back into her chair. "Now tell me all the gossip. How is Mr. Kline? Has he been haunting the place?"

Aunt Eloise giggled delightedly. "I must admit I have been seeing a great deal of him lately. Such a fine man he is, Sara."

"Have you set a date yet?"

"My goodness, no. First we must know what your plans are. As I told you before, if you wish to remain in town, I will stay with you."

"And as I told you, you will do no such thing."

"Only if you are quite sure, my dear."

"Quite," Sara said firmly. "I want no more discussion on that point."

Aunt Eloise looked dubious but decidedly

relieved. "Actually, John has mentioned taking a house in Bath. Many of our friends are there. John would like you to come live with us. It would be an ideal solution. You would enjoy Bath, and we could still come to town for the season."

Sara considered this for a moment. "That is terribly sweet of both of you, Auntie, but I won't impose on a newly married couple that way. It would be distinctly *de trop*."

Aunt Eloise blushed. "No, not at all, my dear. We would love to have you."

Sara laughed. "After you get settled in, I will come to visit and stay until you are both heartily sick of me. Do thank Mr. Kline for me, but I will have to refuse his offer."

"But what will you do? You cannot stay on alone here, you know."

"Why not?" said Sara, a trace of bitterness in her voice. "It seems I have no reputation left to protect now so it could not possibly make any difference."

"Oh, Sara, that is not true. There has naturally been talk, but your friends will all support you and soon this will be forgotten."

She shook her head. "The gossip-mongers have long memories."

"But you cannot live alone," her aunt persisted, obviously distressed. "I would worry about you constantly. If that is your decision, I will stay here with you."

"No, Auntie, no. I am being selfish. Once the doctor gives me permission to travel, I think I will go to Langton for a while. The season is over now and I do love summer in Somerset.

If I decide to return to town later, I will advertise for a companion. I promise to do nothing of which you would disapprove. For now I must get some rest. This has been a tiring day."

After she had gone, Eloise sat for a long time, staring out the window. She was convinced something had happened between Awick and her niece. If only she could find out what. She decided that she needed to talk this over with someone. She rang for Roberts. "Have the carriage brought around, please. If Lady Sara asks, tell her I have gone to visit Mrs. Warrington."

She found that lady in her front parlor working on a piece of embroidery. "Wedding present for Clare and Freddie," she explained, greeting her guest and ringing for tea.

"Have they settled on a date, yet?" asked Aunt Eloise. She sat on the blue-and-gold-striped loveseat.

"I have not heard the day but it is to be in September. I understand Randy is giving them that little estate he has in Devonshire. Mighty generous of him."

"Is Freddie giving up his ideas of a career then?"

"No indeed. The income from the estate will allow them to rent a house in town. There is an excellent bailiff there who can see to the running of the place. Freddie is enjoying his work for Lord Buffield and it seems he'll have a position in the Home Office by Christmas." She paused as the butler entered with the tea tray. She handed a cup to Aunt Eloise.

"Did you visit Sara this morning?"

Aunt Eloise set her cup down on the table beside her and chose a cucumber sandwich from the plate. Nibbling on it, she said, "I did not need to. Sara came home this morning."

"What? I thought the doctor forbade her removal until the bandages came off."

"He did," said Aunt Eloise. "That is what concerns me. It was all so sudden. She just showed up at the door this morning. She did not mention a word about coming home today when I saw her yesterday morning."

"What does it mean then?" Mrs. Warrington said, perplexed. She thought for a moment. "Surely you do not suppose that something *else* has gone wrong. But it must have or she would not have gone home so abruptly." She shook her head. "What on earth is wrong with those two? They seem to be doing their very best to make sure that they are unhappy. Do you have any idea at all what may have happened?"

Aunt Eloise thought about the matter. "When I spoke to Sara yesterday, I told her that there had been some gossip about her staying alone with Awick and that, when he offered for her, she ought to accept him. She said that she did not want him to marry her out of pity."

"What do you mean 'when' he offered for her? Did you have any reason to believe he would?"

"Yes indeed. I spoke to him about it, you know, and he said that he had come to the conclusion that it was the only way out for Sara."

Emily Warrington groaned. "Never tell me

that you told Sara that you had discussed this with Randy?"

"Why to be sure. Why ever not? It was a very sticky situation. Just the other day I heard—"

"But to tell Sara that Randy would offer for her just to save her reputation!" Mrs. Warrington interrupted. "That is the last thing Sara would want. No wonder she flew home in such a rush. She probably wanted to avoid his proposal. Oh dear, what a muddle."

Aunt Eloise looked contrite. "This is all my fault! Oh, I feel terrible! I was concerned when I spoke to Lord Awick, but he said he had already come to the same conclusion and I thought everything would work out." She looked on the verge of tears.

"No, no, dear," said Mrs. Warrington. "You did as you thought best. Do not fret, I beg. I am sure it will all come right." She thought for a moment. "The first thing to do is make sure that Randy does not offer for Sara while this is so fresh in her mind. If he lets her think that he is not offering for her because he feels sorry for her, she may yet come round. Yes, that's it. I will go visit him this afternoon, and convince him to let things alone for a while."

"Do you think that will serve then?"

"I'm certain of it," Mrs. Warrington said with more confidence than she felt. I hope so at any rate, she thought.

When Mrs. Warrington arrived at the Ketcham household a few hours later, she was informed that Lord Awick was out but expected back momentarily. Lady Ketcham was in the nursery, however, and would be delighted to receive company.

Mrs. Warrington made her way up to the nursery, where she found Beth doing her lessons, her tongue between her teeth in an attitude of intense concentration. She sprang to her feet when she saw her visitor. "Aunt Emily," she said and ran to her for a hug. "Lessons are so hard without Sara. She made everything seem like a game. I miss her so."

"She just left this morning," commented Mrs. Warrington, taking a place on the window seat.

"I know, but now that we are going to Kent, it will be ever so long until I can see her again."

"Going to Kent? What is all this?"

"Did Papa not tell you? We're leaving on Tuesday. Sara said it was all right—lots of people go to their estates in the summer so it is not because I have been bad."

Mrs. Warrington looked amused. "No, child, I am sure it is not. I am just surprised, that is all. When did your papa decide to do this?"

"I don't know, Aunt Emily, he just told me this morning. I thought Sara would go with us but then she said she was going to go home." Beth looked perplexed at all this for a moment, obviously not understanding the strange decisions that adults made, then brightened up. "But Sara said that I can go visit her in Somerset. That's where her estate is, you know. She's going to show me all around and we're going to have a wonderful time."

"Somerset," repeated Mrs. Warrington weakly. "You mean Sara is going there?"

"Yes, didn't I just say so? I hope she will invite me soon. Do you think I can take my pony?"

"I'm sure you can," Mrs. Warrington said distractedly. She did not like the sound of this at all. There was something more here than she had feared. A terrible thought struck her. Was it possible Randy had proposed to her last night? The more she thought about this, the more likely it seemed. Yes, that was exactly what must have happened. And he must have made a rare botch of it to send Sara scurrying to Somerset and himself to Kent. Sometimes she thought she would just wash her hands of them.

Beth was chattering on about the delights of Somerset when Lord Awick walked in. He lifted his daughter and gave her a kiss then turned to his godmother. Clasping her hands, he kissed her cheek and asked to what they owed the pleasure of this visit.

Mrs. Warrington decided it was too late now to warn Randy and she had best think of her next course of action. "Oh nothing really, Randy. I was in the neighborhood and thought I would stop by. Beth has been telling me you're bound for Kent next week."

"Yes, it will do both of us good to get away from town for a while."

"Papa," Beth said, "Sara has invited me to visit her in Somerset. May I go? I promise I will behave and not be a problem."

"Somerset? Is she going there then?" Awick asked.

"Yes, Papa, she has an estate there. May I go?"

"We will have to see, love. If Lady Sara invites you, we'll consider it."

"She will," Beth said confidently. "She told me she would. I am sure I can convince her to invite you too, Papa."

"You will not do anything of the kind, Brat. Now I am going to take Aunt Emily downstairs while you finish your lessons."

Mrs. Warrington kissed the child then returned to the main hall with Lord Awick.

"I think I should be going now, Randy. I still have several calls I wish to make before dinner." She looked at him. "Randy, why did Sara leave so abruptly?"

"If you wish to discuss that, Emily, I suggest we go into the library."

Upon reaching the library, Awick escorted his godmother to a chair. "A glass of sherry?"

"Yes, thank you, Randy."

He handed her a glass, poured one for himself, then walked to the mantelpiece and leaned carelessly against it. He sipped his sherry and stood silent for a moment. "To answer your question, Emily, she found life with me distasteful."

"What? Did she say so?"

He laughed bitterly. "Oh no. In fact she was very polite. I asked for her hand in marriage and she said she did not think we would suit. That we had not suited twelve years ago and nothing had changed."

"Exactly what did you say to her, Randy?"

"Oh I don't recall the precise words," he said irritably. "What does it matter now? The point is she turned me down again."

"The exact words matter a great deal, my dear. I believe that *is* the point. Did you, by any chance, stress her unfortunate position?"

"Of course I did. It was the only way I could think to get her to accept. That, and Beth needing a mother."

"And those are the reasons you gave for wishing to marry her?"

"What else could I say? They are the only things that have changed. She ran away from me last time I proposed. I had hoped that those might be the inducements to convince her."

Mrs. Warrington looked at him blankly. "She ran away from you? But she told me that you had abandoned her."

It was the viscount's turn to look blank. "Abandoned her? But I left her a note explaining about my uncle and asking her to join me at Rotham so that we could be married. I even obtained a special license."

"Well, for some reason, she never received it. She told me just the other day that first you had offered for her and then disappeared. Did you send it by a footman?"

He colored slightly as he recalled the exact circumstances. "No, not precisely. I left it in a place where she could not help finding it."

She looked puzzled at this enigmatic statement but decided not to pursue. "For whatever reason, Randy, she obviously did not find it. Now tell me, what was the extent of your proposal?"

"Oh, I gave her the usual bridegroom blandishment of making me the happiest of men." He stopped for a moment. "Come to think of it, maybe I did not say that but I am sure she knew it was implied."

"And what else did you leave her to imply? That you loved her?"

"Would I offer for her if I did not?" Lord Awick was beginning to be agitated with this inquisition.

"My dear, if you told her that you were marrying her to save her reputation and to be a mother to your child, how was she to assume that you loved her? You do love her, don't you, Randy?"

Suddenly he sat down and placed a hand on his forehead. "Oh God, Emily, you know I do. I have loved her since the first day I met her. When she turned me down the first time I thought I would go mad. Then I went to America and met Phoebe. She was a biddable girl and nice enough, but I never loved her. The whole marriage was terribly unfair to her. I think she was happy, though. I did try to offer her a comfortable life. Then, after she died, I returned to England to find Sara. I hoped that her feelings for me might have changed but when we met she was so cold and distant."

"That is only natural, my boy, if she thought you had deserted her without a word."

"Why did she not ask me about it?"

"How could she?" said his godmother. "If you had admitted it, it would have been too distressing, and if you had denied it, she would have thought you had lied."

"Why would I lie to her?" said Lord Awick, offended.

"How well did she know you, Randy? Trust in relationships takes time to develop."

Lord Awick sipped his sherry, looking thoughtful. "I suppose you are right, Emily. I have handled it badly. What should I do now? There must be some way to get this tangle sorted out."

"It is not going to be easy."

"What do you have in mind?" asked Awick. "Should I go to her and explain?"

"No, I do not think so. At least not now. This is going to take some time."

"But how long? I have waited twelve years already."

"I know, Randy, but a great deal of damage has been done. If you go to her now she will think you are feeling sorry for her. Give her a chance to forget your last unfortunate proposal. She is getting ready to go to Somerset as soon as the doctor gives her permission. Let her go. In the meantime, take Beth to Kent."

"Then what?" he asked impatiently.

"Then you will just have to bide your time."

"What is that supposed to mean?"

"That means, dear Randy, that I have many things to do if this is going to come right. Let me just warn you that I expect a standing invitation this summer. I might want to put on a special celebration." She rose. "And now I must be going. I still have several calls to make, as I said. Please do nothing rash in the meanwhile. Just do not be surprised by anything I may call upon you to do." She kissed him farewell. "I feel sure it is all going to be fine."

After she left Lord Awick sat in the library for a long time. He prayed she was right. He loved Sara and he could not imagine life without her much longer. He would abide by Emily's decisions. It was obvious he had not had any success on his own. Maybe she would straighten it all out. He sighed and poured himself another glass of sherry.

Chapter Fifteen

MRS. WARRINGTON'S NEXT STOP WAS THE LIVIS-combe townhouse. She found both ladies in the drawing room. Sara was still looking frail but her color was better. "Ah, Sara," she said as she entered, "it has been an age since I last saw you. How are you feeling? Is there a terrible lot of pain?"

"Only a little. I will be glad to get these cumbersome bandages off. May I ring for something?"

"As a matter of fact, I have been indulging in Randy's sherry. I think another glass would go down nicely."

"And you, Aunt?"

"Sherry would be very pleasant."

As Lady Sara rang for Roberts, Aunt Eloise turned to Mrs. Warrington and whispered, "Did you talk to Awick? What has happened?"

Emily whispered back, "I was too late. He

had already proposed to her and made the worst possible botch of it. Can you imagine he actually told her that—"

"What are you two whispering about?" asked Lady Sara, rejoining them. "Surely I'm not too young to hear the latest gossip?"

Resuming her seat, Emily Warrington said, "No indeed, dear. Your aunt was just telling me that she and John have decided to wed in August. That only gives us two months to get ready, you know." Aunt Eloise valiantly hid her surprise at this announcement. Emily obviously had a plan afoot. She only hoped that John would understand when she told him that the date of their nuptials had been decided.

Lady Sara turned to her in surprise. "Why did you not tell me, Auntie?"

Aunt Eloise looked uncomfortable. "It was decided rather suddenly, dear. In fact, just this afternoon. I did not have a chance to tell you about it."

"Actually," said Mrs. Warrington, contrite over having placed her friend in an awkward situation, "Eloise and I thought that it would be nice if they could be married out of Awick's estate in Kent. It is such a convenient location, you know, close to Bath and London where their friends are. I spoke to Awick this afternoon and he said he would be delighted to make his house available."

"I am sure that is very thoughtful of Lord Awick," said Sara stiffly. "I rather thought that you would be married at Langton, Auntie."

"That was my first thought, dear," said Aunt Eloise, hoping Emily knew what she was about, "but Emily is quite right. Awick's house is convenient and, you know, most of our friends are so elderly. I would not want them to have to travel long distances."

Sara relented, "Of course, you are right, and it is very thoughtful of Awick to offer you his house. Have you set a day yet?"

Emily again leaped into the breach. "As Eloise said, it was just decided this afternoon. We will have to check all our schedules and decide what day is best." She sipped her sherry. "Tell me, Lady Sara, when does the doctor take off the bandages?"

"In a week or two, if all goes well."

"And you are planning to go to Langton?"

"I think I will." She turned to her aunt. "You will accompany me, will you not? Had you intended to stay in town?"

"No, I will go with you to Langton. John is going to Bath to look at houses and I have numerous preparations to make."

The three ladies then fell into a discussion of wedding details. Eventually Emily excused herself. "I must be going now. I have a few more calls to make this afternoon."

She bade the ladies farewell and departed.

Sara turned to her aunt. "Are you comfortable with this plan, dear? I thought you seemed a little uncertain."

Aunt Eloise took a deep breath. "Not at all. It was just that I had wanted to tell you myself. I hated to have it come from someone else. You don't think I was slighting you, do you?"

Sara took her aunt's hand. "Not at all, my love. I just want you to be happy." She paused.

"Are you sure you want to be married out of Awick's house? We can change the arrangements if you wish."

"Oh no, this will be ideal." *As soon as I tell John,* she thought, wondering how her future husband would react to these plans being made in such casual fashion.

A short time later, Roberts announced Mr. Frederick Ketcham.

"Sara, I just heard you had left my brother's house and come here. Was that wise? Are you feeling quite the thing?"

"Yes, Freddie, I'm coming along very well now. And how about yourself?" she asked. She was finding it difficult to have to explain why she had left Awick's house. "I understand you and Clare are to be wed in September."

Freddie glowed. "Indeed we are. I wanted to make it sooner, but Lady Tishford says that three months is the minimum amount of time one needs to prepare for a wedding. She wanted to set it at Christmas but I *did* override that."

"Where is it to be held?"

"Here in town. St. George's, Hanover Square. Again Lady Tishford's decision. Says she has always dreamed of her daughter being married there. All right with me, you know. One place is as good as another."

Sara and Aunt Eloise laughed at the comical expression on his face. "I take it that your future mama-in-law is taking an active role in the proceedings?" Aunt Eloise asked.

"Indeed. There are times when I wonder which of them is getting married. I do like Lady Tishford, though. And she is a big help. Clare does not know quite how to go on yet and she is giving her guidance."

"I hear Awick has settled the Devonshire estate on you," Aunt Eloise commented.

Lady Sara looked at her in surprise. "He did? I had not heard that."

"Just told me the other night," said Freddie. "Randy's a great gun, you know. Do anything in the world for you. Did I tell you I received a letter from Tom Ashnell?"

"Why, no," said Lady Sara. "How is he? Will he be coming back to London soon?"

"He thinks he will be sent sometime this fall. I'm going to recommend he make it back for the wedding."

Aunt Eloise smiled. "Oh, that would be nice. Such a dear young man."

They chatted for several more minutes, then Freddie rose. "I must be going, I fear. Lady Tishford gives me a set of commissions each morning that I have to fulfill by teatime." The ladies looked amused. "If I had known how complex this wedding was going to be, I would have insisted we elope." He turned to Sara. "Do take care of yourself, sweetheart. I want you to dance at my wedding. And we will both dance at Eloise's." He bowed to the ladies and left.

Aunt Eloise wondered if they would ever have a chance to dance at Sara's. Her niece was wondering the same thing.

Two weeks later the doctor removed the bandages, though he insisted that she keep her arm in a sling for an additional week or two.

"Just use your own judgment. When the arm feels strong enough, you can remove it, but try not to be over anxious."

"When will I be able to travel?"

"Oh, anytime. On a long journey you will be stiff and sore, but there will not be any damage." He frowned slightly. "You took a risk in removing yourself from Lord Awick's when you did, but the danger is past now. Where are you planning on going?"

"Into Somerset."

"Two days on the road, eh?"

"Yes," said Sara, "though I can stop over two nights."

"That would be advisable. I will leave you some laudanum. You may need it at night."

The plans for Eloise Farley's marriage to John Kline were firmly under way. There were guest lists to be made, invitations to be sent, a trousseau to be ordered and fitted. Lady Sara, while still restricted to the house, had taken over the paperwork. They had decided upon a morning ceremony, followed by the bridal breakfast. The newlyweds planned to leave for Bath in the early afternoon.

By a stroke of fortune John had found them a house in Laura Place. Because it was so late in the season, the fashionable areas were filled. It just happened that the week John was in Bath, Lady Denton had been called to her son's house where his three children were down with measles, and his wife was breeding. Lady Denton had given up the house, and John Kline took it.

"I think you will like it, Eloise," he told her.

"The furnishings are pleasant and the location is good. It is small, but we shan't need much room."

Aunt Eloise demanded a complete detailing of all the rooms and furniture.

"It sounds wonderful, dear," she told Lady Sara later. "I have never had a home of my own before, you know. I lived with Papa until his passing, then my brother and his wife and those four obnoxious children of theirs, then you were good enough to offer me a home with you. I do appreciate it, do not think I am being ungrateful, but I have always longed for my own place." She paused a moment. "I will miss you though, my dear."

Lady Sara gave her a hug. "You will not miss me for long. You will have John. Oh, Auntie, I am so happy for you. You have deserved this for a long time. And as I said before, I intend to come visit you often."

Mrs. Warrington called frequently. Since she was to be acting hostess at Awick's house, she had to prepare for the decorations, the menu and the delivery of the foodstuffs, wine and champagne. As Awick's ancestral home, Rotham Abbey, was exceptionally large, all of the guests would be staying there.

While the details of her wedding were being attended to by Sara and Mrs. Warrington, Aunt Eloise was having a wonderful time being escorted around the town on the arm of her future husband and selecting her trousseau.

"Oh, Sara. I have never had so many beautiful things," she exclaimed one afternoon, arriving home just in time for tea, a footman with his arms full of parcels staggering behind her into the hall. "John is encouraging me to buy more gowns than I can possibly wear in a year." She sorted through one of the packages that the footman had placed on the hall table. She pulled out a small, narrow box.

"And just look at this!" she exclaimed, opening it for her niece to see the contents. The box held a slender diamond and emerald bracelet. It was one of the most exquisite pieces Sara had ever seen.

"Oh Auntie, it is just beautiful!" she breathed, taking the bauble out of its box and clasping it around her aunt's wrist. "However came he to buy such a thing?"

"He said it would go well with the emerald-green evening gown he chose for me. He declared that it would need dressing up and this would do the trick." Aunt Eloise held up her wrist and the diamonds flashed in the light. "It is lovely, is it not?"

"Indeed it is, Auntie. You are a very lucky lady."

Sara had decided it was time to come out of hiding and put her reputation to the test. Consequently she asked Aunt Eloise to go out driving with her in the Park.

They set off one afternoon in the curricle. Sara had had qualms about the reaction she would receive and in the end she was correct. Her personal friends were more than willing to greet and acknowledge her, but many acquaintances cut her dead. It came as no surprise to her but her aunt was exceedingly upset.

"Do not take it to heart, my dear," Sara said finally. "After all, we knew this would happen. It was only to be expected."

They had been riding for several minutes when they spied Lord Dydlefield and Lady Dydlefield taking the air in their carriage. Sara lifted her hand to wave. Lord Dydlefield did the same but at a word from his mother he lowered it and looked the other way.

As the vehicles passed each other, Lady Dydlefield refused to look in Sara's direction. Her son turned, giving Sara a beseeching look. She merely nodded to him and the two equipages went their separate ways.

"How dare that woman slight you in such a rude fashion!" exclaimed Aunt Eloise. "Why the very idea! As if you were some sort of lightskirt."

Sara shrugged. "As I said, Auntie, we knew this would happen. Please let us not dwell on it."

At that moment they saw Lord Awick bearing down upon them. Sara felt herself color. What was he doing here and at such a moment? It was just not fair that he should have witnessed her humiliation. Maybe he had not seen it?

Her hopes were short-lived. Drawing up beside them he said, "That unconscionable bitch! To deliver a cut direct is really too much to bear. And her precious son as usual showing no backbone at all." He turned to Sara. "I am sorry for such a scene, and for being the cause of it."

"No, my Lord," she replied, "there is no harm done. I knew there would be some unpleasantness and was prepared for it. Do not think you are in any way responsible. As I told you before, I have many friends who will not believe the tittle-tattle. Let us speak no more of it."

"As you wish, my Lady."

"What are you doing in town, my Lord? I thought you had removed to Kent," asked Aunt Eloise, voicing the question that had been uppermost in her niece's mind.

"To tell the truth, Miss Farley, I was summoned here by Lady Tishford. It seems that since I am to stand up for my brother at his wedding, my advice on which wines to serve at the reception is absolutely vital."

"Oh yes, I completely understand," laughed Aunt Eloise. "I fear my poor niece has been facing the same kind of problems on my behalf."

Awick grinned at Sara. "In that case maybe we ought to compare notes. We should be able to plan the August wedding for your aunt and then duplicate it in September for my brother."

She returned his laughter. "As long as we do not invite any of the same guests, of course. How do you think Clare will look in my aunt's wedding gown or had you meant to repeat the affair to that extent?"

He considered this seriously for a moment. "Yes, I can see there might be a few problems.

The flowers, for instance. Might get a little wilted by September."

The three were soon laughing at the absurdities they were conjuring up and Lady Sara forgot the embarrassment that the Dydlefields had caused her.

Lord Awick, however, could not forget. He considered asking for her hand again but then recalled his godmother's advice. She was probably right. She needed time. There had been too many misunderstandings between them in the past. The best course of action now was to prove to her that she could trust him.

"How is Beth?" she asked. "Did you bring her to town with you?"

"No, she is at Rotham. I only came for a couple of days. She is coming along well with her riding lessons. Perkins is a good teacher and she is a quick learner."

"Be sure to give her my love, and tell her that I still expect her company at Langton this summer."

"So you have definitely decided to go back, then? When do you leave?"

Sara smiled. "That depends entirely on Aunt Eloise. As soon as the initial preparations for the wedding are complete, I will be ready. The question is when the ordering of the trousseau is to be finished. At the rate things are going I am not sure it will be done before the marriage. There seems to be a constant procession of parcels and bandboxes passing through my door these days."

Aunt Eloise blushed. "Oh, I know, dear. John keeps insisting I have this, that and the other.

If I live forever I could not possibly wear all those things. But truly it is almost done. I have one more fitting for the wedding gown, and a few small items to purchase and then I will be ready."

"If that is the case," said her niece, "we might be able to go sometime next week. Mrs. Warrington tells me that we are expected at Rotham one week before the date. Why do you not send Beth to me the week before that and then we can bring her with us when we come?"

"She will be delighted. She talks about you constantly. You rank with her pony in her affections. And that is quite an honor."

"When do you return to Rotham?" asked Aunt Eloise.

"Probably tomorrow, if Lady Tishford has no further use for me. Considering the way she issues orders, I think she missed her true calling. She could have won the battle in the peninsula singlehanded."

They chatted amiably for a few more minutes. Arrangements were discussed for Beth's visit to Langton and a date was settled. Then they parted and the Liviscombe ladies returned home.

The next few days passed in a whirl of activity. Sara and Mrs. Warrington finished their preparations for the wedding and put in all their orders. The invitations were sent out and the ladies felt very pleased with themselves. Aunt Eloise and Mr. Kline at long last completed their shopping for her trousseau and their household effects.

One morning, a week after their meeting with Lord Awick in the park, they found themselves alone with no plans made.

"If it is all right with you, Auntie, I will leave for Langton on Friday. That will give us two days to pack and close down the townhouse. Can you be ready by then?"

Aunt Eloise thought for a moment. "Yes, my dear, that should be fine. John is leaving for Bath on Saturday and he will take all of our purchases with him. He intends to stay there until just before the wedding. I have no reason to linger in town and I think a rest would do us both good. You're still looking haggard and the activity of the past few weeks has taken its toll on both of us. Yes, let us plan on it."

They left on schedule early Friday morning. Because Sara was still sore, a condition aggravated by the jolting of the carriage, they stopped overnight at both Cheltanham and Colchester. Thus they reached Langton in the early afternoon on Sunday.

Their days quickly settled into a pleasant routine. Aunt Eloise worked on her embroidery, took leisurely strolls around the extensive grounds and wrote long letters to John Kline. Sara spent a great deal of time in the gardens, and reviewing the affairs of the estate with her bailiff. Being the old duke's only child and the heiress to the holding, she had made sure that she was totally conversant with the proper running of it. Fortunately, along with the house and land, her father had bequeathed her a highly competent set of retainers.

But as busy as she kept herself, for the first time in her life Sara felt that something was lacking. She could not put a name on it, just a vague sort of feeling that there should be something more. Maybe it was Aunt Eloise and her constant talk of John and the life they would share. Or maybe it was just the advancing years and the thought that this would be the pattern of her days. Whatever, she found herself feeling increasingly melancholy and depressed.

About two weeks after they arrived, she received a letter from Lord Awick. It was cheerful and amusing, detailing all the preparations for the two forthcoming marriages and confirming the plans for Beth's trip into Somerset. Sara was surprised and, she had to admit, pleased that Lord Awick had decided to escort his daughter. She convinced herself that she only felt pleasure at the prospect of seeing him because it would be a welcome change to have company around, even if only overnight.

She launched herself into a massive cleaning program for the old house. The maids were instructed to clean and dust, air and wax. Soon the place was shining from top to bottom and the scent of lavender and beeswax was everywhere.

"Good heavens!" exclaimed Aunt Eloise at one point. "I thought we were expecting Lord Awick and his daughter, not the King!"

Sara looked embarrassed. "Oh come now, Auntie, it is not that bad. And you must admit the house was looking deplorable. I have let it go much too long. That is one of the hazards of spending most of the year in town."

By the time Lord Awick and Beth were due to arrive, Langton was immaculate. Sara had cut flowers from her gardens and, with the help of Aunt Eloise, had fashioned arrangements for the rooms.

The two ladies were seated in the drawing room when they heard a carriage arrive at the front steps. Within moments, Roberts appeared at the door.

"Lord Awick and Lady Elizabeth," he announced.

A tiny blonde whirlwind burst into the room. "Sara! Sara! How glad I am to see you! I have missed you terribly!" She threw herself into Sara's open arms.

"And I have missed you, sweetheart. But come, say hello to Aunt Eloise."

As the child made a polite curtsey, Lord Awick entered and approached Sara. "I am sorry, my dear," he said ruefully, "I know she seems a bit of a hoyden but she has been so anxious to see you and I just do not have the heart to reprimand her."

She laughed. "No apologies needed. It is nice to have that kind of adoration. Did you have a good trip?"

"Yes, indeed, very pleasant. Beth is a great traveler. Except for her anxiety to see you, she was not a problem at all." He turned to Aunt Eloise. "You are looking well, Miss Farley. Are you at last ready for the event?"

"I believe so, my Lord. As you know it will be quite a change for me."

Beth again turned to Sara. "Oh Sara, I am so glad to be here. I have so much to tell you!"

"And I am pleased to have you. But before we talk, I think you and your papa might like to go to your rooms and freshen up a bit. I have planned an early dinner and I think that you should join us at table tonight if your papa has no objections."

Beth looked at him expectantly and he smiled warmly at Sara. "Thank you. We would both be honored."

Dinner proved highly enjoyable. Beth was on her very best behavior and regaled her companions with all the highlights of her life in Kent. Lord Awick told them all the latest gossip and they discussed current events. At last, Sara noticed that Beth was having a hard time staying awake and her papa was not doing much better.

"It has been a long and eventful day," she said. "I think it is time we were all in our beds. What are your plans, my Lord? Must you rush off or can you stay on for a while?"

He gazed at her for a long moment. "As dearly as I would love to stay, I fear I must return to Rotham. The first of the guests are due to arrive day after tomorrow and there is still much to be done. Emily is due in tonight but I dare not leave her alone to face the last-minute crises. I had planned to leave at first light tomorrow."

"Oh," she said in a low voice. "I had rather

hoped you could stay longer. But I do understand. We will see you in a week in any event."

They said good night and adjourned to their rooms. Lord Awick was pleased with this interview. Perhaps his godmother had been right. All she needed was some time.

Chapter Sixteen

SARA LAY SLEEPLESS. SHE HAD MEANT WHAT
she said. She had hoped that he could stay for a
while. She berated herself for being a fool. Why
did she persist in loving a man who did not
return her affections? At least she would have
the comfort of his daughter for the next week
and then, after the wedding, they would not be
thrown into each other's way so often and she
would have a chance to forget him.

By the time she descended the following
morning, he had already gone. "Lord Awick
asked me to bid you good-bye, my Lady," said
Fenton, "and to thank you for your hospitality.
He said he will look for you one week from
today and hopes that Lady Elizabeth will not
be a problem."

Lady Sara smiled. "Thank you, Fenton. And
where is the Lady Elizabeth? Is she up yet, do
you know?"

"Not only is she up, my Lady, I last saw her sitting in the kitchen with Cook consuming blueberry tarts and milk. I told her that breakfast was served in the dining room but she said that she loved the kitchens and if I did not mind she would like to go there." He cracked a rare smile. "What could I do, my Lady?"

"You did exactly the right thing," said she, returning his smile. "She is an adorable child."

She made her way to the kitchens where she found Beth perched on a stool chatting with Cook and finishing a tart.

"I see you had no trouble in finding the kitchens, my love," she said, smiling at the child. "Is this how you go on at home, too?"

"Oh yes," replied Beth nonchalantly. "The kitchens are ever so nice and I even get to help once in a while." She suddenly looked self-conscious. "You don't mind do you, Sara?"

"Not at all. I love the kitchens myself though I must admit that Cook only lets me help when we are making gingerbread."

Cook beamed at her. "Yes indeed, M'Lady. I was just thinking that it be high time we made gingerbread again." She turned to Beth. "What do you think, Childie? Do you think you'd like to help us?"

Beth positively glowed. "Oh, I would! That would be wonderful!"

Cook furnished them both with aprons and soon they were all coated in flour and laughing delightedly as they prepared, rolled and cut the dough. Beth stood by the oven as the first batch baked, anxious to see the results. "I have never made gingerbread before," she breathed excitedly. "Can I take some to Papa?"

"Of course, love," said Sara. "I am sure he will want to know how you spent your time while you were here."

Cook removed the steaming pan from the oven and they all admired their creation. To celebrate the occasion, Cook served milk and tea and they sampled their product. All agreed that it was the best gingerbread ever made, and Beth and Sara promised to return the following morning to help make currant tartlets.

That afternoon Sara called for the curricle and took Beth and Aunt Eloise on a drive through the grounds. She called for a stop at one of her tenant farmers whose ewe had littered shortly before. Beth was enchanted with the lambs and found great delight in their antics.

The week passed quickly by. In the mornings, Sara and Beth visited the kitchens, the afternoons were spent in drives through the countryside, fishing expeditions and walks around the estate. Beth was pleased with everything and proved to be a model guest.

At last the day arrived on which they were to set out for Rotham. Since it was a long drive, they had decided to make an early start. Beth and Sara were ready and waiting by the front door at the appointed hour, but Aunt Eloise was not to be seen.

One of the maids informed her mistress that Miss Farley had been up for some time finishing her packing but had no idea where she might be at the moment.

Sara ascended the stairs to her aunt's room and found her sitting on the bed amid a pile of bags and bandboxes, crying softly. She rushed in and threw her arms around the forlorn little figure. "Why, whatever is the matter, love? Are you not feeling well?" she asked worriedly.

Aunt Eloise stifled a sob and sniffed. "Oh, Sara, I just realized that I will never come back here and it has been my home. A portion of my life is ending."

"But a new portion is beginning. You do love John, do you not?"

"You know I do, with all my heart. It is just that things will be so different."

"Of course they will be different," said her niece bracingly. "They should be different. And you will come back, I will invite you and your new husband often. Dry your eyes now. You have the promise of a wonderful life ahead of you. Everything is going to be fine."

Aunt Eloise smiled shakily. "You are right, of course. I think I am suffering from bride's nerves."

Sara smiled back. "It is only to be expected. Come now, let me call a footman to get all this baggage to the coach so we can be on our way. John is waiting for you."

Within twenty minutes they were on the road, the three ladies in the curricle followed by the traveling coach laden with Aunt Eloise's wardrobe. They stopped for lunch at a posting house and reached Rotham in the late afternoon.

Rotham Abbey, the Ketcham family estate in

Kent, had been granted to the first Viscount Awick during the Restoration. Both the title and holdings came in recognition of Charles Randolph Ketcham's efforts on behalf of the monarchy. There had indeed been an abbey at Rotham but it had been badly damaged during the Cromwellian Revolution. Viscount Awick and his sons after him had all engaged in massive rebuilding programs that had resulted in an odd assortment of styles and material which logically should not coexist but had created an atmosphere of remarkable charm. Set around with numerous outbuildings and what remained of the old priory, Rotham had more the appearance of a small hamlet than a private residence.

As the Liviscombe carriage drew up the long drive to the elegant Palladian entrance, Sara was struck by the warmth and cheerfulness this seemingly ungainly building exuded. The main house was a long rambling structure built of blond brick that glowed golden in the late afternoon sun. The grounds were extensive and expertly manicured, and she longed to escape from the confines of the carriage and explore them further.

The horses drew to a halt and the peaceful atmosphere was shattered by the sudden eruption of a stream of people through the front door. The first to reach the carriage was John Kline, looking very much the impatient bridegroom. Even before the footman could open the door, he was leaning through the window to plant a kiss on his fiancée's cheek. Aunt Eloise blushed and laughingly admonished him. Right behind him was Lord Awick dressed in buckskin breeches and a leather jacket, followed by upward of twenty elegantly clad ladies and gentlemen all laughing and talking at once. Several servants appeared to hand the ladies down and remove the luggage.

"Welcome to Rotham," greeted Lord Awick as he kissed Sara's and Aunt Eloise's hands. "As you can see a few of the wedding guests have arrived. There are several more here but they have gone out riding. You shall see them all this evening at dinner."

He picked up his daughter and gave her a kiss. "Amazingly enough I have missed you, Brat. Did you behave yourself for Lady Sara?"

She laughed delightedly. "Oh, yes, Papa, and I had the most wonderful time. Sara taught me how to make gingerbread. I brought you some. And we went fishing and we—"

"All right," he laughed. "That is enough for now. You can tell me all about it after we get the ladies safely installed inside." He again turned to them as a large motherly woman reached his side. "This is Mrs. Porter, my housekeeper. She will show you your rooms. I suspect you would like to freshen up a bit before tea."

They made their way into the house, exchanging greetings with the numerous guests as they passed. Sara was pleased to see how many of her aunt's old friends had been able to attend. By the time the day of the wedding arrived, there should be quite a crowd.

The interior of Rotham was as much of a hodgepodge as the exterior and just as inviting. The entry hall was tiled in black and white, and a long refectory table, a relic of the old abbey that had somehow escaped destruction, stood along one wall. A large pot of freshly cut flowers had been placed on it. The back wall contained a massive stone fireplace built by a Ketcham with a penchant for things medieval. The curving staircase leading to the upper floors was lined with family portraits. As they reached the landing, Sara was particularly struck by the painting of a young girl dressed in the fashionable style of thirty years earlier. Her large green eyes held a wistful expression. Her face was framed in ringlets of white-gold.

"My mother," said Awick, pausing beside her.

"She was a lovely woman," replied Sara. "And Emily was right, Beth is going to look just like her."

Awick studied the picture for a moment. "Isn't that odd? I never before noticed the resemblance. But it is quite marked. Strange how sometimes we do not see things that are so obvious to others."

"Yes, it is strange," she said thoughtfully, wondering if he were implying anything.

They continued on to the second floor where Awick took Beth's hand to escort her to the nursery wing. "Mrs. Porter will make sure you have everything you need. I have requested tea to be served in the drawing room within the hour, so join us when you are ready. I am going to the nursery with Beth so that I can hear the tale of her adventures in Somerset." He smiled and bowed to them.

"Thank you, Lord Awick," said Aunt Eloise. "I can see you have gone to a great deal of trouble on my behalf and I want you to know that I deeply appreciate it."

"It has been my pleasure, Miss Farley," he replied. "I have not had a house party in years and I must admit I am enjoying it immensely. Go along now and freshen up. I know that Mr. Kline has many details he wishes to discuss with you."

The two ladies set off after Mrs. Porter and found themselves being led down innumerable interconnecting passageways twisting and turning this way and that. They exchanged worried glances.

As if in answer to their unspoken thoughts, Mrs. Porter said, "Great rambling old pile, but don't you be concerned. For the first day or two, ring for a footman to show you the way but you'll soon catch on and know all the ins and outs. Just ask Lady Beth for a tour. She'll have you all straightened out in no time."

Mrs. Porter stopped and pushed open a door. "This is your room, Miss Farley," she said.

They entered and found themselves in a confection of pink and white. The carpet was worked in a field of tiny pink roses, as were the lacy draperies and bed hangings. The furniture had been painted white. There was a frothy, frivolous air to the room which greatly appealed to Aunt Eloise. She had never had much chance in her life to be frivolous.

"How enchanting!" she exclaimed. "Oh, Sara, have you ever seen anything like it?"

"No indeed," her niece replied truthfully. "I cannot say I ever have."

Mrs. Porter noticed the wry expression on the girl's face and smiled to herself. Oh, yes, she thought, I know now why the master is making such a fuss.

She advanced to the clothespress and pulled it open. "Your things have been put away and the girl will be up shortly with hot water. I have asked Molly to attend you and she will help you dress. If you need anything at all, just ring." She turned to Sara. "Your room is just across the hall, my Lady."

She led her into one of the most beautiful rooms Sara had ever seen. It had ornately carved furniture and deep gold and rust fabrics. Bowls of fresh flowers were set about, adding a touch of femininity.

Sara breathed deeply. "This is perfect," she said quietly.

The housekeeper beamed. "Yes, isn't it? Lady Awick had it redone when she came here. I have always thought it to be the best of the bedrooms."

Lady Sara looked at her and blinked in surprise. "Lady Awick? I did not realize she had ever been here. I had understood that they had stayed in America until her death."

"Oh no, my Lady, not the master's wife. His mother redid this room. No, the last Lady Awick never did come here. His Lordship was gone a good many years."

She pulled herself up. "As I told Miss Farley,

the girl will be up shortly. You just make yourself at home and ring if you need anything."

An hour later Aunt Eloise entered her niece's chamber wearing a freshly pressed lavender gown, her hair caught up in a lace mob cap. "Are you ready, my love? A cup of tea would be refreshing right now."

Sara, dressed in a simple blue-and-white-striped morning dress, nodded her agreement and rang for a footman. Within moments they were being led back down the intricate passageways trying to fix landmarks to orient themselves.

By the time they reached the drawing room, it was already filled with people. Upon seeing Aunt Eloise, the crowd pressed closely around them, all offering congratulations and best wishes. They were finally rescued by Mrs. Warrington. "Come now. There is plenty of time for that. They have just arrived from a long journey and need a little air and sustenance." Supplying them with tea, she led them through the French doors that opened onto the patio. "Come," she said, "it will be cooler out here and we can have a little private conversation. Such a perfect day it is. I only hope that the wedding day will be this fine. If it is we can hold the bridal breakfast on the lawns."

The ladies chatted for a while, going over the wedding details and making sure everything had been taken care of. They were soon joined by Mr. Kline who seemed to have an endless supply of pressing issues to discuss with his future wife.

Lord Awick joined them. "How are you liking Rotham, Lady Sara?" he asked.

"It is lovely, my Lord. I understand your mother had a great deal to do with the refurbishing."

He laughed ruefully. "It seems one of the prerequisites in this family to redo Rotham. As you have probably noticed everyone has had a hand in it at one time or another. I must admit though that I find the overall effect pleasing, but then I was raised here and it must appear different to others."

"On the contrary, my Lord," she replied. "I find it to be one of the most marvelous homes I have been in."

"I am glad," he said. "I hope you will be comfortable here."

Mrs. Warrington, delighted with this conversation, decided to interrupt. It was much too tentative at this point to leave it in the hands of amateurs. "The last of the guests should be here by Thursday," she said. "The rehearsal will be on Friday and the wedding of course on Saturday. I had thought that instead of the usual bachelor dinner we would have an estate party Friday night and invite all the local neighbors for an early dinner, giving the servants the night off to have their own celebration. What do you think, Randy?"

"That sounds splendid," replied her godson. "I will work out the details."

The next few days were filled with activity. There seemed to be endless calls on the time of the Liviscombe ladies. Aunt Eloise was totally caught up in her guests. Sara found herself spending a great deal of time with Beth. Increasingly enchanted with the child, she made a point to be with her during the better part of each day.

They were alone in the nursery one day when Beth turned to her and exclaimed, "Oh, Mama, look!"

Sara, startled, suppressed her surprise and turned to the child. Beth, obviously unaware of what she had said, held up the piece of embroidery on which she had been working industriously for the past several days. She smiled proudly. "It is finished!" she said.

Sara took the work from her and studied it closely. Set in the outline of a heart were the names of Eloise Farley and John Kline and the date of the wedding, now just three days away. There were two doves at the top and flowers bordering the whole. "Why, darling, it is beautiful. I know Aunt Eloise will be delighted. You did a lovely job."

"Do you really think so? Will Aunt Eloise truly like it?" asked the child.

"Yes indeed. Any woman would be delighted with such a gift."

"Then I shall make one for you," said Beth, smiling brightly.

"I fear you will have to wait until I find someone to marry."

"Oh, that's all right. I will find someone for you. I had better get started right away. I wonder what date I should use?"

Sara laughed. "Maybe you can just leave the

names and date blank for now. I do not think there is any hurry."

"Any hurry to do what?" asked a voice from the doorway.

The two looked up to find Lord Awick smiling at the charming picture that they made holding their embroidery with bits of brightly colored thread scattered liberally on the carpet, sofa and even their gowns.

"To get Sara married," said his daughter casually. "I was just telling her I will do a sampler for her like the one for Aunt Eloise when she gets married but I don't know what date I should put."

Lady Sara stood up, shaking the bits of thread from her gown. "And I don't know whom the groom will be, so I think we can consider the subject closed now. Show your papa your handiwork."

He was appropriately pleased and proud of his daughter, and was anxious to reopen the earlier discussion. He had suggestions for both the groom and the date—himself and anytime before tomorrow. It was a topic he had every intention of bringing up again. But he still felt that the time was not right.

"Would you like to go for a ride, Beth? You have been inside most of the day. A little fresh air might be good."

"Yes, please, Papa. Perkins is teaching me how to jump now. Will you come, too, Sara?"

"I think perhaps I will. In fact, I have been giving some thought to having Perkins teach me to ride. With everyone out on horseback all the time, I am beginning to feel an outsider. What do you think, my Lord? Am I too old for riding lessons?"

"Not at all, my dear. In fact I think you would enjoy it immensely. I don't suppose you have a riding habit?"

She shook her head.

He thought for a moment, looking her up and down. "Yes, the perfect thing. I will have one of my mother's brought down for you. I fear it will be terribly old-fashioned but it should fit you well. Did you want to start now?"

"I think I had better. If I wait and think about it I know I shall change my mind. Will it be much of a bother to get the habit for me?"

He walked over to the bell cord. "It will be in your room in fifteen minutes."

"In that case, Beth and I had better get changed. Shall we meet you in the stables in, say, half an hour?"

"That will be fine. I will go down and talk to Perkins and see which of our horses are in right now. I presume you will not want a spirited animal, your first time up."

She laughed. "You presume correctly. And remember, it is my second time up. I just hope this attempt will be more successful."

Perkins had the perfect mount for Sara, an older mare with steady paces and no bad habits who was considered much too tame by the other members of the house party. Lord Awick had her and Beth's pony saddled and led into the exercise paddock.

The ladies arrived a few minutes later. The

habit that Awick had obtained for Sara was black with a lacy white cravat. The hat sported one long ostrich plume that swept her cheek. Beth was dressed in a sky-blue habit, her curls caught up in back with a wide blue ribbon. The two made an enticing picture as they strolled across the yard, Beth clinging to Sara's hand and pulling her along excitedly.

Awick could hear her chattering as they approached. "You are going to love it," he heard her say. "It is the most wonderful feeling flying along with the wind on your face. And truly there is nothing to worry about. Papa will give you a gentle mount."

He strolled forward to meet them. "Beth is right. I *have* found a gentle mount. Her name is Daisy. All you have to do is follow Perkins's instructions and relax."

Soon Sara was seated on Daisy and Perkins was leading them around the ring. Beth had mounted her pony and was working on the low jumps in the center. After several minutes, Perkins handed the reins to Sara and suggested she try a few rounds by herself. She found she rather enjoyed the experience and kicked Daisy into a trot.

She was beginning to believe her terror of horses had been totally irrational. Riding was not that hard and a great deal of fun. She gave herself over to the pure enjoyment of the experience.

Lord Awick was proud of her and clapped as she passed, bestowing encouraging smiles on her. Perkins, watching her closely, said that she had a good seat and light hands and would be able to handle some of the friskier horses in no time.

She was on her fourth circuit of the paddock when the afternoon riding party pulled into the yard. The quiet afternoon was suddenly shattered by thundering hooves and the yelping of dogs. Daisy, who was not used to the commotion, became fidgety and reared up. Her tentative rider, caught unawares, found herself falling. She grasped for a hold but to no avail and felt a jolt as she hit the ground. Expecting the worst, she closed her eyes and lay still.

Lord Awick was at her side immediately. With the recent accident fresh in his mind, he bent over her and lifted her head, cradling her in his arms.

"Oh, my dearest love, I should never have allowed this to happen," he whispered in a husky voice. He was frightened by how pale and still she was. He made a quick search of her bones and decided nothing was broken. He then lifted her up and took her into the house. Beth was beside him demanding to know if Sara was all right and exactly what had happened.

He assured her that Sara would be fine and sent her to the nursery. He then carried his burden up to her room. Carefully laying her on the bed, he felt her pulse and found it strong and normal. Pulling the bell cord he requested that a doctor be summoned.

Sara, who had been nothing more than a little shaken from her spill, roused up. "There is no need for a doctor, my Lord. Truly I am fine."

He turned at the sound of her voice and rushed back to the side of the bed. "Are you certain? There is no pain?"

"A little winded, that is all." She realized she was trembling but was not sure if it was a result of her fall or of the words she had heard him murmur while he thought she was unconscious. She whispered, "Did you mean it, my Lord?"

"Mean what, Sara?" he asked, seating himself on the edge of her bed.

"About my being your dearest love."

He took her hands in his and smiled. "So you heard that, did you? Yes, Sara, I do love you and have since the first time we met twelve years ago. I guess I have made a terrible botch of things with you, haven't I? Do you think we can get it all sorted out?"

By now he had her in his arms, her head resting against his shoulder. She murmured, "There is only one little matter to sort as far as I can see."

He looked down at her. "And what might that be?"

"You have yet to ask me to marry you."

He gazed at her seriously. "And what would your answer be?"

"So far, you have proposed to me twice. Once I said yes and once I said no. You have never explained why it was that you left me so abruptly after I said yes the first time."

He arose and sent for his valet. After a brief

discussion, the man left to return in a few moments with a white envelope. Awick took it from him, then returned to her side. Silently, he handed it to her.

"What is this?" she asked.

"Just open it and read it."

She looked at the unmarked envelope for a moment, a fleeting memory stirring in her mind. She read the contents, then her eyes flew to his face. "But I don't understand."

"Believe me, my love, I did not either. Then I realized that I had forgotten to address the letter in my haste to visit my uncle. My servants in London found it and sent it here, but I had already left for America when it arrived. I did not discover what had happened until I returned here a few weeks ago. And now, my girl, for the third time, what is it to be? A simple yes will suffice."

"A simple yes," she replied demurely.

He raised her head to give her a long, lingering kiss. "That wasn't so hard, was it?"

She smiled at him. "Almost as easy as falling off a horse and considerably less painful."

He kissed her again. "And now there only remains one question. Beth will need to know the date so she can start on her sampler."

She considered for a moment. "There are so many preparations to complete."

"It seems to me we have completed the preparations. How about the day after tomorrow?"

"Surely you are joking. That is Aunt Eloise's wedding day, and we still have to post the banns and invite the guests and . . ."

"I am not joking. I just happen to have a special license that I have been carrying for twelve years and we have plenty of guests and you can wear my mother's wedding gown. This work should be used for more than just one wedding." He stood up and drew her off the bed. "Come, let us break the news to your aunt and Beth."

They found Beth in the nursery working on a piece of embroidery. She jumped up when they entered and ran to Sara.

"Oh, Sara, you are all right!" she exclaimed. "I have been so worried."

"Yes, I am fine, thank you, dear."

"Are you going to try riding again?"

Sara smiled at Lord Awick. "I think I will. I always seem to have better luck the third time around." She turned back to Beth. "And now we have something we would like to discuss with you." She sat on the little sofa and drew the child down beside her. "As you know, Beth, your papa and I have known each other for a very long time, longer than you have been alive, in fact. We have found that we have much in common and have decided to marry." She paused to take a breath.

"Oh, I already knew that," said the child airily. "I told you so earlier. I have just been waiting for the date so that I can finish the sampler."

The adults laughed and Sara gave the child a hug.

"I knew everything would work out, Mama. I just wonder what took you so long."

"Out of the mouths of babes," quoted her father and also gave her a hug. "You will like to have Sara for your mother, I presume?"

She laughed at him. "You silly. I told you that ever so long ago. Now when is it to be? I have work to do." She looked dismayed when they announced it would take place three days hence. Donning a very serious expression, she told them to run along and let her get busy.

They discovered Aunt Eloise and Emily Warrington in the library, gossiping and sipping sherry.

Emily took one look at their glowing faces and clapped her hands delightedly. "You have finally decided to wed!" She jumped up and embraced them both.

Aunt Eloise did the same. "Oh, my dears, I cannot tell you how happy this makes me. We must ring for champagne at once."

They discussed all the details for the upcoming celebrations. When the champagne arrived, Eloise Farley proposed a toast. "To the two most stubborn people I have ever met. May you be very, very happy." She turned to Emily and laughed. "He proposed to her twelve years ago and they are going to be engaged for two days."

Emily Warrington smiled in return. "Believe me, Eloise, the sooner they are married the better. I do not think any of us could stand it if anything else went wrong."

From the look of the two, who were holding hands and exchanging lingering glances and soft words, there was nothing now that could keep them apart.

About the Author

Adrienne Scott lives in a small town just outside of San Francisco with her husband and two cats. Employed as a facilities planner, she is currently involved in the design and construction of an eleven-building office complex. She finds time to write while cooking dinner and commuting. Her other interests include travel, needlework, tennis, and aerobic exercise.

Tapestry
HISTORICAL ROMANCES

Next Month From
Tapestry Romances

GLORIOUS TREASURE
by Louise Gillette
GILDED HEARTS
by Johanna Hill

POCKET BOOKS

Home delivery from Pocket Books

Here's your opportunity to have fabulous bestsellers delivered right to you. Our free catalog is filled to the brim with the newest titles plus the finest in mysteries, science fiction, westems, cookbooks, romances, biographies, health, psychology, humor—every subject under the sun. Order this today and a world of pleasure will arrive at your door.

POCKET BOOKS, Department ORD
1230 Avenue of the Americas, New York, N.Y. 10020

Please send me a free Pocket Books catalog for home delivery

NAME _____

ADDRESS _____

CITY _____ STATE/ZIP _____

If you have friends who would like to order books at home, we'll send them a catalog too—

NAME _____

ADDRESS _____

CITY _____ STATE/ZIP _____

NAME _____

ADDRESS _____

CITY _____ STATE/ZIP _____